Rescuing Finley

A Forever Home Novel
Book 1

Dan Walsh

Praise for Some of Dan Walsh's Other Novels:

Part I

Two Years Ago

1

She could get arrested for this.

Amy knew that, walking into the mall. Signs were everywhere. *Shoplifting is a crime! Shoplifters will be prosecuted!*

But Amy Wallace didn't need a sign to tell her she was doing wrong. She'd been raised a church girl. *Thou shalt not steal.* She'd stolen plenty before now. The worst kind. Not just stores, but from family. And not just once, many times. One too many. They'd finally gotten sick of it, all her lies, and threw her out of the house.

That was over a year ago. Since then, she'd been on her own.

At the moment, Amy considered herself a recovering meth addict. Clean five days now, ever since she'd lost her job after failing a drug test. The temptation to start using again had gotten really bad recently. Today it had been especially strong.

"Are you ready?"

Amy looked up at Sandy's face. Sandy was the ringleader of their little trio. Standing beside her was Chloe. The two of them were close friends; Amy was the outsider. Neither of them were users, and that was a good thing.

"I'm ready." She stood and looked around. "Are you sure we

should do this?"

"Yes," Sandy said. "I've done it just like this five times already. Never got caught. Never even had to run. Just do like I told you. You'll be fine."

Sandy was so confident. But her confidence did nothing to calm Amy's nerves.

The three of them stood outside the department store entrance dressed in expensive outfits they had stolen from this same store last week. This time the stakes were higher. They were going for jewelry, the high-end kind. The kind you could turn into quick cash. Sandy had said they needed to dress the part. Look like girls who belonged in a place like this. She needed to look even better; like a girl who could afford to buy sapphires and diamonds.

They walked past a full-length mirror attached to one of the mall pillars. Amy barely recognized her reflection. Sandy could do wonders with hair and makeup.

"Okay," Sandy said, "Time to split up. You all know what to do, right?"

Chloe nodded.

"Can't I change places with Chloe?" Amy said. "Be the distraction?"

"No, it's all set. Besides, you run faster than Chloe. You need to be the one that gets the ring out of the store. Anyway, I got the hardest job. I have to do all the talking."

Amy nodded. Not like she had a choice. It wasn't just how much Sandy intimidated her. Amy really did need the money. Her bank account was nearly empty. The only food she had left were some leftovers in the fridge. If she couldn't come up with two hundred dollars by Friday, she'd be out on the street again.

That happened, she'd be back on meth in no time.

They split up, but stayed within eyesight of each other as they walked into the store. Amy went left, Chloe went right. Sandy walked slowly down the main aisle toward the jewelry section. After she arrived there, Chloe relocated to a spot two aisles away.

Amy pretended to care about something at eye level on a nearby shelf. She watched Sandy walk up to the sales clerk at the jewelry counter. A tall brunette. In no time at all, Sandy had her laughing about something. She was good at small talk. After a minute or so, Sandy said something else. The two women walked down toward the glass case with the diamonds. Sandy leaned over slightly and pointed at several diamond rings.

Amy knew she was picking out one that cost well over a thousand dollars. That was the plan. In a few moments, the clerk had unlocked the cabinet and set the ring down on a square of satiny blue cloth. Sandy picked the ring up, looked at it closely then held it to the light, as if checking the quality of the stone. All the while, chatting away and flashing her photogenic smile. She asked the clerk a question. Amy couldn't hear clearly, but she knew what it was. Could she try on the ring? The clerk nodded yes.

That was the first cue.

Chloe knocked something off the shelf. Whatever it was, it made a loud noise. Startled Sandy and the clerk. Chloe made an even louder fuss, apologizing profusely. The sales clerk said something to Sandy, then left the counter to see what Chloe had done.

That was Amy's cue.

She came out from where she'd been standing and walked quickly toward Sandy. Sandy palmed the ring and stuck her hand behind her back. As Amy went past her, she took the ring, shoved it into her pocket and kept walking. She turned left down the main aisle toward the exit leading to the parking lot.

Sandy waited until Amy was safely out of sight then began to scream, "That girl, she just stole the ring!"

Amy couldn't see what happened next. She dared not turn around. She just kept walking. Sandy had explained how this scheme worked the other times they did it. The clerk would instantly leave Chloe and rush back to Sandy. Chloe would then slip away and head for another exit. Sandy would act all frantic and upset. When asked which way the thief went, she'd point toward the exit that led back into the mall. By the time security arrived on the scene, Amy would be safely out the door and headed for the car.

The double-glass doors were just up ahead. She was so nervous but did her best not to let it show. She walked quickly but tried not to appear in a hurry.

Calm down, you're almost there.

A few more steps and she reached the first set of doors. She walked through the middle section, and was just about to push open the door to the parking lot when she felt a strong hand grip her shoulder and pull her back.

Then a deep voice. "Where you think you're going with that ring?"

2

Amy was trembling inside. She didn't know if it showed. In handcuffs, she sat in a straight back chair next to a metal desk. The security guard who'd put her in this little room said he'd be right back. He was not a nice man; shoving her and squeezing her arm as they walked through the store. She was sure she had bruises. And he scolded her like a child, though he wasn't more than a few years older than she was.

Where were Sandy and Chloe? Hopefully, they'd made it out of the store okay. It wasn't concern for their welfare, but her own. They weren't really friends. Amy was certain if either of them had gotten caught they'd make the whole thing out to be her idea.

She heard footsteps. The door opened. Two men entered. The original security guard and another guy dressed in street clothes.

He spoke first. "That was a pretty stupid thing you did out there." He stepped closer. "My name's Alec. I'm in charge of security at the store. The police are on their way. It'll go better for you if you cooperate."

Amy held up her handcuffs. "If you're not the police, what gives you the right to put these on me? Am I under arrest?"

"We can't arrest you," he said, "but we can detain you until they get here. And we can use whatever means we feel is necessary to keep you from escaping custody."

"Don't you have some papers for me to fill out? It'll be hard to do that with these on."

Alec leaned against the desk. The uniformed guard remained standing near the doorway. "So you've done this before," Alec said. "You know the routine."

"No, my friend told me what happens when people get caught shoplifting." Amy was lying. She had gotten caught in another store last year. They had her sign some papers and agree to pay a fine and restitution. The police got involved, but she got off with community service.

"That's good. So you're willing to admit you were shoplifting. That's a start, anyway."

"Well, it wouldn't do any good to deny it. I had the ring in my pocket."

"That's right, you did. And we've got more evidence than that."

"Why don't you show her?" the other guard said. "I've got the video queued up."

"Good idea," Alec said. He looked at Amy. "Stand up."

She did. "Where are you taking me?"

"Not far. Just to another security room."

They led her out of that room down a cement hallway to another room with several flat screen TV monitors hanging on the wall. Each showed a different section of the store. The uniformed guard sat in front of a keyboard. Amy instantly recognized the picture paused on the screen above it. It showed a perfect angle of the entire jewelry area. Sandy was standing in front of a glass case with the sales clerk; the ring, resting on the blue satin square. You couldn't really see Sandy's face.

"I was in here watching you and your friends the whole time," the guard said.

"And I was watching you from just a few aisles away," Alec said.

Amy tensed up. She should've listened to her gut and turned Sandy down.

"Go ahead and play it," Alec said.

The guard pressed a button and Amy watched the whole thing unfold. Near the top of the screen, she saw an arm push a silver teapot set off the shelf. Sandy and the clerk jumped at the noise. But you couldn't see Chloe's face, just her arm. The clerk turned toward the noise, said something to Sandy, then walked over and bent down near the fallen merchandise. Sandy put the ring behind her back and held it out, palm up.

"Freeze that," Alec said. He pointed to the picture on the screen. "Clearly, you were working as a team. My guess is, the girl that knocked that teapot over was part of it, too. Who are they?"

So they had escaped. Amy didn't answer.

"You know who they are," he said. "Why should you take all the blame for this?"

Still, Amy didn't answer.

"Suit yourself. Keep going."

The video continued. From the other side of the screen, Amy watched herself come down the aisle in front of the jewelry counter, right behind Sandy. She took the ring and put it into her pocket. She noticed now how much she had picked up her pace. Once she had pocketed the ring, she turned left down the main aisle."

"Did you see that?" The uniformed guard said, pausing the screen. "You can see the blonde girl who just handed her the ring looking right at her as she walks away. And look how long she waits before she says anything?"

Alec looked at Amy. "She was giving you time to get away. But as you can see, it didn't work. She's the one who got away. You're sitting here with us. Who is she? And who's the other girl, the one that knocked the teapot over?"

Amy didn't say anything. Alec stared at her more sternly. "Why should I tell you? You've got me, and you've got your ring back. Getting them in trouble's not gonna help me. Just give me whatever papers you want me to sign, and let's get this over with."

"You don't get it, do you?" Alec said. "This isn't like you stole a pack of cigarettes, or even an expensive blouse. That ring sells for twelve hundred dollars. In Florida, it only takes three hundred dollars to move shoplifting from misdemeanor to third-degree felony. We've got you with the ring in your possession, and we got you on video. I'm not going to give you any papers to fill out. You're not gonna pay some fine and get a slap on the wrist here. You're going to prison for this. The only question is…how long?"

Amy felt like she was going to be sick.

"When the time comes, the judge can either throw the book at you and give you the maximum, or he might show some mercy, give you a lighter sentence. That's why I suggest you tell us who your friends are. That kind of cooperation could help you out."

Amy didn't know what to do.

"Look," Alec continued, "what kind of friends are they anyway to take off and leave you to catch all the heat by yourself? I can tell you're not the leader of this little group. My guess is, it's that blonde, the one at the counter. And I'm also guessing by the look on your face, she didn't tell you that going after such expensive merchandise made this a felony, did she?"

She did not. Sandy had said it was no big deal whether they stole some clothes or jewelry. Big stores like this had insurance to cover shoplifting losses. But if she gave up Sandy and Chloe to the police, Amy would be a snitch. Everything she'd always heard said that snitches get beat up in prison. "When the police get here," she said, "they're going to read me my rights, aren't they?"

"They are."

"One of those rights is the right to be silent. So I'm all done talking."

The guard's radio squawked. He picked it up, pressed a button and said, "Go ahead."

A scratchy female voice responded. "The police are here. I just sent them back."

3

Finley

Why'd she leave him closed up in this little room again? He could barely walk or even stretch without bumping into something. His legs ached to run. He kept listening under the door. All he heard was the irritating hum of the exhaust fan over the tub.

The mother put Finley in here. She was starting to do that now every time she went out. Chaz was Finley's owner. He would never do this to him. Chaz and the mother argued about it many times.

But here Finley was again.

He wished he saw it coming, but he fell for it every time. The mother would start talking to him in that high-pitched, happy voice. Using his name instead of *"that dog."* She'd get out a treat and start waving it in front of his nose. He felt powerless. Then she'd lead him down the hall. Like a fool, he'd follow. Even wagging his tail. In some vague, undefined place in his mind, Finley knew where she was taking him. But it was always the same. At that moment, it didn't matter.

That soft, chewy beefy treat was amazing.

Finally, she would stop at the doorway, turn the light on in the small room, bend down and face him. Once again, she'd wave the treat right in front of his nose. "You want this? Do you want this?"

Of course he did. More than anything else in the world.

She'd toss it on the floor. He'd watch it glide across the tile and bang into the back wall. He'd tear off after it and just as he'd reach it, the same thing would always happen. The fan would turn on and the door would close behind him. He'd gobble down the treat and try not to think about the fact that he'd fallen for it again.

The last thing he'd hear was her voice through the closed door, as she walked down the hall. "I won't be gone long. You be good in there, Finley. Don't bark!"

But she'd always be gone long. Being stuck in a closed room for five minutes was too long. She'd be gone for hours. It felt like forever.

A sound.

Finley sat up, ears up. Were those footsteps? Voices? He waited, listened. They were muffled, but there could be no doubt. Someone was nearby. No, two people. He cocked his head. Two male voices. He stood, his tail began to thump against the cabinet.

Jingling keys at the front door.

He pawed at the floor.

The front door opened. "Mom, I'm home."

It was Chaz. Finley couldn't help himself. He began to bark and scratch at the door. The mother would scold him harshly whenever he did. But she wasn't here. Chaz was here. Chaz was everything. Chaz would get him out of this place.

"Mom?"

"She's not here, Chaz. Can't you hear Finn barking? But maybe that's a good thing. Give you more time to figure out what you're gonna say."

"Did she shut you up in the bathroom again? Poor boy."

That was Chaz. The other voice was Alonzo, Chaz's friend. Chaz was walking this way. Finley couldn't stop himself. He barked louder. A few howls slipped out.

"I'm coming, Finn."

The doorknob turned. The door opened and banged into his head.

"You need to back up, boy. Let me get the door open."

Finley understood *back up*. He was just too excited. The door was squeezing him into the tub. Pulling back a few steps, his head and body broke free. He leapt onto Chaz, who'd bent down to hug him. Finley couldn't stop jumping. He knocked Chaz over. Chaz began to laugh. There was only one thing to do. Finley licked his face.

"Okay, okay, Boy. That's enough."

"You'd think you been gone a month," Alonzo said.

"I know. He's always excited to see me, but especially when he's been shut in the bathroom. I wish she wouldn't do that."

"Why does she? Isn't he housebroke?"

"For the most part. But if he gets left too long, sometimes he slips. The other thing is the chewing. When he was younger, he destroyed some of her shoes and the corner of that stuffed chair."

The boys walked toward the living room, Finley right by his side. Finley had to go the bathroom in the worst way, but he wanted Chaz to know how grateful he was for letting him out of that room.

"So why doesn't she just put him in your room? Why lock him up in the bathroom?"

"She says he barks. Some of the neighbors complained. But I asked the people on either side of us. They said he barks sometimes, but not enough that it bothers them."

"Think she's making it up?" Alonzo sat on the sofa.

Finley followed Chaz out to the kitchen. "I don't think so. I don't know. She's just not a dog person."

"That's gonna be a problem, Chaz. Especially after what we just did. You thought about that?"

Finley wondered what they were talking about. He looked at Chaz. He didn't answer Alonzo, but Finley could sense him tensing up. Chaz's heart began to beat a little faster. He opened up the fridge and pulled out a can of soda. "You want a Coke?"

"Sure. But I'm serious Chaz. That recruiter said we could be heading out to boot camp within six weeks. They don't allow pets."

"I know." Chaz popped the top on the soda can. "I know."

"What are you going to do with him? I don't think your Mom will—"

"I'm gonna ask Celia if she'll take him."

"Does she even know you joined up?"

Chaz shook his head no. "I didn't even know I was going to do it, till we walked into that recruiting place in the mall."

"What do you mean? We been talking about it for months?"

"I know, but I should've waited till I thought all these details through. Now I gotta figure out how I'm going to tell Celia…and my mom." He walked into the living room, sat in the chair next to the couch.

"And see if Celia will take Finn."

Chaz released a sigh. Something had made him sad. Finley went to his side, sat against his leg.

"I hate to bring this up," Alonzo said. "But I'm not so sure that's a good plan, even if Celia says yes."

"Why?"

"I mean…Celia's a nice girl and nice looking but, c'mon, she's kind of an airhead."

"She is not."

"She is, too. She forgets stuff all the time. I don't think I'd feel too good about leaving Finley with her all that time. We could be gone two years."

Chaz sighed again. Heavier this time. He scratched the top of Finley's head. Something was bothering him. Finley thought about jumping on his lap, at least halfway, but he couldn't wait a minute more. It was being shut up in that room for so long, then all this excitement. He was about to explode. He ran over and grabbed his leash off the hook on the wall above his water bowl.

"Think Finn's trying to tell you something," Alonzo said.

Chaz laughed. "You gotta go out, boy? Alright. I'll take you out." He pulled the leash out of Finley's mouth. "Let's go."

Finley ran ahead of him to the front door, started spinning in circles.

"I'll be right back," he said to Alonzo.

Finley's eyes focused on the crack of the door. He heard the familiar clicking as Chaz fastened the leash to his collar. The door opened. Finley pushed through and stepped out onto the balcony. Finally, fresh air. He loved being outside. Especially with Chaz. Chaz always paid attention to Finley, and he always felt secure whenever Chaz was around.

Chaz loved him. Chaz was everything.

4

About an hour later, Chaz and Alonzo were playing Xbox in Chaz's room. Finley tried napping on the edge of the bed. Every few minutes, one of the boys yelled out something and woke him up. The look on their faces said they were in no real danger, but his instincts wouldn't let him ignore their cries.

Just then, a new sound. Finley lifted his head. The front door was being unlocked. He looked at the boys. They couldn't hear it over the explosions in their game. He jumped down to investigate. Bracing himself in the hall at the edge of the living room, he released his best angry bark as the door opened. He was about to charge it when he recognized the mother.

That would've been a big mistake. He ran up to greet her, tried to suppress the urge to bark.

"How did you get out of the bathroom?" she said, as she walked through the doorway. She set some packages down on the coffee table. An explosion came down the hall, followed by Alonzo yelling out something. She stood with her hands on her hips, staring down the hallway. "That's how."

The front door was still open. Finley took a step in that direction, but stopped. An open door always felt like an invitation, but he knew she hadn't left it open for him.

"Chaz!" The mother yelled. She walked down the hallway and yelled again, "Chaz, I need your help with the groceries!"

Finley followed but kept his distance. The noise in Chaz's room stopped. His bedroom door opened the rest of the way. "Mom, you're home."

"I am, and the trunk's full of groceries. I carried what I could up the stairs, but my back is killing me. Can you get the rest?"

"Sure. Alonzo, give me a hand."

Finley stepped out of the way as the mother walked back into the living room. She brought her packages into the kitchen. The boys hurried out the front door. Their apartment was on the second floor. Finley followed them as far as the outdoor balcony. He wasn't allowed any farther. They carried the groceries from the car in one trip. Finley ran down the corridor and met them as they came up the stairs.

Alonzo stopped halfway to the front door. "After we put these down, I'm gonna go."

"Why? We're not done with our game. You've gotta gimme a chance to even things up." Finley sat beside Chaz.

"Because your mom's home, and you need to have a talk with her. And I don't want to be here for that."

"I'll talk with her during dinner."

"You really wanna do that? You know what'll happen. The longer you wait, the more nervous you'll get. You'll say something wrong when she gets upset and make it worse. Besides, no way you were gonna catch up with me."

"You think she's gonna get upset?"

"Of course she is. This isn't gonna be a nice surprise."

Finley heard Chaz sigh again. He didn't know what they were talking about. Whatever it was, Chaz was no longer happy. He nudged his hand with his head. Chaz patted him a few times. The three of them walked back toward the front door in silence. The boys brought the rest of the shopping bags into the kitchen and set them on the counters. Finley watched from the dining area.

"Well, I gotta be going," Alonzo announced.

"You don't want to stay for dinner?" the mother asked. "I didn't mean to chase you out."

"No, that's okay. It's not you." He started walking through the dining area into the living room. "There's just some things I've gotta do. I'll see you later, Chaz."

"Yeah, see you later."

"Thanks for helping with the bags," the mother said.

"No problem."

Finley followed Alonzo to the door then turned back toward the kitchen after he closed the door. Chaz sat at the dining room table, so Finley laid beside him on the carpet.

"Before you start fixing dinner, Ma, can we talk?"

"Can't we talk *while* I'm fixing dinner? I'm kind of hungry, aren't you?"

"Actually, I'm not."

The mother put something into the pantry, then closed the bi-fold door. "What, have you and Alonzo been snacking back there while you played your game?"

"No, not this time. I'm just not hungry."

"Not hungry?" She walked over to him, put her palm gently on his forehead. "You don't feel hot."

"I'm not sick. I'm just not hungry. Could you sit down?"

She did. "Is something wrong? What's wrong?"

"Nothing's wrong. Not exactly. It's just something's come up. Something we need to talk about."

"Okay...what is it?"

Finley could sense it now; both of them were tense. It made him feel uneasy. He sat up, leaned against Chaz's leg, wanting to comfort him.

There was a long pause.

"Chaz? What is it, son?"

"I joined the Marines today."

"What? You did what?"

"Joined the Marines. Alonzo and I both did, along with a few other friends. We signed up down at the recruiting office in the mall."

"Why? Why now? Why didn't you ask me first? Something this important, we should've—"

"You know I've been talking about it, right? For quite a while now."

"I've heard you talk about it, but I didn't know you were serious." She leaned back in her chair.

"Of course I was serious. I told you I wanted to join up as soon as I graduated high school. That was over a month ago."

Another long pause.

"Mom, c'mon. This is a good thing."

"How is this a good thing?"

The mother was clearly upset.

"I'll be serving my country. Doing my duty. You've heard me and the guys talking about this. These jihadists have to be stopped. If we don't stop them over there, they'll be coming over here. We'll have another 9-11 all over again."

"What about your duty to me? To our family?"

"Aww, Mom. Don't be that way."

Finley moved away from the table, so he could see both of them. The mother leaned forward again, resting her elbows on the table. "What other way can I be? You just told me you're going to leave me. For how long?"

"I don't know, two years I think."

"Two years?"

"It'll go by fast, you'll see."

She started to rub her forehead. "I'll be here all alone."

"No, you won't. Finley will still be here. He'll keep you company, right boy? And Maria doesn't live that far away."

Finley didn't know what Chaz was saying, but he recognized *Maria*. Maria was Chaz's sister. She didn't live here anymore.

"Maria lives on the other side of the state. And he won't keep me company," she said, looking at Finley. "He'll be nothing but trouble. Think of all the things you do for him now. Who's going to do all that if you leave? Me? He's a big dog, Chaz. The few times I walked him he almost yanked my shoulder out of its socket."

Finley hated the way the mother looked at him just now. He lowered his shoulders, then lowered to the ground completely. Had he done something wrong?

"When you begged me to let you have a dog, I said you could have a small one. Look what you came back from the Humane Society with? He's part golden retriever and part...some other big dog."

"He wasn't big when I brought him back. He was just a puppy."

"But you could tell he was going to be big. His paws were humongous."

"I didn't know," Chaz said. "But you're not gonna have to look after Finley all by yourself. I'm going to ask Celia to help out."

"Celia," the mother said. "She's a nice girl, but after you're gone, do you really see her coming over here every day to take care of Finley? How long do you think that will last?"

"Maybe she can take him off your hands completely till I get back. Watch him at her place."

"Chaz…how do you think her parents will feel about that?"

"I don't know, Mom. Why are you being so negative about this? Guys my age have been signing up for the military for ages. It's just something I've gotta do."

There was another long pause.

Finley looked up at the mother's face, mostly at her eyes. He saw something besides anger there. She was sad. Deeply sad. He felt drawn to her. He had to find a way to help her if he could. He walked over and gently nudged her leg with his nose. She didn't respond.

"It's not Finley," she finally said. "It's not even having to take care of him by myself. It's you. You going away. Far away. Not across town for a few days. Not even across the state like your sister. But on the other side of the world, to an evil place…where people hate you and will try to kill you."

Chaz reached his hand across the table and held hers. "Mom, I'm going to be fine. The war's winding down. You can see it on the news. Hardly anyone gets killed anymore."

"But some of them do. Chaz, I don't know what I'd do if…" She stopped talking. Tears fell from her eyes.

Finley leaned against her, wishing there was some way he could ease her pain. He watched Chaz get up, walk across the room to grab a box of tissues. As he walked back, he pulled a few out and handed them to the mother. Then he reached down and gave her a hug.

They didn't talk for a little while. Finley wished he knew what they had said. Whatever it was, it left him feeling sad and confused.

5

Chris

Helmand Province, Afghanistan
(near Marjah)

Officially, he was known as US Marine Corps Lance Cpl. Christopher Seger, 2nd Battalion, 8th Marine Regiment, Regiment Combat Team 6.

Friends called him Chris. They called his job, route clearance. It's what he did on pretty much every mission. Chris was a minesweeper.

The Taliban liked to hide IED's along roadways throughout Afghanistan, see if they could blow up any military vehicles driving by. These roadside IED's were big and generally built to pack a wallop. Since the war started, they accounted for over three thousand military deaths and had seriously wounded thirty-three thousand more. The military had formed special patrol units and manufactured special equipment for snooping these things out and disarming them.

Out here in the rural areas like Marjah, the IED's were much smaller. They buried them in the hard-packed dirt paths that ran through the poppy fields. They functioned more like the old-fashioned mines used during World War 2. Their aim wasn't to blow up a military vehicle but a single soldier on foot patrol.

The guys feared these mines more than a sniper's bullet. Almost everyone knew someone who'd become a victim. Some of the guys had made their friends promise to shoot them if they ever stepped on one. They'd rather be dead than go home with no legs.

Chris hated hearing them talk like this.

Because of this constant danger, whenever a patrol was sent out on foot, guys like Chris would lead the way, waving a handheld metal detector back and forth as they walked. Though more expensive and sophisticated, these detectors looked pretty much like the devices you'd see middle-aged men fiddling with on weekends, hunting along beaches or through the woods for old coins and buried treasure.

Treasure hunters got all excited when their detectors sounded off. Usually meant they'd found something valuable. Historical trinkets or antique coins. What Chris longed for on patrol was silence. It was a good day if the detectors didn't make a peep.

He hoped today was a good day. Yesterday wasn't.

Thinking about what happened ruined his sleep last night. Even now, as he sat leaning against a dirt wall waiting to be sent out again, he was thinking about it. The problem wasn't something his detector had found. They'd started taking sniper fire barely a fourth of the way through a poppy field.

Everyone hit the deck. Chris remembered thinking how odd it was to be laying there in a beautiful field of pink and white flowers, as bullets ripped through the sky inches above them. Like fighting a battle in the Land of Oz.

Some of the guys returned fire, giving the rest a chance to crawl back through the flowers to a dried out drainage ditch thirty yards away. Just as Chris made it over a dirt pile and dropped into the ditch, a trio of bullets smacked into the ground behind him. Right where he had been. If he'd crawled a few seconds slower through that field, he'd be a dead man.

It didn't feel like Oz after that.

The battle raged on for another twenty minutes. Finally, the lieutenant spotted little gray puffs of smoke through his binoculars, coming from just above a wall across the field a few hundred yards away. The mortar unit was able to suppress the fire long enough for two Apache helicopters to appear. Everyone cheered as their rockets made quick work of the insurgents.

After they had flown off, the battle was over.

That's when they'd discovered two of the guys providing covering fire had been hit. One was KIA, the other seriously wounded. He was airlifted out. Chris knew both guys, though not well. It was painful to think about losing them. They had sacrificed everything for the unit without a moment's hesitation. It unsettled him even more thinking how close he'd come to being casualty number three.

"Better get on your feet, Chris. Sarge said to come get you. We're moving out."

Chris looked up at Kyle. Kyle and he did everything together. Kyle's the one who helped Chris get over being dumped by his girlfriend last month. "She ain't worth it, man," he'd said. "The kind of woman who was worth it would wait." Chris didn't know why, but those words somehow broke him free of her spell. He reached up his hand.

"Hopefully," Kyle said, pulling Chris to his feet, "we'll get across that field today without getting shot at."

Chris bent down, grabbed his gear, including his detector.

"Well, at least we'll know there won't be any shots coming from the stone wall across that field. The Apaches pretty much leveled it."

"Hope you're right."

They walked toward the rest of the guys forming up near the same drainage ditch they had fought from yesterday.

"Okay guys," Sarge said, "you know what we gotta do here today. Pretty much complete the mission we started yesterday. Only now, after we get across this field we'll explore all the buildings around where the shots came from. We heard from some of the locals that the Taliban have cleared out. They're probably right, but we need to make sure. Chris, Kyle...you guys head out, clear the dirt path. We'll be right behind you. I got sharpshooters eyeing all the borders of this field. You worry about the ground at your feet."

Chris and Kyle walked up the dirt embankment to the edge of the poppy field. The rest of the guys started lining up behind them.

"Wish we had a tank out here," Kyle muttered. "Remember when we had tanks to cross these fields for us?"

Chris did. Tanks could absorb these small IED's way better than a man's legs. "Today it's just you and me," Chris said. He turned on his detector and started down the path, covering the same ground as yesterday. Back and forth, back and forth. Nice and slow. Kyle was behind him, far enough back that he wouldn't be injured if Chris stepped on a mine. The further Chris walked, the more tense he became. He tried to focus on the ground, on his job, tried to keep his tension from turning into fear.

It didn't work.

He and Kyle were sitting ducks out here. He kept walking but looked up, just for a second. Had to be a hundred places snipers could be hiding.

"You okay, Chris?"

"I'm fine."

"At least we know this part of the path is clear," Kyle said. They were covering the same ground as yesterday, before the ambush started.

They kept walking, the detectors moving back and forth. Chris's eyes focused on the metal detector's head. He wished the newer models had come in already. These could only detect metal. The Taliban had begun making mines with metal and plastic. The new detectors came with ground-penetrating radar, supposed to be able to detect everything.

He looked around. They were now beyond the spot they had stopped at yesterday. So far so good. He'd done this so many other times before, always without incident. The poppy farmers had been working in this field just a few days ago. They didn't have any problems. This was just another routine run, like all the others. Stay focused on that.

He glanced up again. They were halfway through the field now. "Hear anything?" he yelled back to Kyle over his shoulder.

"Not a sound."

A moment later, Chris did hear a sound. A click. It didn't come from his metal detector.

It was down by his left foot.

6

He was just about to shout "Mine!" when the ground erupted beneath his feet. A deafening explosion. Chris flew up and back, landed flat on his back in a patch of flowers. The impact knocked the wind out of him.

"What was that?" someone yelled.

"A mine," Kyle yelled. "Chris is down. Medic!"

Several others yelled medic.

"Nobody else move," Sarge said. "Chris, you all right?"

He couldn't speak. He was fighting for breath. Footsteps nearby.

"Kyle, stay put," Sarge yelled.

"I'm staying in his footprints. I gotta help him."

Chris was looking straight up into the sky. His left leg felt on fire. His right leg throbbed. He tried moving them. He could, but just barely. Kyle bent over him.

"Oh, man, Chris. I'm so sorry." He rested his hand on Chris's shoulder, looked down at Chris's legs, then back at his face.

Chris finally found his voice. "How bad is it?"

"Don't worry about it. Medic's on his way. We'll get you patched up."

It had to be bad. Kyle started applying a tourniquet to his left leg. He heard the Sarge yell, "You two, follow the medic with a litter. Footprints only. The rest of you men, back outta here slowly. Retrace your steps back to the ditch."

Soon the medic arrived, a corporal named Sam. Everybody liked Sam. He set his pack beside Chris, started pulling out rolls of bandages. Kyle helped him. Chris's pants were already ripped by the blast. Sam ripped them some more, above his knees. "You'll be okay, buddy. It hurt anywhere else beside your legs?"

"I don't think so. My back hurts a little. I think from the fall."

The medic looked over his shoulder. "Good, there's the purple smoke in the road. They've already called in the chopper. We'll get you patched up. They'll fly you out of here in no time."

"Did you even hear anything on the detector?" Kyle said.

"Nothing. Not a sound."

"Plastic mines," Sam said. "I been hearing about 'em. They figured out how to make 'em now with no metal at all."

"Then these things are useless," Kyle said, pointing to his metal detector. "They shouldn't send us out here anymore till we get those new ones."

"After this," Sam said, "maybe they won't." He started wrapping Chris's left foot, carefully. He'd already given Chris some morphine.

Kyle looked at him. "Course, what do you care, right? You just got a permanent ticket home."

He was smiling, but Chris could tell he was upset. He tried hard not to look at what Sam was doing down by his legs. The other two soldiers arrived with the litter. Kyle moved out of the way. They told Chris how sorry they were. Kyle told them about the mines being totally plastic.

Sam looked up at them. "He's as good as I can make him here.

Let's get him on the litter, so he's ready to go as soon as the chopper comes."

They carefully lifted Chris onto the litter. He was aching all over now, not just his legs. He tried not to groan out loud, but he couldn't help it.

Kyle walked out in front of them. "I'll lead the way. You guys walk in my steps." He looked at Chris. "You'll be all right. We'll get you back to the road in a sec."

They began walking back through the dirt path in the middle of the poppy field. Chris started to feel dizzy, like the sky was moving, so he closed his eyes. He must've passed out. The next thing he knew, he was in the road. Four guys were holding the corners of the litter, one of them was Kyle.

Off in the distance, he heard a helicopter coming.

He must have been moving in and out of consciousness. Chris didn't remember the copter landing, but he did remember being lifted onto it, seeing Kyle's face, as they slid him inside. He looked so sad. Kyle said something, but Chris couldn't hear it. So much noise. Dust and sand everywhere. Guys started strapping his litter down.

"We gotta get an IV in him," one of the medics said. He looked at Kyle. "We're about to pull out. You need to back away."

Kyle obeyed. "I'll check in on you, man" he yelled, as the chopper began to lift off the ground. "You're gonna be okay, Chris. You're gonna make it."

They were in the air. Chris looked up at the metal roof. It was vibrating, or was it him? Was he trembling? He glanced at the IV hanging from somewhere, then at the tube running down into his arm. He didn't even know they'd put it in.

He was thirsty. Felt someone tugging at his thigh. He didn't feel too much pain now. The meds must be working.

"Tourniquet's good," the medic said, looking at Chris. "That's good. That'll help."

Chris nodded but didn't know what he meant. He faded out for a few minutes. When he came to, the helicopter was banking heavily. He felt his weight shifting toward his feet. Suddenly, the green foil blanket they had wrapped him in came loose and started flapping in the wind. One of the medics fought with it and finally wrestled it back under the strap.

"We're almost there," he said. "We'll have you on the ground in a minute or two."

Chris felt weak, like he was going to pass out again. "How am I doing?"

"You're doing fine."

"Am I gonna make it?"

The medic nodded his head. "Definitely. Your vitals are pretty strong, considering." He looked down at Chris's legs, and his confident expression changed.

"How about the leg? Am I...am I gonna lose it?"

The medic looked out the window, as if he didn't hear.

"Please tell me. I gotta know."

"The right one's fine. Just cut up pretty good. And you've got some pretty good shrapnel wounds on your hands and arms."

"What about the left?"

He glanced at it, made a face. "I'll have to let the surgeon get back to you on that."

Part II

The Present

7

Kim

Humane Society
Summerville, Florida

Kim Harper got up from her desk and moved around. She'd been staring at the computer screen too long, working on a new training brochure. She needed to be around the animals again. "I'm going to walk through the A-kennel," she announced to Roger Hannon, her boss. They shared the same office space, one of the many challenges of working in a small, non-profit organization.

Roger banged away at the keyboard. He was developing a fundraising event planned for that weekend. He didn't seem to hear her.

She walked passed his desk. "Hey Rog, in case anyone stops in to see me, I'm going to check things out in the A-kennel. Marsha called me a little while ago, asked me to look in on a few of the dogs they just brought down there."

He swiveled in his chair. "Sure Kim, anyone shows up, I'll let 'em know." Then swiveled back.

Kim was the Animal Behavior Manager and dog trainer for the facility. Besides all the private and group training classes that involved, she was also responsible for a team that evaluated each dog that came in and assessed its ability to interact successfully with humans and other dogs.

She headed down the carpeted hallway past the copy room and the other administrative offices, then out through the door leading into the main part of the facility. Instantly, the muffled sound of barking dogs filled the room. It came from the double set of doors on her left. She was just about to open the door when she noticed Marsha standing at the other end of the room, holding the door open to the main lobby for the adoption area. She waved at Kim, a concerned look on her face. Then again, Marsha wore that look half the time.

Kim headed her way. "What's the matter?"

Marsha waited till she got closer then let the lobby door close by itself. "I just called you. Roger said you were headed this way."

"I was going to check on those dogs you called me about earlier."

"They can wait." She looked through the glass panel in the upper half of the door toward the lobby. "See that Hispanic woman there sitting in the waiting area?"

Kim looked where she pointed. "The one holding that nervous-looking retriever mix?" Kim said.

"That's her."

"That's not one of ours." Kim would've known if they had a dog that nice getting ready to be adopted.

"No, she came into the adoption area by mistake. She's here to surrender the dog. I was just about to send her over to Intake, but then we started talking. We weren't even talking a few minutes before she starts crying. And I don't mean a few tears. I thought she was going to start sobbing if I pressed any further."

That wasn't unusual behavior for people getting ready to give up their pet. Some people did it without an ounce of emotion. Like they were totally done with the dog and relieved to finally be free of it. But most people really struggled to let go when that moment finally arrived. Some lost it completely. "So, what's her story," Kim asked.

"I was thinking I should let you hear it for yourself. You're so good with these one-on-one things. There's some special circumstances with this situation, and I'm—"

"Good special or bad special?"

"Sad special," Marsha said. "The dog's not really hers. Well, it is now. She's been watching it quite a while. But clearly, she's not a dog person. And now..."

"I guess I can get with her," Kim said. "Why don't you introduce us, and I'll take her into the counseling room?"

"Great."

"Is the dog friendly?"

"Totally. Maybe too friendly."

Just then, an older couple came through the front door and the dog lunged at the man, almost knocking him down. Kim noticed, though, his tail wagged the entire time.

"As you can see," Marsha said, "he's a little out of control.

Kim opened the door to let Marsha through, then followed right behind her. They walked past the counter on the left, where several workers sat interviewing a number of people interested in adopting dogs. The waiting area was up ahead. It was nothing more than a row of padded chairs lined up along the outside window. The woman and dog were the only ones there.

As they approached, the dog started jumping toward them, but Kim didn't see an ounce of aggression in him. He was just a loving goofball, probably starved for attention. He almost pulled the woman off her chair. Kim came closer but didn't acknowledge him, just the woman. This was intentional. She was sending the dog a calming signal.

"Hi, Ma'am," Marsha said. "I'm so sorry, I've already forgotten your name."

"It's Alicia, Alicia Perez. Finley, calm down. Sit!"

The dog ignored both commands. His whole body trembled with excitement. *You don't have a clue why you're here, do you boy?* Kim thought.

"Alicia, this is Kim Harper. She's a certified dog trainer, and—"

"I'm not here for training," Alicia said. "I told you why I'm here." Tears welled up in her eyes.

"I know. I remember. That's why I got Kim. I think she can really help you through…what you're dealing with."

Alicia looked at Kim, who held out her hand. Alicia shook it but said, "You're not going to try to talk me into keeping him, are you?"

"No, Ma'am. Not if you're sure of your decision."

"I am sure. I don't want to be. I mean, I wish I didn't have to do this, but I have no choice." The tears now rolled down her cheeks. She wiped them with her hand.

"I'll tell you what, Alicia. Is it okay if I call you Alicia?"

Alicia nodded.

"Why don't you and—what did you say his name was?"

"Finley."

"Why don't you and Finley follow me to this room down the hallway? We can talk better in there without all the noise and distraction going on here in the lobby."

"I guess I can do that."

Kim stepped back and Alicia stood. "I just want to hear your story, that's all. Whenever an owner surrenders a dog, we always try to get as much information as we can. It will help us better care for your dog while he's here, and help us find the best possible home for him in the future."

"The future? So you're saying if I leave him here, you won't be putting Finley to sleep? My daughter said that's probably what's gonna happen with an older dog like him."

Kim reached down and patted Finley's head, since he had calmed down and was now sitting at her side. "How old is Finley?"

"He's almost three."

"I don't think you have a thing to worry about," Kim said. "We only euthanize dogs as a last resort, when there are absolutely no other options. I can already see, that's not going to be Finley's story. He's going to make somebody a wonderful forever friend."

Alicia sighed audibly. "I'm so relieved."

"I'm going to leave you two," Marsha said. "You're obviously in good hands."

"So," Kim said. "If you'll just follow me down the hall here, I want to hear all about Finley's story."

8

Finley

When they first came here, Finley was feeling nervous about this place. So many conflicting scents. But now that this other woman was here, he started to relax. Something about her was different. She made him feel calm.

The mother had brought him here. As a general rule, she was often tense but, on the drive over, Finley sensed her tension was much higher than usual. The odd thing was, how kindly she had talked to him the whole way here, even patted him on the head several times. She rarely took him anywhere in the car.

Chaz used to take him everywhere he went, back when he was here. But Finley hadn't seen Chaz for so long. His scent was even starting to fade in the apartment.

Although she had been nice to him, Finley was confused. It was obvious she wasn't happy. Several times when he looked at her, he saw tears in her eyes. She cried again just a few moments ago, talking to this new woman they just met. She and the mother had exchanged names, but Finley hadn't heard it enough times to remember. The other woman they'd first met had just walked away. Now they were going somewhere else, following this new woman down a hallway.

"We can talk in here," the new woman said. "If you shut the door, you can let Finley off his leash. And if he's thirsty, there's a bowl of water on the floor in the corner."

The mother sat in a chair. "Maybe I should keep him on his leash. I don't want him jumping on you."

"That's okay. I'm used to that." The woman sat also. "I actually know how to make him stop."

"I can't even imagine that," the mother said. "Finley not jumping on people. He's never mean when he does it. He just gets so excited."

"I can tell he's not an aggressive dog."

Kim. Finley felt drawn to this woman. He came a little closer to Kim.

She leaned forward and scratched his head behind his ears. "He's a total sweetie, aren't you Finley?" She turned around in her chair, put her hands on the table. "Are you okay with me taking a few notes as we chat?"

"That's fine."

"Looks like he's mostly golden retriever," Kim said.

"That's what we were told. My son brought him home as a puppy. I think he got him from here."

"That's possible," Kim said." I don't remember him, but so many dogs come through here. Whose name was he adopted under? He's probably in our system."

"My son, Chaz."

"So, let me guess...your son can't keep him anymore, and he's a little too much for you."

Finley heard the mother sigh. Something had just upset her.

"I'm sorry. Did I say something wrong?"

Finley walked around the table and sat next to the mother. She was crying again.

"It's not your fault." She reached for a tissue from a box in the center of the table." The mother reached down and actually patted Finley on the shoulder, then left her hand on him.

This was so unlike her. He leaned against her chair.

"You're right. My son can't keep him anymore. He was killed in Afghanistan a few weeks ago."

"Oh, no. That's terrible. I'm so sorry. I feel awful now. That was so insensitive of me."

"No, don't feel bad. You couldn't know. The worst part, I think, was he was due to come home in a few weeks. All these months I was so worried about him being killed by the Taliban. But his tour was all done. He was supposed to be out of danger. He was killed in a helicopter crash."

"Was he a pilot?"

"No, just a regular soldier. They were being transported somewhere, supposed to be away from a dangerous place to a safer one. I don't know all the details. They don't tell you very much when these things happen."

"I'm so sorry, Alicia."

"Me, too. I've actually been watching Finley here are for a good while, ever since Chaz left for boot camp."

Chaz. Finley's ears perked right up. That's the second time she said his name.

"His girlfriend was helping me the first few months. But then she started seeing somebody else, I guess. I thought about bringing him down here so many times. It was so hard taking care of him myself. I'm not even a dog person. I was just doing it for Chaz. He sent me money every month for Finley's expenses, and every time we'd talk on the phone, the first thing he'd ask about was Finley.

How's Finley doing? Is he eating okay? He'd even want to talk to Finley on the phone. Then before he'd hang up, he'd apologize a hundred times for me having to watch him, and he promised me he'd take him off my hands the minute he got home. So, I'd say yes and promise him I'd hold out a little longer."

The mother turned in her chair. She was looking right at Finley. She looked so sad.

"But now," she continued, "I can't hold out any longer. It's not just all the extra work to keep up with him. It's hard to even look at him." She looked back at Kim. "Every time I see him, I think of Chaz. I know it's normal to be grieving now. But I'm not sure I'll ever get over this. Somehow, having Finley around makes my loss feel even more painful. I don't know if that makes any sense."

"I can see why that would be a challenge," Kim said. "It sounds like he and Chaz were very close."

Finley kept hearing Chaz's name. They were definitely talking about him. Was he coming here? Was that why the mother brought him to this place, to see Chaz? But why was she so sad then? The few times Chaz had come home since he'd been away, the mother was always very happy.

"Chaz absolutely adored this dog. And Finley loved him just as much. I'm afraid he hasn't had much of a life with me, and it's not going to get any better from here. Are you sure you can find him a home?"

"I know we can."

"Even though he gets out of control sometimes? Looking at him now, you'd never know it. But he's usually quite a handful."

"Believe it or not," Kim said, "problems like that are fairly fixable with some training. In fact, most of the reasons people give for surrendering their dogs stem from problems we can fix with training. I'm not saying that to change your mind. I perfectly understand why you're doing this. I'm just saying the problems you've had with Finley aren't serious enough to keep us from finding him a good home."

"I'm glad. Because he is a good dog. I think it'll ease my mind at least a little if I know he's happy living with someone who can really take care of him."

No one said anything a few moments.

"So what do we do now?" the mother said.

"Well, normally I would take you both down to our Intake area. But I don't want to put you through that, or make you share this all over again with someone else. I can take care of that for you, if you want."

"Thank you. I appreciate that."

"Then you two stay right here for a minute. I'll go get the paperwork and be right back." Kim got up and left the room, closing the door behind her.

Finley waited there a few moments then walked back to the mother. She was wiping her eyes with tissues. He sat and leaned against her, but she didn't acknowledge him.

Some time went by then the woman, Kim, returned. The mother still hadn't touched him or said anything to Finley, so he was happy when Kim returned. She instantly spoke his name and looked right at him. When she sat, he hurried around the table to see if she would pet him, and she did. They talked for a few more minutes, while the mother filled out some papers.

After, she said, "So, is that it? Is there anything else I have to do?"

"No, that's it," Kim said. "I'll take care of everything from here. We probably should put the leash back on him."

"Can you do that?"

"Sure, I can do that. Do you want me to give you a minute or two, to be alone with him and say goodbye?"

"No, I think that would be too hard. I can tell he'll be in good hands here with you." She stood up and extended her hand. "Thank you so much. You made this a lot easier for me than I expected."

They shook hands. Finley watched as the mother opened the door, walked out and closed it behind her. She never even looked at him. He didn't understand her mood. Where was she going? What should he do now?

9

Kim

She stood in the hall a moment as Alicia walked away. Kim could tell even from the back that she was crying. This was always such an emotional time, which is one of the reasons why Kim didn't work in the Intake area fulltime. Occasionally, she was called in to offer counseling when one of the workers believed an owner wasn't fully committed to surrendering their dog.

People often brought their dogs to the Humane Society as a last resort, believing that their problems were insurmountable. Most dog behavior problems are fixable. And often the one who needed the most training were the owners themselves.

But Kim knew that wasn't the case here with Finley. It broke her heart to hear Alicia's story. A mother's worst nightmare, losing a child. She couldn't imagine how she'd ever get over the loss or the grief.

As Alicia left the facility through the glass exit door, Kim noticed that she never looked back. That wasn't surprising. Finley instantly reacted to her departure, whining and stretching to the end of his leash. As she disappeared down the sidewalk, he began to pull even harder toward the door.

Kim didn't yank him back. Instead, she tried to entice him back with some cheese and called his name in a high-pitched, happy voice. Neither trick got his attention. That wasn't surprising, either. She knew a dog like Finley would struggle with this separation almost as much as Alicia did. Probably more. Finley couldn't understand what was going on. There was no way to tell him what had just happened, no way to help him process what he was going through.

Scientific studies had proven dogs experience intense emotions, not unlike humans. They could become very excited during happy events but also very depressed when experiencing a significant disappointment. Of course, Kim didn't need to see scientific evidence to know this. She'd studied dog behavior long enough and had spent enough time being around dogs to know how deeply affected they could get from situations caused by their owner's decisions and choices.

She called out Finley's name once more and gently tugged the leash in the opposite direction. Finley resisted at first but reluctantly complied. She quickly walked down the hall toward the Intake area. The thing to do now was to get his mind on something else as quickly as possible. It wouldn't help his disposition on a deeper level, but the temporary distraction might do a little to ease his pain.

As they walked through the door into the Intake area, Finley's ears instantly perked up. There were two other dogs standing by the counter with their owners and one sitting in the waiting area. Kim tried not to make eye contact with any of the workers, lest they try to suck her into dealing with their situation. She really needed to get back to the A-Kennel to check on Marsha's request, then get back to her desk and finish that training brochure.

She did notice Chuck, the Intake manager, was just finishing up with someone and heading back to his desk. "Hey Chuck, can I talk to you a minute?"

"Sure Kim, what's up?" He turned and walked toward her. They connected at the end of the counter, away from the others. He looked down and noticed Finley. "Who do we have here? Some dog you're working with?"

"No, at least not now. His name's Finley." Hearing his name, he looked up at her, so she patted his head. "He's a new surrender. I just met with his owner a few minutes ago."

"Really?"

"I know. That's not something I usually do, but the woman came into the adoption area by mistake. Marsha was just going to send her over here, but then they got to talking, and I happened to walk by. It's kind of a long story. I took some notes, so I'll fill in the details on the paperwork myself. But I was wondering if you'd take care of him yourself. He's kind of a special case. His real owner was a soldier killed in Afghanistan a couple of weeks ago."

"Oh my."

"Yeah. His mom was keeping Finley for him, for quite a while now I think. He was supposed to be coming home in a few weeks. But now that he's not, she just doesn't think she could take care of him anymore. She's not really a dog person, and seeing him just—"

"Brings up the pain," Chuck said. "I get it. You don't want me to skip the normal intake procedures with him, do you?"

"No. Still have the team do the normal assessment they do with any dog that gets turned in. But I can already tell, it'll just be a formality. He's gonna pass with flying colors."

Chuck leaned over the counter and patted Finley's head. "Yeah, you can see, he's got a really sweet disposition." He opened the top to the counter and walked through. "I'll go ahead and take him back for you. If you want, you can use my desk to finish up the paperwork. I've got a few things to take care of back there."

"Thanks. I think I'll do that." She handed Finley's leash to Chuck. She looked down at Finley, who seemed confused by the exchange. The poor thing. Nothing he experienced for quite a while would make any sense to him.

"So you figure," Chuck said, "after we do his assessment we'll just leave him in the stray kennel for twenty-four hours, then bring him over to the adoption kennel?" The stray kennel wasn't just for stray dogs. That's where all the dogs were brought when they first came into the facility.

"That's what I was thinking," Kim said. "There's no reason to leave him over here any longer than that. There's virtually no chance of the owner changing her mind."

10

Amy

Brookins Correctional Facility
15 Miles west of Summerville, FL

After spending almost two years in the general population without a moment's privacy, Amy couldn't believe what she was seeing. It wasn't much bigger than the cell she had lived in, but there was only one bed, and the room had its own small desk and chair. They even called the rooms dorms over here, not cells. Best of all, it had a window. "This is mine? This room, is all mine?"

"You and your dog's, if you get one," Rita Hampton said. Inmates called each other either by nicknames or their last names. Amy didn't like it much but went along with it. In her head, she always used their first name. Hampton, or Rita, was showing Amy around. She was a seasoned vet in the Prison Paws & Pals program. Rita had trained over twenty dogs so far and was one of the first inmates to qualify for the program.

"*If* I get one?" Amy said. "I thought everyone in the program got a dog."

"You're right, Wallace. I should have said *when*. That's where he'll sleep, in that crate at the foot of your bed."

Amy looked to where Rita was pointing. "He's gotta sleep in a cage? That doesn't seem right."

Rita took a few steps inside the room. "We don't call 'em cages. They're crates. Anyway, dogs aren't like us. We never put them in their crate for a punishment. To them, it's a good place. A place where they feel safe. A place all their own."

Amy hadn't felt safe since she'd been in prison, something she prayed about every day. But she had felt the tension in the air drop by half as soon as she came into this place. "Do you...ever feel safe? I mean here, now that you're in this program?"

"Yeah, I do," Rita said. "And you will too...eventually. I know what you're going through. It was a few years ago, but I still remember. Takes a while to realize how different things are around here. You know how hard it was to get approved for this program? Every girl in here went through the same thing. And they know what it's like out there." She pointed toward the main prison area. "And they know if they want to stay in here, they gotta keep earning their place, keep doing the things that got them here in the first place. I'm not just talking about how well we train the dogs. I'm talking about how we treat each other, and the people who run this program."

Amy liked the sound of this. It shouldn't be that hard to start treating people decently again. She'd had to learn how to act like such a totally different person for so long now. Pretend to be somebody hard, somebody that wasn't afraid all the time. It left her exhausted every day. What Rita just said sounded almost too good to be true. "You can call me Amy," she said. "When we're alone, I mean."

Rita looked at her a moment.

"I don't mean anything by it. It's just out there I had to call everyone by their last name. In here—"

"I'm okay with that, I suppose," Rita said. "When we're alone. It's Amy, right?"

Amy nodded. "Where are all the other girls, all the dogs they're training?"

"They're here, just outside. It's graduation day. I think if you look out your window to the right, you can just see the edge of the tent they set up out in the yard."

Amy walked over and looked. She saw the corner of a big white tent. Well, it was more like a tarp or a canvas pavilion. It didn't have any walls, just a roof to block the sun. She could just make out the last few rows of chairs. The people she saw weren't wearing prison garb. "Who are they, people here from outside? The ones getting the dogs?"

Rita came over and looked. "Some of them. Most of the dogs we train are for military vets. I can't see any one that looks like a vet from here. They might be sitting toward the front. Those look like city or county officials. Some of them come out for graduation day. Sometimes even news people."

"How come you're not out there? Didn't you train a dog this time?"

Rita walked back toward the middle of the room, stood on a little brown throw rug and faced the doorway. Amy heard her sigh out loud.

"What's wrong?"

"I did train a dog. Amber."

"Did something happen to her?"

"No, she's fine. She graduated with flying colors."

"So why aren't you with her out there?"

Rita turned around, forced a smile. "She's gone. The vet I

trained her for moved to Tampa. He had to leave two days ago. Amber was all ready. All the dogs really graduated last week when we finished the program. Today is just the ceremony. So me and Amber said our goodbyes on Wednesday. When Miss Bridget mentioned this morning you were coming over today, I volunteered to give you the grand tour."

"I appreciate that."

"I'm glad, but I didn't do it for you." She sighed again and looked out the window.

"Must be hard," Amy said. "That's one thing I wondered about, coming over here. Spending all that time with a dog, getting really close to it, then having to give it away to somebody else. Must be hard."

"It is. I loved Amber. I loved her like...well, I never had any kids, but if I did. I've loved all the dogs I trained. If it were possible, I would've kept them. Any one of them. But it's not possible and, to tell you the truth, I wouldn't want to keep them shut up in here with me. They should be free, be able to go for long walks in parks, take trips in the car."

Amy leaned up against the metal headboard of her bed. "So do you just get used to it? Swallow the pain?" That's something she had learned to get pretty good at, living here.

"Pretty much," Rita said. "It definitely helps getting to spend time with the military vets we give these dogs to. We overlap with them the last few weeks of our training, so they'll know what to do with the dogs when they get home on their own. But you can really see the difference these dogs make in their lives. Some of them write you a few months later, and you just know you're doing the right thing." Rita looked out the window. "I think working with these dogs is the only thing I've ever done right in my life. Certainly since I got put in here." She walked into the hallway.

"You want to watch the rest of it?"

"Can we go out there now, even though it's already started?"

"No. The only door into the yard from here is right near where the podium is. We'd catch it for being such a distraction. But the main training room down this hall is closer to where everyone's sitting. There's several windows in there. You can pretty much see the whole thing."

"Sure, I'd like that."

They entered a large open room. Against the far wall, trays of subs, desserts and bottles of soda were laid out on folding tables. As Rita said, there was a row of windows along the outside wall on the left. Through the shears you could see the whole ceremony.

They stood there a while and watched.

"So how long you in for?" Rita asked.

"Got a three-year sentence," Amy said. "Served two. Waiting to find out how much gain time I'll get being accepted into this program. But I think I could be getting out in six months or so." It was hard to believe, even hearing it out of her own mouth.

"That so? You might only have time to work with one or two dogs then, depending on what kind of training they get. You ever trained one before?"

"No. The truth is, I never even owned a dog. I've always loved them and always wanted one, but my brother had bad allergies growing up, so we could never get one. When I got out on my own, I always lived in apartments that didn't allow them." She looked at Rita. "They're going to teach me how to train them, right?"

Rita nodded. "They'll show you everything you need to know. When I first started, I was clueless. But it's amazing how much these dogs can learn when they get the right kind of training."

They got quiet again as they looked out the window. Talking

about her brother's allergies made her feel sad. Last she heard, he was better now, but she'd pretty much lost all contact with him and her parents three years ago when they threw her out.

She'd written them a few times when she got to the prison. For the first time in a long time, she'd have a stable address for a few years.

They never wrote back.

The only letter she'd gotten was from her brother's new wife, Cassie. She didn't even know he and Cassie had gotten engaged, that they were even a couple. Cassie was one of her friends back in high school. Another casualty of Amy's meth addiction. But her letter had given Amy a little hope. Cassie had become a Christian, urged Amy to try and hook up with a prison ministry she'd read about. One that helped drug addicts get freed up while inside.

So Amy did.

Those people had helped her get right with God again, and turn her life around. She was sure God had opened up the door for her to get into this dog training program. The only sad thing was...that was the only letter she'd gotten from Cassie.

Months later, Amy had written her back to thank her and tell her how she was doing, but the letter came back with a sticker saying no one by that name lived at that address.

Guess she had moved. That was almost a year ago.

11

After the graduation ceremony, most of those in attendance piled into the room where Amy and Rita stood, including all the female inmates with the dogs they had trained. Standing with them, Amy supposed, were the veterans who would soon bring the dogs home. None of the vets wore uniforms, though a few wore camo pants. The dogs were all excited but did their best to behave and remain seated beside their trainers.

Several of the vets were squatting down, engaging their new pets. Talking to them, patting their head, itching behind their ears. The dogs were certainly friendly and responded well to them, but it was also obvious most of their attention was centered on their trainers, not their new owners.

Although there were plenty of smiles in the room, Amy could feel the inmates' tension and see it in their eyes. A few of them blinked back tears.

Just then, Captain Bridget Cummings, the woman in charge of the program and the emcee during the ceremony, spoke up in a loud voice. The inmates called her either Miss Bridget or Boss Lady. "Excuse me everyone. As you can see, we have some wonderful food laid out on these tables for lunch. The subs were donated by a local deli. There are three or four different kinds. We cut them in smaller sections, so feel free to try a few different ones. To start off, let's have the trainers hand the leashes to the dogs' new owners, then get in line for their food. Then you can switch places."

Rita walked up to Amy and said quietly, "You better get in line, too. This is our lunchtime."

Amy followed Rita's cue and got in at the end of the line. "I can't remember the last time I ate food brought in from the outside." Several of the other inmates already in line greeted Rita with a nod or a few words. They all looked at Amy, but no one said anything.

Halfway through the line, an inmate with dirty blonde hair standing in front of Rita said, "So, you're the new girl. Wallace, right?"

Amy nodded.

"She's taking Hogan's place," Rita said.

Amy didn't know Jenna Hogan personally, but she did know she had been released from prison recently after serving seven years of a ten-year term.

"Hogan was good people," the inmate said. "You've got some big shoes to fill. She was especially good with the dogs."

Amy picked up two small sections of a turkey and swiss cheese sub. She didn't know how to respond. She didn't know the first thing about training dogs. When the captain had interviewed her, she said that didn't matter, that they would train her themselves. A retired couple who'd worked with dogs all their lives, the Maloney's, were actually the ones who'd put this program together. They were supposed to be the ones who trained Amy. She hadn't met the Maloney's yet, but she knew who they were. Miss Bridget had introduced them during the first graduation ceremony.

Right now, they were sitting in two metal chairs close to the front door, talking with a veteran. He held the leash for a mostly-white pit mix with big brown spots. Amy had always been afraid of pits. Not from any personal experience, just from their reputation. The captain had told her she needed to get over it if she wanted to be in the program. At least a third of the dogs were pit mixes. She'd also said much of their bad reputation was undeserved, and that the ones that they brought in the program had all been thoroughly evaluated.

Amy hoped so. Glancing at the dogs in the room, at least a third of them *were* pits, and their faces and body language looked anything but fierce. The facial expression of the brown and white pit sitting next to the vet by the front door almost resembled a human smile.

She and Rita finished getting their food and found two empty metal chairs to sit in. Amy said, "Have you ever trained a pit?"

"Sure, I have. Amber was a pit mix. She had the sweetest disposition a dog could possibly have. And they're smart, too. Way above average. And loyal. You can't find a more loyal pet."

"Where does their bad reputation come from? Seems like every time you hear about someone being attacked by a dog on the news, it's a pit."

"I know that's how it seems," Rita said. "But it's not really what's going on. You're too young to remember this, but when I was your age and even younger, Dobermans were the bad dogs. They were the ones always attacking people in the news. I was terrified of them. I saw one coming down the sidewalk, I crossed the street. Back then, you never heard of pits attacking people. Now it's all you ever hear. So what happened, Dobermans started being nice and pits started being mean?" She took a big bite out of her roast beef sub. "Brenda showed us a video about it," she said, still chewing.

"About pits?"

She nodded. "About the bad rap they always get. In the video, there was a World War I Army poster of a pit in uniform. He was, like, the military mascot back then. The video showed all kinds of clips from old black-and-white movies. Pits in every one of them. Did you ever hear of Spanky and Our Gang?"

"No."

"It's a kids' show made back in the thirties. We used to watch reruns of it when I was a kid. The main dog in the show was a pit. Can you imagine people using a pit in a kids' TV show today? Some people want to ban them altogether, because they think they're so vicious. But they're not. Not unless they're raised that way."

Amy thought about it. What Rita said kind of made sense. She just figured pits were some new kind of breed, and that's why you never used to hear about them before. But if they've been around all that time... "So, why do you only hear about pits anymore? Why are they the only ones in the news?"

Rita set her sub back on her paper plate. "Because a bunch of jerky guys started breeding them to fight, so they could make money betting off the dogs. Think the video said it started back in the eighties. As the reputation for being fight dogs grew, other jerky guys, like drug dealers and gang members wanted them for guard dogs. And they all had this attitude about them. You know, my dog can take your dog. So these dogs, bred to be mean, got out of the yard sometimes and do what they were trained to do. But if you look at these dogs in here, they couldn't be any sweeter. And none of the dogs we've ever trained, pits or otherwise, have ever come back because they attacked someone."

Amy felt relieved to hear this. She looked around the room at each of the pits. They acted just like every other dog here. Affectionate, calm and obedient. It was hard to think, as ignorant as she was now, that she'd ever be able to get a dog to act this way.

Still, she had to admit if she was being honest…she hoped her first dog wouldn't be a pit.

12

Chris

The sense of danger was palpable.

All around him, people went about their business as though everything was fine. Maybe for them, it was. They didn't know what Chris knew, hadn't seen what he'd seen.

In a single moment, everything could change.

Snipers didn't wear a uniform. They dressed like everyone else. As he crossed the intersection, his eyes involuntarily scanned every window and doorway, especially in the upper floors around him. Looking for a curtain that moved, a shadow out of place, or even the barrel of a gun.

On the sidewalks, it wasn't just the men you had to watch out for. In this war, the women, children, even the elderly could turn on you, would turn on you. This kind of religious fanaticism transcended rational boundaries. War was always terrible and scary, and there were plenty of ways a soldier could get killed. But at least there were some basic norms in other wars you could count on, a few things that made sense.

Not anymore.

"Hey man, you getting on?"

Chris turned his head toward the voice. A teenager with long blonde hair holding a skateboard.

"The bus is here. You getting on?"

Chris looked at where the kid was pointing. At the curb, a city bus had just pulled up and opened its doors. Some people were beginning to board. "Yeah, I am. Thanks."

The kid went ahead of him.

Chris remembered where he was; the tension and sense of impending danger temporarily subsided. He looked both ways, then behind him. It seemed okay, so he carefully climbed the bus steps.

Steps were still a challenge with his prosthetic leg. He knew it was firmly attached, so it wasn't going anywhere, but lifting it so high made him nervous. He quickly surveyed the scene on the bus, individually checking out the handful of passengers.

"You have to take a seat," the bus driver said, "so I can get going."

"Sure," Chris said. "Sorry."

The teenager with the skateboard sat in one of the front rows. The aisle was clear now, so Chris headed all the way to the back. He was relieved to find the back row empty. Made him feel a little more secure. He hated leaving his back exposed. Anything could happen behind you.

Thankfully, he rarely had to take the city bus. He was on his way to pick up his car, which he'd dropped off yesterday to his mechanic. Like his nerves, his brakes were shot. It was a hassle, in some ways, going to this guy. But he'd known him since high school. Chris knew little about car engines. He could trust this guy not to take him to the cleaners. But his shop wasn't big enough to offer the use of a rental car while you waited. That morning, he'd gotten the call. His car was ready to pick up whenever he was.

Just a few more miles to go until they reached the street. He should be fine until then. Everybody in the bus seemed legit.

Since he'd come home, he didn't venture out too much. Going out and mingling with the general public always made him tense. His conscious mind knew he wasn't in any harm. Not anymore. But these feelings would come over him. Some days worse than others.

But for now, he was doing all right. He'd pick up his car, maybe drive-through a McDonald's for a Big Mac and fries, and just make it in time for his job interview at the golf course.

Suddenly, the bus stopped. The doors opened.

Chris sat up, eyeing the doorway, trying to get a glimpse of who was getting on. Maybe he'd get lucky, and it would just be an old lady. Somebody he didn't have to worry about.

13

Summerville Oaks Golf Course

Chris was starting to tense up as he sat in a straight back chair waiting for his interview to start with the Maintenance Manager. He needed this job. Not so much for the money. These days it was just him and he lived simply, so he could pretty much make it every month on his disability pay alone.

He needed the job for sanity's sake.

Between his physical therapy sessions, he mostly sat around all day with nothing to do but think. Thinking wasn't healthy. Not these days. It never led him anywhere but down.

The inside door to the manager's office opened, startling him. Another thing he couldn't seem to control...overreacting to sudden noises. He did it all the time. He'd had some counseling and watched a number of videos, enough to know he was wrestling with PTSD. They hadn't determined his final rating yet, but his physical therapist said it was often high among vets with amputation injuries. He was told his disability check would increase once the rating was finalized. But Chris didn't want a high rating. He didn't want to stay dependent on the government, or become even more so.

He wanted to beat this thing.

Chris looked up into the smiling face of Tom Korman, the man he was there to see.

"You ready?" Tom said.

Chris nodded. "Sure."

Tom waited a moment. Chris understood he was supposed to get up and follow him into the office. He did his best not to limp. He'd been working on smoothing out his stride for months. His physical therapist assured him he was getting closer every week. The goal was that no one would know he even had an artificial leg if he wore long pants.

Tom walked around his desk and sat in his chair. It squeaked as he leaned back. "Have a seat." He lifted a manila folder and opened it. "I've been looking over your application. You filled in all the blocks, but your answers were a little short."

"Short? There wasn't a whole lot of space to write. At least with some of them. Feel free to ask me if you want any more info."

"I will. Actually, I need to."

Chris wondered what he meant.

"Before we get into this, I want you to know most of the guys that work here are ex-military. Those two guys you passed on your way in here, for example. One was an Army ranger, the other used to work on A-10s."

The office they were sitting in was actually an enclosed area tucked in the corner of a larger, metal maintenance building. To get here, Chris had walked by a guy washing golf carts and another guy repairing a large ride-on lawn mower.

"You don't *have* to be from the military to work here," Tom said. "It's not a requirement, of course. I just said that to put you at ease. The golf course owner's a retired Marine colonel. For a lot of good reasons, he prefers to hire vets whenever he can."

That was reassuring.

Tom sat up a little straighter. "I was a tank commander in Iraq during Desert Storm. Retired from the Army in 2010, started working here shortly after."

Chris guessed that Tom was in his mid-forties. He spoke like he was still a commander.

"Quite a few of the guys on our maintenance crew have some measure of disability, mostly varying levels of PTSD. You'd be the first one missing a limb. I know it's probably hard to talk about, and I won't ask you to talk about it much beyond this interview, but I'd like to know what happened, at least a little. And maybe a little about what you've been doing since. Looks like this'll be your first job after your medical discharge."

"It is," Chris said. "And I don't mind you asking. I don't like talking about it much, but I know talking's supposed to help." Chris didn't particularly get this aspect of the therapy. He knew lots of guys with injuries far more severe than his, who talked about it freely. Even displayed their war wounds openly as badges of honor. He wasn't quite there yet.

Really, not even close.

"I lost the leg stepping on a mine two years ago. We were on patrol in Helmand Province, near Marjah. I don't know if you've heard of it. We weren't in the mountains or the desert. It was mostly poppy fields, where they grow their opium. Worst part of it is, I was a minesweeper. I was actually using my detector when I stepped on the mine."

"It wasn't working?"

"No, it worked fine. Problem was, it's a metal detector. The Taliban started making mines with plastic."

"So you were the one who actually stepped on it," Tom said. "I thought maybe you were just nearby, since you only lost the one leg. I've talked with guys who lost both, some even an arm from taking the full hit from one of those anti-personnel mines."

"I know. I got to know some of them pretty well when I first got home. Compared to them, I was lucky. You asked what I've been doing since I got home. They sent me to Brooke Army Medical Center in San Antonio. Stayed there for over year. I think I was the only guy there who'd stepped on a mine and only lost a leg."

Tom looked down at the application a moment. "Do you think you're really ready to start work, Chris? I mean, physically. There's nothing here about your limitations. I know their goal is to get you to where you can do everything you're capable of doing. How far would you say you are on that spectrum? If I was to hire you on our maintenance crew, there's a whole range of jobs and tasks. Some of them are quite strenuous. Some, not so much. I'm going to need to know what you can and can't do."

"I think I can do quite a lot," Chris said. "I still experience some pain in my bum leg. Even the one that's still mine. It got banged up pretty good in the blast, too. But it's healed up a lot. I'm getting used to the pain levels, and they're getting less as time goes by."

"I'm glad to hear that. But I think I'm going to need something more specific. What I'd like to ask you to do is get in touch with your doctor, or at least your physical therapist, and ask them to give me something in writing that spells out your medical restrictions. As time goes by, if things improve, they can always reevaluate you."

"I can do that," Chris said. "If I get that, are you saying you'll give me a job?"

"If there's enough things out here that they will qualify you for.

I can think of one thing you can probably do even now. Did you drive a car here?"

Chris nodded. "Fortunately, I lost my left leg. So I can drive an automatic."

"Well, then you can probably operate our main ride-on mowers. You only need one foot to work the pedals. Mostly you'll use your hands. Lots of grass to mow out here."

"I'm sure I can do it," Chris said.

Tom leaned back on his chair again. "I think you probably can. I can hire you part-time to start off. But if I get that medical paper back saying you can do more, we can talk about increasing your hours."

"I'll call them right after I leave here."

"Can I ask you why you decided to apply for this job? Reading over your application, I don't see where you've ever done this kind of work before."

Chris hesitated to answer. But Tom had been pretty upfront with him, so he decided just to say it. "To be honest, I'm struggling with some PTSD symptoms myself. Most days, I'm fine." That wasn't entirely true. "But sometimes things get to me. I did some reading about it on the internet, about the kind of jobs people with PTSD are best suited for. One of them was this, working outside with your hands. Landscaping, yardwork. They say it keeps your mind busy, besides that..." He thought maybe he shouldn't say the next part.

"You don't have to be around people very much," Tom said.

Chris nodded. "That never used to be a problem for me before this." He tapped his leg. "I was almost always a people-person before. But now...I don't know why, I just prefer being alone more."

"You don't have to explain," Tom said. The other guys are the same way. Guess it just goes with the territory."

Chris nodded. He didn't really want to agree. He wanted to be the way he used to be. But he didn't see how he could ever be that guy again.

14

Kim

Summerville Humane Society

There, that was the last one. For now at least.

Kim set the phone down on her desk. For the last hour, she had been returning phone calls. Her ear felt numb and her left hand ached. At some point during the cluster of calls, Ellen, who worked in the stray kennel, dropped a note on her desk. It had to do with Finley; the retriever mix who came in last week.

Kim had taken a particular interest in him. Not just because of his heartbreaking story, but because she had promised the mother of Finley's owner they would find him a good home. So far, things were not going as planned. She picked up the note and read:

Finley still not doing well -
Need to speak with you.

She pushed her chair back from her desk and got up, still holding the note. "Roger, I'm heading back to the stray kennel to take care of this. You need anything while I'm up?"

It took Roger a moment to disconnect from his computer screen. "What? Oh, sure. Go right ahead. If you don't mind, could you stop by the printer?" He held up a colorful flyer. "I just printed out ten of these. Could you pick them up on your way back?"

"Sure." She walked into the hallway, through the office area then into the main facility. She hoped she wouldn't be stopped along the way, though she'd come to expect interruptions.

When she first came to work here, it wasn't that way at all. They'd never had a dog trainer on staff before or anyone who really understood dog behavior, except the CEO, who had been paying attention to the latest trends in the animal care industry. He realized that in recent years there had been major strides in studying dog behavior. College curriculums had been formed to train and certify people to work with dogs on an entirely new level.

It wasn't just about getting dogs to sit, rollover or walk properly on a leash anymore. Those things still mattered. But it was actually possible to understand how dogs thought, why they did what they did; even how they communicated with each other. Kim had attended one of these dog training colleges and received her certification. Part of her curriculum required a certain number of hours volunteering at a local shelter.

That's what brought her here to the Summerville shelter. By chance one day, she and the CEO had gotten into a conversation. When he found out who she was and what she was studying, he began paying close attention to her progress. In time, he was convinced she was exactly what this shelter needed. He appealed to the Board of Directors to create a position for her that had never existed before.

That was almost five years ago.

Opening the door to the stray kennel, Kim thought about the moment he had asked her into his office and offered her this job. It was like a dream come true. How many people got to drive to work every day and do something they love to do?

Of course, things didn't go silky-smooth at first. Most of the shelter staff and volunteers weren't totally on board with all these new ideas. She walked through the main lobby, remembering some of those early encounters. It was definitely a "dues-paying" season. Turns out, lots of people who love and work with dogs have lots of different ideas about how to solve dog problems. In reality, most of these homegrown "solutions" don't work. But that doesn't stop people from forming strong opinions and freely sharing those strong opinions.

At other times, Kim found people would simply give up on a dog with behavior problems they couldn't fix, declaring the age-old popular myth: *"You can't teach an old dog new tricks!"*

That was certainly true, on occasion. Some dog problems were beyond remedy. But Kim had learned most of them were not. Many dog behavior problems had practical and effective solutions that a person of average intelligence could learn and even teach their dog.

It seemed to Kim the bigger part of her job was learning how to work with the people who work with dogs—shelter workers and dog owners—not the dogs themselves. But over time, and with a good dose of patience and diplomacy, the lights had started to turn on.

Now, five years later, she had the opposite problem: people asking for help and advice constantly throughout the day. She tried to remember that these moments were not a hindrance to her job. They *were* her job, or at least a big part of it.

She reached the door to the stray kennel and saw Ellen standing midway down the concrete aisle between the two rows of kennels. Right about where Finley's kennel was located.

The first few slots in the stray kennel were actually reserved for stray dogs brought here by the Animal Control Officers (what people used to call the dogcatcher). Or else by individuals who found a stray dog wandering in their neighborhood. But many of the dogs in this kennel were not strays. They were just dogs who, for some reason, weren't ready to be adopted.

Kim had found all the different dog stories fascinating. The owners of a few of the dogs were in the county jail, but only for short periods of time. Their dogs were brought here until they could be reunited. Kim felt especially bad for these dogs. It was like they were serving time though they had done nothing wrong. Other dogs were here because they'd bitten someone. The law mandated a ten day quarantine to make sure they didn't have rabies. Some of the dogs had mild aggression issues, the kind that could be modified with time and training. These were the hopeful dogs, the ones Kim expected one day to move over to the A-Kennel, the adoption kennel.

And then there was Finley.

She walked up to Ellen, who had just bent down by Finley's kennel. "Still not eating?" she said.

Ellen looked up. "Oh, hey Kim. No, he's not. Well, he's eating enough to barely survive. But that's it."

Kim looked at Finley. He was laying in the back of his pen, his head resting on his front paws. His face looked totally sad. He hadn't even noticed her. She called his name. He lifted his head. His ears perked up a little, even his tail started to wag, slowly.

"That's the most I've seen him react to anyone in the last few days," Ellen said.

Kim bent down, reached her fingers toward the cyclone fence

door. "Hey Finley," she said in her friendliness voice. "How you doing, boy?"

He actually stood and walked toward her. His ears dropped as he licked her fingers. The sweetest expression came over his face. Through his deep depression, he was trying to be happy to see her. It saddened Kim to see him this way.

"It's not that strange to see dogs get depressed for the first day or two," Ellen said. "But this has been going on for almost a week. We tried to find a foster home, but they're all full. He's passed all the tests and evaluations. But I don't see how we can move him over to the adoption kennel as long as he's like this."

Kim remembered what Finley was like the day he was brought in. "You should've seen him when he got here. He was happy and energetic. So much so, his owner was concerned he wouldn't be adopted because he was acting so crazy."

"I can't even imagine that," Ellen said. "I've only seen him like this."

"No, this isn't Finley. This is Finley with a broken heart and totally confused. He needs to be with someone. Someone he can love and who will love him back. Someone who can invest some time in him. If that happened, I think Finley has the potential to be an amazing dog."

"If that happened," Ellen repeated. "But who's going to take him as long as he's like this?"

Kim remembered an appointment she had a few hours from now. She stood up. "I just thought of something that might work."

15

Someone from the lobby had just called Kim to let her know that Brenda Maloney had arrived. Brenda and her husband, Bill, were the ones who'd started the Prison Paws and Pals Program. They were kind of pioneers in this business. Most of the programs that trained service dogs to work with military veterans only used purebred dogs. The dogs by themselves, as well as the cost to professionally train them, often set the price tag at many thousands of dollars. By using mixed-breed dogs from shelters and teaching prison inmates how to train them, they could offer the dogs to vets for free.

Kim got up. "Hey Rog, Brenda's here. It's time to show her the next class of dogs for the prison, so I'll be with her for the next hour or so."

"Tell her I said hi," Rog said, without looking up.

Kim headed out the door to meet Brenda near the entrance to the A-kennel. She arrived to find Brenda already peeking through the glass window.

Brenda turned and greeted Kim with her usual warm smile. "Are you ready for me?"

Kim bent over a little and they hugged. "I am. I've put a hold on a number of dogs I think will be perfect for the program."

"I can't wait to meet them. Bill's going to be here in a few hours with the van. You have enough dogs for all the girls?" That's what she called the inmate dog trainers, *the girls*. "If so, we'll have to make a couple of trips to transport them all."

"I do," Kim said. "And all but one of them are in here," she pointed to the A-kennel.

"Where's the other one?"

"He's in the stray kennel. He's got a rather unique story, and there are still a few challenges. But I think he's ready."

"Well, I definitely want to meet him. But I trust your judgment completely." She opened the door leading to the kennel, and they both walked in. "Ever since you began to supervise dog selection for us, the quality level has dramatically improved. We used to have a fairly high number of dogs being returned by the vets after going through our program. We could never quite figure out why. But now that hardly ever happens."

Kim was pretty picky about the dogs she selected. Veterans with PTSD and other physical disabilities presented a unique set of challenges and needed a dog with the right temperament and character traits to meet those challenges. Kim had developed a profile that helped evaluate a dog's fitness, regardless of their mixed heritage. A checklist that helped insure only the right kind of dog made it into the program. Even so, after that point they still needed to be trained properly.

"I'm really glad to hear that," Kim said. "Dogs getting turned back in is never a good thing, for the people or the dogs. I'm glad we've been able to cut down that number." Kim walked toward the first kennel of the first dog she had picked. The dog came right up to the fence door, sat and began wagging his tail. "This is Champ. We haven't done a DNA test but, as you can see, Champ is part collie and part something else."

"He's beautiful."

"Yes, he is. And I want you to know, it took some effort to keep him from going home already. Two or three people wanted to put a hold on him. But I think he'd be a perfect companion to a vet." She walked down a few more kennels. "And here we have Titus."

"That name definitely fits him," Brenda said. Titus was a pit-mix, on the larger side. "He's a strong looking fellow."

"He is strong," Kim said, "but he's a total marshmallow. As sweet as can be. The problem is, when people see his size they don't even give him a chance."

This continued on from one dog to the next, until Kim had introduced Brenda to every one of the dogs she had selected for the program.

All except one.

"I love them all," Brenda said.

"Well, I have one more to show you. Follow me." They left the A-kennel through the back door and walked across the grass to the back door of the stray kennel.

As Kim opened the door, Brenda asked, "Is this last dog fairly new?"

"Fairly. But he's been here about a week."

"A week? Don't you usually move them over to the adoption kennel after a few days?"

"We do. But Finley isn't quite ready yet." Kim led her about midway down the aisle to Finley's kennel. As before, Finley was laying in the back looking sad. His head lifted slowly as he recognized Kim. "Hey Finley." Now his ears perked up.

"Really? You think this dog is right for our program?"

"I know he doesn't look like it. But you should have seen him the day he was brought in. He was happy and energetic, constantly wagging his tail. He's just very depressed right now. He's barely been eating, so he has very little energy."

"Why, what's his story?"

Kim explained everything to Brenda. When she'd finished, Brenda said, "That is very sad. Heartbreaking even."

Kim opened Finley's door. When she did, he stood and his tail began to wag slowly. She stepped inside his kennel and bent down to pet him. He instantly came to her and sat beside her.

"You poor thing," Brenda said.

"And if you think about it, Finley's suffering on a totally different level than we do when we hear this kind of news. No one can even explain to him what's happening. All he knows is this young man who loved him and treated him like a best friend suddenly stopped coming around. It sounds like, after that, he was just left shut up in a room every day by himself, for months, while the soldier's mother was at work. She said herself she wasn't even a dog person. And now she's brought him here and left him. And he has no idea why. No idea if he'll ever see them again, or what will happen to him now."

Brenda started getting teary. "You better stop, or I'm going to lose it completely."

"I'm sorry," Kim said. "But I really think that's why he's so sad. I know I'd be too, if all that happened to me."

Kim stepped out and Brenda stepped into his pen. She bent down and began to pet him. His ears went back and he licked her hand. "Do you think he'll be able to snap out of this depression?"

"I definitely do," Kim said. "I think if we put him with the right girl, and she starts to love on him and work with him, I think it's just a matter of time before he becomes the dog he really is on the inside. Because this is not who he is. I think Finley has the potential to be an amazing dog. I'd really like to bring him out to the prison myself and meet the girl who'll be working with him. If I'm wrong, and it doesn't work out, I'll come back and get him. What do you say?"

"How can I refuse an offer like that?" Brenda said.

16

Finley

After the two women had left, Finley walked to the back of his pen, circled a few times until things felt right, then laid back down. It was nice seeing Kim again. He hadn't seen her for a few days. He felt good whenever she came around. But the feeling didn't last long, because she would always go away and leave him here.

Since he'd come to this place, different people had been looking after him, but he didn't know any of their names or feel any connection to them. Kim was the only one who reminded him of the love he felt from Chaz. Chaz was everything. He hadn't seen him for so long, Finley was beginning to believe he would never see him again.

Which was one of the reasons he felt so sad.

The main kennel door opened. Instantly, most of the dogs started barking. Finley didn't join in. Didn't see any point in it. No one hardly ever stopped by his door. It wasn't time for food. Even if it was, he'd barely touched what they'd put down this morning.

The footsteps grew louder. So did the barking, especially from the dogs nearest him. Suddenly, the footsteps stopped. Right in front of him.

"Aww, Finley. Don't look so sad."

He looked up. It was that young lady who worked in here sometimes, the one who had come in with Kim a few hours ago. He couldn't remember her name.

"Things are looking up for you, boy."

He noticed a leash in her hand. Were they going for a walk? She unlatched his door and stepped inside.

"They're coming to take you out of here. Do you know that? In just a little while from now." She bent down.

He lifted his head to allow her to click the end of the leash on his collar.

"Kim said I needed to get you ready. How about we start with a walk?"

He stood. Involuntarily, his tail began to wag. He understood two words from all she had just said: *Kim* and *walk*. Both were good words. Was she taking him to see Kim? Was Kim going to take him for a walk?

She led him out of his pen and down the aisle toward the back door. He followed behind a few paces. "That's it, boy. Keep coming. You're going to like this. I promise."

The dogs on either side of him barked furiously as he walked by. He couldn't blame them. He knew how tough it was sitting in a kennel all day. But he refused to acknowledge them. Why should he? It wasn't his fault. He was on the end of a leash.

She picked up her pace as she walked through the back door. Finley tried to do the same. The sunshine felt good on his face and back. The barking faded as the door closed behind them. Finley looked around but didn't see Kim anywhere. They were heading away from the building across a field, mostly covered by patches of dirt and weeds. Close to the ground, the air was filled with dozens of conflicting smells. As they walked, he tried lifting his head above it, to catch moments of fresh air.

Up ahead, he noticed a fenced-in area. He'd been in there once before, the first day he'd gotten here. It wasn't a big space but certainly big enough for a dog to cut loose. Back then, he ran like crazy all over the place and had so much energy. Seemed like they were going there now.

Finley didn't feel much like running, though.

The young lady unlatched the fence door, and they walked in. As she re-latched it behind them, a host of new dog smells rushed through his nostrils. Some were pretty fresh. He quickly eyed inside the perimeter to make sure they were alone. Finley wasn't in the mood to make friends.

"You don't have to be afraid, Finley. It's just you and me." She bent down and unhooked him from the leash. "Go ahead. You're free. You can run now."

Finley wasn't sure what she was saying, but by the way she was waving her arms it looked like she wanted him to go away. This confused him, because her face seemed happy not angry. He looked in the direction she pointed and even took a few steps in that direction. But he didn't understand what she wanted him to do.

She picked up a ball and threw it across the yard. "Go on, Finley. Go get it. Get the ball."

Finley understood *get the ball*. Chaz often played ball with him, and he loved it when they did. More than almost anything. He just wasn't in the mood.

"You can do it, Finley. Bring it. Bring the ball."

The ball. She wanted it for some reason. Finley walked toward it, slowly. Halfway there, he lost interest. He looked back at her.

She was standing with her hands on her hips, staring at him.

"Don't you want to get it? Says on your card that you love playing ball."

He sat. What else could he do? She walked toward him. He looked at her face, her eyes, sensed her mood. She wasn't angry. What was it?

She walked past him. "Okay, I'll get it."

He watched as she walked to the other side, near the fence and picked up the ball. She stood for a moment, held up the ball and said, "You sure you don't want it?"

What was she saying? Now she was coming back.

"Okay, guess we're not playing ball. We'll move onto the next thing."

She still didn't seem upset, more like confused. He was, too.

She reattached his leash. "I'm supposed to get you all cleaned up. Let's head back in, and I'll give you a bath. You look like you haven't had one in a while. We'll take a look at your nails, too. Get you all spiffed up."

He still had no idea what she was saying or where they were going. He followed along. Looked like they were heading back inside. Guess they weren't meeting up with Kim after all. He wondered why this girl had mentioned her name.

They walked through a side door of the building into a room he didn't recognize. That wasn't much of a walk. Whenever Chaz had taken him for a walk, they'd be gone a long time.

He looked up at the young woman's face. She looked so happy. He wished he knew why.

17

Amy

It was after lunch, and Amy had a little free time in the afternoon. They were told Brenda and Bill would be arriving sometime soon with the next group of dogs from the Humane Society. For the last thirty minutes or so, Amy had been straightening up her cell, her dorm. It was already pretty clean. She was mainly moving around the handful of things she owned, trying to make the room feel like her place. At least a little.

The effort ended with her holding onto a shoebox she had gotten from a prison ministry last Christmas. At the time, it contained mostly bathroom and toiletry items like deodorant, toothpaste and a nice hairbrush. Now she used it to hold little personal things. Like the last, and only, letter she had gotten from Cassie, her brother's wife.

For now, she set the shoebox on the floor and slid it under her cot near the headboard. Something tugged at her heart, so she pulled it back out a moment and lifted the lid. There was the letter folded, sitting on top. It was really the only connection she had to her family. No photos. No little gifts or mementos. Just the one letter and, really, if you thought about it, Cassie wasn't even family. Not blood anyway.

She opened the letter and read it again:

Dear Amy,

Heard things weren't going so well for you. I mean even worse than they had been going. Your brother told me about you getting arrested and going to prison. He didn't know if it was for 3 years or 5. I'm guessing you hadn't heard he and I got married, almost a year ago now.

I know we haven't been close since, well, since you got hooked on meth. I want you to know I forgive you for stealing from me. Guess it wasn't just me. According to your brother, you robbed them blind. He said it was so many times they finally had to cut you off completely. I guess you already know this, but they want nothing to do with you anymore. I didn't even mention I was writing you. It would probably have started a fight.

But I had to write you, at least this once. Cause there's something else you probably don't know. I became a Christian shortly after high school. A real one (read my Bible every day and everything). Jesus changed my life completely, I know he can help you too, no matter what you've done. I looked it up, and there's a really good prison ministry going on out there where they're sending you. I wrote the name and website on the back of this page. Don't know if they let you use the internet in prison. If not, ask somebody out there about them.

Well, better go.

Your new sister-in-law,
Cassie

Amy folded the note back over, blinking back some tears that were making their presence known. It wasn't anything Cassie had said. Not especially. She knew her family had given up on her long ago. And she didn't blame them. But she wished there was some way she could let them know she was different now. Some way she could tell them how sorry she was for what she had put them through.

But there wasn't. She had better just accept it. She didn't even know why she kept this letter anymore, or the envelope it came in. Wasn't like the return address was any good. And reading it like this only made her sad.

She looked over at the small trashcan next to the desk. Then she set the letter back in the shoebox, closed the lid and slid it back under her bed.

While Amy waited for the dogs to arrive, she decided to use the remaining time to read some of the dog training materials Miss Bridget had given her. She'd been told each of the newer inmates in the program was assigned a more seasoned inmate-trainer to get them up to speed. She was glad to find she'd been assigned to Rita.

At the moment, Amy was on her cot lying on her back holding the booklet over her head. She was fascinated by what she read. She was thinking the training would be all about things like teaching a dog to sit and stay and walk on a leash. That was certainly part of it, but this booklet was about things she'd never heard about before, the way a dog thinks, about its behavior.

Rita walked in. "Are you understanding that? I know it's quite a lot to take in. Ask any questions if something doesn't make sense."

Amy set the booklet down and sat up. "Is this stuff for real? Have you really seen it work with dogs?"

Rita pulled out the chair from the little desk and spun it around, sat. "Course it's for real. There's all kinds of science behind this stuff now. Dogs can't talk, but they sure have a lot to say. Once you understand how they communicate. One of the biggest problems I had at first was having to unlearn so much crap I believed about dogs."

"Like what?" Amy said.

"Just the usual stuff. People think they know dogs because they love 'em and spend so much time with them. And because dogs seem so eager to want to be with us and make us happy. I think the biggest mistake I made, and I see others make when they start out in this program, is thinking dogs think like people do. But they don't. They got their own way of looking at life, and it's not the same way we do. Half the time we wind up treating them like we treat kids. But they're not kids."

"Can you give me an example?" Amy said. "I'm not really following you."

Rita thought a moment. "Here's one. Like when dogs bark. People yell at them to stop barking, like you yell at a kid. If you say it loud enough, and the kid thinks he may get punished, he might even stop. That's because he knows what you're saying. Dogs don't. We yell at them to stop barking, and they usually keep right on barking. So we yell louder. They look at us, and if you're paying attention, you see this confused look on their face. Then they bark some more. You know why? It's not because they don't want to obey us, they don't understand what we're saying. They think we're barking, too. That's what our yelling sounds like. So they bark some more."

Amy smiled. "I never thought about this before. But it makes sense."

"Course it does," Rita said. "You keep reading. There's all kinds of good stuff in there."

"So how do you make them stop barking, if yelling at them isn't the answer?"

"You distract them with something else, or redirect them. They're barking because they think there's a problem. Yelling just makes them think you agree. It's okay to tell them to stop barking, once, but then you give them something else to do to get their minds in a new direction. Tell them 'Enough' and pat your leg. When they come, give them a treat or a toy. You make coming to you a whole lot more rewarding than barking. In a few moments, they'll forget all about what they were barking at."

"Wow," Amy said. "Does that really work?"

"I've seen it work," Rita said. She tilted her head like she heard something, then stood and looked out the window. "Thought so. That's Bill's van getting checked in at the gate."

Amy stood up and walked to the window.

Rita turned and walked past her toward the door. "The new dogs are here. This is always interesting."

Amy looked out the window, saw a big white passenger van being inspected by a guard. Her first dog was probably in there. Not just the first dog she'd ever trained, but the first dog she'd ever had.

Lord, don't let it be a pit. At least not this time.

18

Amy followed Rita down the hall through the main room, where the graduation luncheon had been held. Most of the other inmates had gathered there already. They were all looking out the window as the white passenger van pulled into a paved area near the building.

"Can all the dogs fit in that?" Amy said quietly.

"No," Rita said, "only about half. Bill will drop them off then go back for the other half.

"How do they decide who gets what dog?"

"Well, you and I won't be getting one out of this batch."

"Why's that?"

"Because our team lost the last round."

"Am I on a team?" Amy said.

"Not you so much. The girl whose place you're taking. She was on our team. We divide up into two teams for the Top Five Contest."

"What's that?"

"It's just something the program directors came up with, to spice things up I guess. The idea is, they pay extra attention to how we're doing the last month before graduation. You'll see them sometimes taking notes. They decide which dogs make the Top Five but don't tell us. Not until graduation day. I guess they're thinking if the girls know they didn't get picked, they won't try so hard. During graduation, they announce which dogs made it. The girls who train the dogs win, too, because the team with the most girls in the Top Five get first pick of the new dogs that come in the next round."

"I see," Amy said.

Just then the door connecting to the yard opened up and Miss Bridget walked in. "Okay, the winners can line up in order. Soon as you do, you can head out to the yard near Bill's van. Your dogs await."

The ladies instantly responded, formed a line and headed out into the yard. They all looked pretty excited. Once they had left the room Miss Bridget told the "losers" they could watch things unfold outside from the picnic benches if they wanted. The benches were set up in rows on a concrete slab. During the graduation ceremony, this is where they had set up the white tarp for shade. Today, it was cloudy and not too hot, so most of the girls headed outside, including Rita and Amy.

Amy watched where Rita sat and sat nearby. "You said the winning team is the one with the most dogs, or trainers, in the Top Five. Why did Miss Bridget just tell the winners to line up in order?"

"Oh," Rita said. "I didn't mention...one of the five dogs is named Top Dog. That dog and trainer are selected to give a public demonstration during the graduation ceremony, sort of show off everything we've taught the dogs. And that trainer gets her choice, first pick, of the new dogs when they come in. See the girl in front? That's Jane. Her dog was Top Dog, so she's at the front of the line. The rest of the team picks numbers out of a hat."

Amy looked across the grass area at the line of girls waiting by the van, each one holding a leash. The leashes had been sitting in a plastic tote bin on the last picnic table. Bill opened the back door of the van then the side doors. He said something to the girls and stepped off to the side. As soon as he did, the dogs began to bark. Amy couldn't see them from where she sat, but she could tell by the tone of the barking they were all fairly big dogs.

That was confirmed as the dogs were let out from their cages in the van onto the grass, one by one. Half of them looked like pit-mix dogs to Amy, but she had to admit they looked very friendly. Wagging their tails, playfully jumping up on the girls who just put them on a leash, even licking their hands. The rest of the dogs behaved just the same way. Some looked like they were part Labrador retriever. One had curly hair like a large poodle. It was half-poodle anyway. The last one coming out of the van had to be part German Shepherd.

"Now, that's a beautiful dog," Rita said, pointing to the Shepherd mix. "I would've loved to work with him."

The surprising thing to Amy was, that the Shepherd wasn't picked first. That's the one she would've picked. The girls who had won the first several slots and had their pick of all the dogs in the van had all picked pits.

"All right, ladies," Bill yelled to the inmates sitting on the picnic benches, "I'll be back before you know it with your dogs." He said something to Miss Bridget, closed the van doors, got inside and headed back toward the gate.

Amy watched as all the girls with dogs began spreading out across the grass area to let their dogs go the bathroom.

"Don't forget to bag it," Miss Bridget yelled, "if any of them poop."

For the last forty minutes, Amy had been laying on her cot reading more of the dog training booklet. The whole dorm area had been abuzz with activity. Mostly related to the dogs and trainers getting acquainted. She could hear the trainers introducing the dogs to their new rooms and crates, and dog toys being squeezed, tossed and squeaked. The atmosphere resembled nothing of the prison life she had known for the last two years, and the inmates sounded nothing like hardened criminals.

More like…well, happy college girls in a dorm.

She turned the page to the next chapter, which was all about how to get a dog to walk properly on a leash. Before she finished the first paragraph, Rita stuck her head in the door.

"Bill's here with the van. Ready to meet your dog?"

"Definitely." She sat up, set the booklet down on the bed. Rita had already headed down the hallway. Amy stood, then walked over to the window. Sure enough, Bill's van was inside the gate getting inspected. She felt mostly excited about getting her dog, but a little nervous.

Rita had said she'd help train Amy herself. That's how they did things around here. The newer trainers were taught by the more seasoned ones. Bill and Brenda would also conduct group training classes. Besides all that, Rita had said, dogs were extremely patient and forgiving animals, so it would be pretty hard for her to screw this assignment up. A few more inmates walked past her doorway in the hall toward the main room and the door leading out to the yard. Amy decided it was time to join them.

When she got outside, she noticed the other inmates, the ones who hadn't received their dogs yet, the "loser" group she was a part of, gathering in front of the picnic benches. She headed over there. As she did, she noticed they were picking numbers out of a hat, like the first group had, to determine who got the dogs in the van and in what order. She stood next to Rita.

Rita turned and whispered to her, "They decided not to include you in this, since you haven't done anything yet."

"I still get a dog though, right?"

"Yeah, but you get whichever one doesn't get picked by everyone else. But don't worry, all the dogs now are good picks. We haven't had any duds ever since that lady Kim at the Humane Society started selecting them."

Amy was glad to hear that. Oddly enough, she wasn't that disappointed to learn she would get the dog no one else had wanted. Although, it reminded her of being back in high school or middle school, every time team captains would select teams in PE. She'd get picked last every time. And it wasn't because her last name was Wallace. Usually, the captains could pick whoever they wanted in whatever order they wanted. Amy just wasn't any good at sports, and everyone knew it.

She sat at a nearby picnic bench and watched the scene unfold. Apparently, Rita's number had put her in third place. That was the position she held in the line now forming near the van. Over the next ten minutes, just like before, Bill opened the van doors, the girls began checking out the dogs inside, picking their favorite, and leading them out into the yard.

Rita came out with a husky/pit mix, white with brown spots. She had the biggest smile on her face. Amy decided she should get up and get in the last place in line. When it was just two of them in line, the girl in front of her walked up to the van and looked inside. Amy couldn't see, the view was blocked by the back door. The girl looked all around the van with a confused look on her face. Still wearing that look, she glanced at Amy, then back inside the van. "Guess it's just me and you, girl," she said, then bent over and opened the cage door.

Amy heard the leash click, the sound of an excited dog exiting the cage then watched her fellow inmate as she led a black lab-mix onto the grass. She made a facial gesture to Amy as she walked by that Amy didn't understand.

It was her turn. She wondered what she'd find on the other side of that door. She had mentally prepared herself to be okay if it was a pit.

She clicked the leash in her hand a few times and stepped up to the back of the van. Now she understood why the other inmate had looked so confused.

The van was empty. All the dogs were gone.

19

Kim

Kim set her phone down. The last call she had to make, for now. She looked at her watch. It was time. Actually, she was running a little late from the time she had given Brenda. Bill had left the facility quite a while ago headed out to the prison with the second load of dogs.

She stood up and turned to see Roger, her boss, coming in from the hallway with some folders in his hand. "I'm going to head out to the prison," Kim said. "The last dog for the upcoming class wasn't quite ready, so I told Brenda I'd bring him out there myself."

Roger looked up at the clock on the wall in between their desks. "Guess that's your last task of the day. Don't expect there's enough time for you to come back here after you're through."

"I don't think so. I may need to spend a little more time out there, not just drop him off. He didn't look too ready when Brenda came by earlier to look at the dogs I'd picked. I told her I was certain he'd work out but agreed to bring him out there myself, in case I'm wrong. That way I can bring him back, if needed."

"Which dog are we talking about?" Roger asked.

"Finley. Remember the one I told you about? The one whose original owner got killed in Afghanistan a few weeks ago?"

Roger sat at his desk. "Kind of," he said. "A golden retriever mix, right?"

"That's the one."

"Well, see you tomorrow."

"Thanks. See you tomorrow then." She headed down the hall in the direction of the stray kennel. She greeted several coworkers along the way but did her best not to make eye contact. She needed to look like a woman on a mission to avoid getting sucked into anything. After walking through the Intake area, she ducked inside a room to pick up a spare leash.

Opening the door to the kennel set off an onslaught of barking dogs, all hoping she had come there to set them free. That part of the job was hard sometimes, knowing you couldn't really help all the dogs that needed it. But this afternoon, she was definitely able to help one of them. She hoped that Finley would think he was being set free, though she knew at first she'd probably just be adding to his already confused state.

His kennel door was up ahead but she didn't see him near the front. That wasn't strange for Finley; he tended to lay all the way in the back. Then she looked up at the clear plastic folder hanging on the fence door. Each dog had one. It held all their paperwork.

Finley's was empty. A few moments later, she realized…so was his kennel. Finley was gone.

This didn't make any sense.

Ellen had sent her a voicemail over thirty minutes ago, saying she had just finished giving Finley a bath. He was ready to go. She walked down to the end of the aisle, inspecting every kennel. He wasn't in any of them. She hurried back out to the Intake area and found Chuck.

"Chuck, do you know what happened to Finley? That golden retriever mix Ellen was getting ready for me? She called me before she left saying he was all set."

Chuck looked up. "No, I would've thought he should still be back there. I'm guessing he's not."

"Any idea where he might be?" Kim said. "Did anyone take him for a walk?"

"I doubt it. We're pretty slammed up here. Did you check the adoption kennel area? They came here to get a few of the dogs that were ready to be moved about ten minutes ago. Maybe they mixed things up, brought Finley over there by mistake."

That could be it. "I'll head over there right now."

Finley didn't understand any of this, so he huddled on a wrinkled throw rug as far back in the pen as he could. This place seemed a lot like the place he had been staying in for several days now. A long aisle, lots of kennels on either side. Dogs in every one of them, none who wanted to be here. They seemed a little nicer than the ones he had been with before, and a lot more people walked by. But Finley had hoped all this new activity today meant something better was coming his way.

He had even been brought outside for a while, then washed in a big tub and dried off. His hair had been brushed. Several different women had been petting him, calling him by name, saying nice-sounding things to him.

All of that, just to put him here? He didn't understand and had no idea what to expect, and he didn't want to think about it. He closed his eyes pretending to sleep.

Kim walked through the Adoption lobby, around the counters then down the hall toward the adoption kennel. She could have stopped and asked one of the workers which kennel Finley had been moved to, but it probably would've taken longer than just looking for herself. She opened the door and quickly glanced at the individual pens as she walked down the aisle. Several dogs barked and called out to her, but she was only there to see one.

Up ahead, halfway down the aisle, a couple with two children had stopped in front of one of the pens, but she didn't see the dog they were looking at. Sure enough, when she got closer, there was Finley laying in the back. The husband was reading the information on Finley's card. The wife had bent down to the height of her children who were all saying things to Finley. Finley was looking at them but not responding, and he made no attempt to get up and see them.

But as soon as Kim reached his kennel, his ears perked right up and his tail began to wag. A moment later, he stood and stepped closer to the front of the pen, his eyes zeroed in on Kim's face.

"Well, he certainly knows you," the woman said. "He's a beautiful dog, but he doesn't seem very friendly."

Kim noticed he looked even more handsome all cleaned up.

The husband stopped reading the card and turned to face Kim. "Can you tell us anything about him? He's the kind of dog we were looking for. He's mostly golden retriever, right? Aren't they usually pretty good family dogs?"

"I'm sorry," Kim said. "Finley's been brought over here by mistake. He's not really ready to be adopted just yet. In fact, he's been selected for a prison program."

"Finley's going to jail?" the little girl said.

"Kind of, but not really," Kim said. "Not because he's done anything wrong." She turned her attention to the parents. "We work with a program out there that trains selected dogs for a number of weeks, so that they can help military veterans coming home from Iraq or Afghanistan with disabilities or PTSD."

"Oh, wow," the mother said. "I saw something about that on TV."

"Well, that's what Finley's going to be part of. He was brought over here by mistake. I'm actually here to drive him out to the prison right now."

The mother looked at him. "He's a beautiful dog. I guess if we can't have him, at least it's for a good cause."

"Sorry for the confusion," Kim said. "But I'm sure you'll find a good dog in here. All the dogs in this kennel have been carefully checked out by our staff to make sure they'd make good family pets. Some aren't as good with kids as others, so it's a good idea to do what you are doing," she said to the husband. "If they have any kid issues that we know about, it will be written on their card."

"Otherwise, they're okay for kids?" The mother said.

"Hopefully. As best we can tell, but we don't know for sure. We haven't found any parents willing to let us use their kids to test the dogs."

The mother laughed; she could tell it was a joke.

"Well, I'm glad we got to talk with you," the husband said. "Come on kids, let's keep looking. We'll find a good one."

They started walking down the aisle. When they had cleared a few kennels, Kim opened Finley's door. "Look at you." He was wagging his tail so hard his rear end was shaking. She patted his head and scratched behind his ears. "You ready to get out of here? Can you give me a sit?"

He knew that word and instantly obeyed. She clipped on the leash. "Good boy." She led him out of the kennel, stopping only to grab his paperwork from the clear plastic sleeve. He walked briskly by her side, more energetically than she had seen him all week. "We'll just stop by the adoption counter and clear up the confusion, then you'll get to ride in a car."

She knew he didn't have a clue what she was talking about, but she said it in a high-pitched happy voice, and he acted like he did.

It was so nice to see him looking cheerful. She wished there was some way she could tell him that things should be looking up for him from this point on.

20

Something was definitely going on.

Finley had no idea what it was, but it had to be something new. The one person who'd treated him the most like Chaz had come to take him out of this place. They were walking on a sidewalk out to a parking lot. Whatever she was saying, she sounded excited. That made him feel excited too.

He understood the phrase, *car ride*. Is that what this was, a car ride? Finley loved car rides. Chaz had rarely taken him on them but, whenever he did, it was always a good thing. After, he would usually wind up back in the apartment. But he still enjoyed them. Especially sticking his head out the window. There was just something about having all that air rushing into your face. It was as much fun as playing ball or chewing a steak bone.

Kim stopped in front of a car. "Are you ready, Finley? Want to go on a car ride?" She opened the back door and Finley hopped in.

He could barely contain himself. It wasn't a large area, but he just had to spin around a few times. He watched as she came around to the driver side and opened the door. Good, she was getting in. This was definitely going to be a car ride.

She sat in her seat. "I hope you don't get car sick. I probably should have put down some towels. But this won't take long. Maybe fifteen or twenty minutes."

Whatever she said, he enjoyed the sound of her voice. So pleasant and calming. He felt the car begin to back up and turn. He looked out the back window as they drove away. They *were* leaving this place. That was clear. It was getting smaller and smaller. Would he be coming back after the car ride? He hoped not.

Where was she taking him?

He tried to block the thought out of his mind. Stay in the moment. It was a good moment. He looked out the side window. Everything was rushing by so fast. He was certain the wind on the other side of the glass was blowing hard. He had to find a way to get the window open. He pawed at the panel and armrest, then lifted his nose toward the top, as close to the edge as possible.

"Are you okay back there?"

He turned and looked at Kim. She was staring straight ahead, but then he saw her eyes looking back at him through a mirror. He repeated the same behavior, pawing at the side panel and pressing his nose against the glass.

"You want the window open, boy? What am I saying? Of course, you do. Alright, give me a sec."

Suddenly, a humming noise. The window began sliding down. Instantly, the wind rushed in. He stood tall and lifted his nose to greet it. In a moment, it was down enough to poke his head through, so he did.

What a feeling. So cool and refreshing. As good as he remembered.

For a dog, it doesn't get any better.

Kim turned off the main road then traveled one block and turned left, down the long winding road that led to the prison. She'd been out here many times. It still gave her an odd feeling as she drove past the tall double-cyclone fence with the coiled razor wire on top and bottom, saw the occasional inmate walking around inside the perimeter in their prison garb.

She had never felt any danger, though she knew some fairly dangerous ladies were spending the rest of their lives in this facility. She'd felt even less concern being around the inmates involved in the Prison Paws and Pals Program. They had all gone through a thorough evaluation and had to have squeaky clean behavior records to be accepted.

It gave her a strange feeling, realizing she could come and go freely from this place, but these ladies could not. Only a tiny portion of Kim's time was spent here. For them, it was every day all day and all night, for months and years on end. They couldn't go shopping, go to the movies or meet their friends at a restaurant. They couldn't go on dates or sit on a couch with their boyfriend munching popcorn as they watched Netflix.

Well, neither could she for that matter. The last serious boyfriend she'd had was over a year ago. But that was beside the point. For her at least, it could happen.

She rounded a tight curve, heard Finley slide across the back seat. "I'm sorry, Finley." The whole drive over she had paid such careful attention at every turn and every time she applied the brakes, trying to make it easier for him to hold on. "We're almost there."

Although the dog training program was technically part of the prison, she had to drive all the way around the complex and take a different road leading to a back entrance. The whole look of the place was different, made to resemble more of a college dorm than a prison barracks. But, of course, it still maintained all the high-end security procedures. And it was still enclosed by the same double-cyclone fence and razor wire.

She quickly found a parking place and turned off the car. Finley pulled his head back from the window and focused on her. She reached back and patted the top of his head, scratched behind his ears. Finley looked at the place through the windshield. The look on his face suggested he was trying to process what kind of place it was. "You've never been here before, Finley. But for at least a while, this should be your new home."

Should be, she thought. She certainly hoped it would be, that it would work out for him. She'd hate to have to bring Finley back to the shelter. "You want to check it out?"

His tail was wagging. A good sign. He was definitely doing better now than the day he got dropped off. She got out of the car. Finley followed her to the side door. She opened it slightly and grabbed the leash, then let him out the rest of the way.

She reached into the front seat, got Finley's paperwork then shut both doors. "Let's go, Finley. Somebody very special is waiting to meet you."

21

Amy was sitting in the chair by her desk reading the dog training booklet. The other girls were busy getting acquainted with their new dogs. Her disappointment at not getting a dog yet was short-lived. Miss Bridget quickly informed her that she was most certainly getting one. Apparently, the last dog slated to be with the group had been kept in a different part of the shelter, and he wasn't quite ready to be released when Bill left with the van.

Have no fear, she was told, the main dog trainer for the Humane Society was bringing him here herself. In fact, she was on her way to the prison now.

Amy had asked if Miss Bridget knew what kind of dog it was. She said she didn't. Brenda did, but she and Bill had already left for the day and Bridget had forgotten to ask her. Amy would just have to be patient. She'd find out soon enough.

One thing at least, Miss Bridget did say the dog trainer was bringing a *him*. So, her dog was a male.

A few minutes later, Rita stuck her head in the doorway, her new dog right beside her. "Your dog's here. Well not here, here. He's on the property. Someone said they just saw Kim drive into the parking lot and get out of the car walking a dog on a leash."

"Who's Kim?" Amy asked.

"Kim's the dog trainer at the shelter. She's the one picks out all our dogs, makes sure we get one's we can train. Anyway, she should be here any minute."

"Thanks." Amy stood up and looked out through the curtain. Trees blocked her view of the parking lot closest to the gate. Her eyes zoned in on the spot where the trees ended. She was so excited.

Here comes someone.

It was a female guard. False alarm.

A few minutes later, a dog came into view. She couldn't see it clearly through the multiple cyclone fences, but it had to be him. He was on a leash. A moment later, Amy saw the woman holding the leash. Must be Kim. Her eyes locked back onto the dog. Whatever it was, it wasn't a pit. It was taller and the hair was too long, and it was reddish-brown.

She couldn't wait any longer. Maybe she could get a clearer view in the yard. She set the booklet down and headed that way.

Once outside, she quickly got to the best place to view the security gate. Sadly, the woman and the dog had disappeared. Then she realized, they were probably just inside going through security procedures. Sure enough, a few moments later both the dog and presumably Kim came out of the gate area and walked across the roadway toward her.

Now, with just one fence between them, Amy saw the dog clearly. She couldn't believe her eyes. He was absolutely beautiful. Maybe a golden retriever, or mostly like one. He was almost prancing as he walked next to Kim, his head held up high, tail wagging. Several inmates were already outside working with their dogs. They all stopped to watch the scene unfold. Amy hurried toward the gate.

"Are you Kim?" Amy asked.

"I am. And you are…"

"My name's Amy. I think that's my dog. I mean, I'm the one who's supposed to train him."

Kim unlatched then opened the gate. She was about to walk through, but Finley got a confused look on his face as he peered inside. Suddenly, he sat down. "What's the matter, boy? It's okay," she said softly. "Everything's okay."

Amy noticed that Kim didn't drag him through the gate. Instead, she bent down and patted his head, left her arm around his shoulder then looked at Amy.

"Would you do me a favor?" Kim asked. "Could you come here, but stay a few feet away from us, on the other side of the gate? I want him to see you without a fence between you. Then bend down like I am, hold out your hand and call his name in a gentle, happy voice."

Amy did what Kim had asked, except for the last part. "I don't know his name."

"Oh, I'm sorry. It's Finley."

"Finley," she repeated. When she did, his ears perked up and he looked right at her. What a perfect name for this dog, she thought. She already loved him completely. "Hey Finley. How are you? You are such a beautiful dog." She held out her hand. "Here Finley."

Finley stopped looking around and stopped smelling all the smells floating in the air. He focused on the face of the young woman who just called him, the woman Kim had been talking to. He didn't understand most of what she'd said, except his name, but he liked the way she said it. She had a kind face and nice eyes. He liked the look in her eyes.

"What do you think, Finley?" Kim said, "Want to meet Amy?" Kim stood, so Finley did, too.

"Finley, stay. Stay right here." Still holding the leash, Kim took a few steps in front of Finley and held out her hand toward Amy. "Here, take these. They're treats. A kind Finley loves. You'll be giving out lots of treats during your training."

"I read about that," Amy said. "Positive reinforcement, right?"

"Yes. Good. You've been reading up on it. What I want you to do is stay put and hold out a treat to him. He'll want to come, even if he's shy at first. I'll encourage him to come to you, too. I think he's starting to trust me. After he takes the treat, back up a little bit. When he comes, give him another treat. Then say the word, *Good*. Then give him another treat and add the word *Come*."

"Won't that confuse him? If I'm saying *come* after he's already done it?"

"It might seem like that," Kim said, "but that's not how dogs think. He already knows *come* a little. But doing this will strengthen his association with the word. The treats tell him that *come* is a good thing, especially coming to you. He's been shuffled around a lot lately and has some fear issues. For the first few days, I really want you to overdose him on treats. Give them to him for everything he does right or anytime he does anything you ask. And talk to him just the way you did now."

"Okay," Amy said. "Should we try it now?"

"Sure."

"You mentioned overdosing him on treats. Do we have these treats in here somewhere?"

"No. You do have treats for training in there. I'm sure Bridget or Brenda will show you where. They're good ones, but these are better. Here, I have a whole baggie full of them in my jacket pocket. They're really for Finley. I always like to use high-end treats when I'm working with a dog who's been having a hard time."

"Has he been having a hard time? He seems pretty upbeat right now."

"He does. That's because he just got done having a car ride. It's obvious he loves car rides. And having these treats so close to his nose are certainly helping. But you should have seen him this morning. Really, the last few weeks. He was going through some serious doggie depression."

"Aww, that's so sad."

"I know. But the way he's acting right now is a whole lot more like he was when I first met him, before his owner dropped him off. I'd love to keep this momentum going. He might struggle a little bit after I go, but I'm thinking with all the attention you're going to be able to give him, plus a steady dose of treats, I'm hoping he'll pull out of his depression completely."

Finley watched this exchange between Kim and this new woman. The only word he understood was *come*. But he was confused. They kept saying it, over and over, but they weren't asking him to come. Were they telling each other to come? Couldn't be that, because neither one of them moved. He could certainly smell those treats, those wonderful treats. First in Kim's hand then in the other woman's hand. He still didn't know her name.

What was happening now?

Kim handed the new woman his leash and was stepping back behind him. She had also given the new woman all the treats. He could see loose ones in her hand and she was holding a whole bag full of them.

The woman held out one to him. It looked and smelled so good.

He looked up into her face. She was smiling. And she was holding out that treat. And Kim had handed her the leash. Kim must be okay with him going to her.

So he did. She gave him the treat, and he ate it. Then she gave him another, and another. All the while, saying *Come*. And saying his name in such a pleasant voice. And patting his head and rubbing his shoulders.

First, the car ride. And now this.

He looked at Kim. Kim wasn't coming. She was standing still. She was saying something to the woman. Now she was talking to him. She was saying a word he understood, *goodbye*. And waving goodbye. Now she turned and started walking away.

Finley couldn't help himself, he began to pull and whine. He liked Kim. A lot.

Now Kim was leaving him at this new place. He kept watching her as she walked away. Several times she waved to him but kept walking toward the car. He thought about being sad, but this new woman was being so nice.

She handed him another treat and began walking toward some tables, gently calling his name. He glanced around the yard and noticed other dogs on leashes with other women. None of them seemed aggressive. He sent calming signals just to be safe as he followed this new woman.

What would become of him now? Whatever it was, it was certainly a nicer beginning than the place he had just left.

22

Chris

Chris pulled into the parking lot of the Summerville Golf and Country Club in one of the spaces near the metal maintenance building. He'd gotten the job. Tom, the maintenance manager, had called him a few days ago saying his paperwork had come in and everything looked good. He was to report in today, bright and early at 6am.

Besides the money, it would be such a relief not to have so much time on his hands. Time, especially time alone, wasn't his friend. Being around people didn't help his mental state much, either. He always felt an extra level of tension being around people he didn't know.

That's why this job seemed like a perfect fit. Tom said he'd mostly be operating the ride-on lawnmower. At the start of the day, there'd be a little interaction with the other facility workers but, after that, he'd mainly be seeing people from a distance. Golfers mostly. The main thing was to do his best to stay out of their way.

This suited Chris just fine.

He got out of the car, leaning heavily on the door to steady himself. He was still pretty weak on that side. It wasn't just because of the prosthetic limb, though that was a good part of it. The muscles affected by his shrapnel wounds were mostly on that side, too, and still on the mend. His physical therapist assured him that one day getting in and out of a car or up and down from a chair would come as easily as it used to. One day.

Once he got his bearings, he set out across the small parking lot toward the office door in the maintenance building. Inside the garage, a brownish-blonde haired guy checked out the engine on a ride-on mower. A much larger rig sat in the corner. More like a big tractor hooked to some kind of huge mowing apparatus.

The guy noticed Chris and straightened up. "Are you Chris?"

"I am."

"Tom told me to keep an eye out for you. I'm Jed. I do all the maintenance on the yard equipment and golf carts. I'm almost ready for you. Go on in there to Tom's office. He's got some things for you to read and sign. When you're done with him, come on out here and I'll show you how to work this mower."

"Great," Chris said. "I'll do that." He walked into the side entrance of Tom's office through the garage area.

Tom was sitting behind his desk, tapping away on his keyboard. He stopped and looked up. "Chris, there you are." He glanced at the clock on the wall. "Right on time. Good." He handed Chris an off-white card. "This is your timecard. It's pretty straightforward." He stood up and walked back through the door Chris had come in. "Follow me."

Chris did. They walked down to the corner of that same wall. Chris saw a gray timecard machine. Hanging next to it, a metal rack containing about eight or ten cards just like the one in his hand.

Tom took a few minutes, explained the procedures. "Any questions?"

"Not about this. Just about the work. I know I'm supposed to mow. Where do you want me to start?"

"Jed will show you all that. But first, I have something I need you to read for me, then a paper for you to sign. It's the safety section of the employee manual. It's back on my desk." They walked back into his office and Tom sat in his chair. Chris sat in one of the chairs in front of his desk.

"It's sitting there on the edge of the desk," Tom said. "Every employee has to read it before they start, then sign a form saying they did. I put a post-it by the right chapter. Shouldn't take but five or ten minutes. You can sit right there, if you want, and I'll keep answering these emails. When you're done, just sign that sheet next to it."

"Sure." Chris leaned forward and picked up the booklet.

After reading the safety section Tom had marked, he signed the form. "All set," he said.

Tom looked up again. "Good. I'll bring you out to Jed. He'll train you on the mowers. Right now, we're just going to have you mow the wide open spaces, no-frills or tight spots. Until you get real familiar with how the mower works. We'll start you off on the smaller mower, the one we use with the rough and general areas. After a while, he'll teach you how to use the big guy. You probably saw it there in the corner. We use that on the fairways. Its' a bit more complex. But let's face it, we're talking mowing grass here, not rocket science. Jed can help you with all that. He did it his first two years here."

"Sounds great," Chris said. "And thanks again for giving me the job. I really needed it." He held out his hand.

Tom shook it. "Glad we could work it out. Jed's also going to give you a walkie-talkie. Don't hesitate to buzz me if you run into a snag."

Chris walked over to the mower. As he did, Jed was screwing the cap back on something.

"Why don't you hop up in the seat there, and we'll get started," Jed said. "There's all kinds of things about this mower I'll need to show you eventually. But I'm thinking since we're a little backed up on our mowing, I'll just go over the basics. I'll tell you enough so that you can operate everything you need to get going."

"And I guess, where you want me to mow," Chris said.

"Right. That part'll be easy. We do it in a certain order, but it's all gotta get mowed, and often. We don't mow like most people do, or most businesses. They wait until the grass gets too long. Golf courses are all about the grass being a certain height. There's one height for the rough, another height for the fairway, another for the greens. We mow to keep everything at a certain height. On this guy, you'll just be mowing what we call the rough. Mostly wide-open spaces. See that pad?" He pointed to a notebook resting in a wire mesh sleeve.

Chris nodded.

"Take it out and start flipping through the pages."

Chris did. They were thick like cardboard and laminated. Each page was the layout of a different hole on the golf course.

"See how they're color-coded? Each color is for a different height. The orange is for the rough, where you'll be mowing. At first, you'll need to look at this often. After a while, it'll all be in your head. Besides that, the grass is already pretty close to its proper height, so you can tell which areas are which. Now let's go through how to operate the mower."

He took Chris through all the different steps. It was more complicated than driving a car, but not much. When Jed got to explaining about the foot pedals, he stopped a moment.

"I guess I need to ask, do you have any limitations here?" He pointed to Chris's prosthetic limb.

"Some, I guess," Chris said. "But I'm getting stronger all the time with it. How often do I have to use that left pedal?"

"Not constantly. Just when you have to shift gears. It requires more pressure than your average gas pedal on a car."

"Like driving a stick shift, right?" Chris said.

"Sort of. But there's no traffic lights out here, no stop signs. And barely any traffic. You have to use the pedal sometimes and, when you do, you'll have to be able to use it with your left foot. But there should be long periods of time when you'll get it in the right gear and just leave it there as you mow."

"I guess we'll have to give it a try," Chris said, "see if I can do it. I'm pretty sure I can."

"Well, I'll grease it real good. If that doesn't work, I suppose we can make some kind of rig that would let you push down on it with your left hand."

Chris hoped he didn't have to do that, but he was happy to see how eager Jed was to make it work.

Jed went on with his talk, explained all about shifting gears and using the brakes. About all the safety features for lowering the mower blades and backing up. When it seemed like he was all done explaining things, he stepped back out of the way. Chris thought he was going to tell him to turn the key on.

Instead he said, "So how'd you lose the leg anyway? Tom didn't mention it, just that it was in Afghanistan. I served there in 2008."

"That was a while ago." Chris figured Jed was maybe five years older than he was. Maybe a little more.

"A lifetime ago," Jed said. Then he shifted into that stare Chris instantly recognized. "And sometimes, it feels like yesterday." He shook his head, broke the stare and focused on Chris again. "We were fighting in the mountains, the Korengal Valley. Heard of it?"

"Yeah. We were far from there, though. Much flatter ground, in Helmand Province near Marjah."

"Guarding the poppy fields?" Jed said.

That made Chris laugh for some reason. "You could say that. That's where I lost this." He pointed to his leg. "I was working a minesweeper out in front. It didn't make a peep. Walking through a trail in a poppy field, stepped right on a plastic mine, and that was that. You suffer any injuries in Korengal?"

Jed sighed. Looked away a moment, then looked back. "Just in here," he said, pointing to his head.

Chris instantly understood.

23

Jed continued to explain the finer points of the mower operation to Chris, then had Chris ride it slowly out to a large patch of grass near the maintenance building. There, Chris got a chance to put everything he'd learned into action. After a few bumpy moments, he was soon going back and forth in mostly straight lines and turning fairly well.

After Jed was satisfied Chris could depress the clutch pedal with his prosthetic leg, he turned him loose to begin mowing the highest level of grass, the rough surrounding the nearby ninth hole. When he'd finished, Jed told him to keep mowing the rough on as many of the back nine holes as he could before lunch.

That's how Chris spent his morning. And he kinda liked it. He'd mowed the grass in his own yard as a kid growing up, but always with a push mower. This felt more like riding a big, powerful go-kart. Hardly felt like work at all.

More than enjoying the go-kart connection, he enjoyed even more having his mind engaged in something productive. And the scenery was certainly pleasant. Like riding around in a theme park. His instructions were to avoid all the water hazards and sand traps for now. After he had a few more days mastering the machine, they'd trust him with areas that required more skill.

The only moment of excitement came when a golfer's drive bounced two feet in front of Chris on the tenth hole. Chris was wearing a sound-muffling headset, so he didn't hear the man yell, "Fore!" Unfortunately, at the speed he was going he wasn't able to react fast enough and ran right over the man's ball. The mower tore it to pieces.

When the elderly golfer arrived on the scene, Chris was very apologetic but the man wasn't angry. Mostly embarrassed the ball wound up so far from where he was aiming.

Chris headed back to the maintenance building. It was lunch time. Since he only got thirty minutes, he'd packed a sandwich and a baggy full of chips. The sandwich was in a cooler in his car.

After parking the mower where Jed had shown him, Chris fetched his cooler and found a picnic bench under a tree behind the building. He was disappointed to find Jed was already there eating his lunch. He was tempted to head back to his car, but Jed had already seen him.

He set his cooler on the picnic table and opened it up.

"What hole were you on?" Jed said. "How far did you get?"

"The twelfth hole," Chris said.

"Not bad for your first day. Forgot to tell you, if you know you're going to be far away from this place when lunchtime hits, you could just bring your cooler with you on the mower, so you don't have to head all the way back here. There's a metal basket behind the seat. Pretty sure that cooler would fit in it. If not, you could strap it down with a bungee."

"Thanks. I'll do that tomorrow."

They didn't talk for a minute. Jed kept eating. Chris started unwrapping his food.

Jed broke the silence. "How's the leg holding up? With the

shifting, I mean. Giving you any trouble?"

It was giving Chris some. In fact his left knee was pretty sore. "Not much. I'm sure I'll get used to it."

"How often you go in for physical therapy?"

"Down to twice a week," Chris said, "unless something goes wrong."

"I'm actually seeing somebody again. A shrink at the VA. I quit going for a while, but Tom thought it might do me some good to go back."

Chris could tell Jed had more he wanted to say. He wasn't sure he wanted to hear it. But the counselors he'd talked to all agreed...talking helped, especially with someone who understood. "Things starting to bother you again? I mean, since you stopped going for a while and now you're going back."

"You could say that."

"Anything in particular?"

Jed seemed to think about it. "Guess it started back when the president pulled everybody out of Iraq. Before a year was up, look what happened. The whole thing reverted back to the way it was, even worse than it was once ISIS took over."

"But that's Iraq," Chris said. "I thought you fought in Afghanistan."

"I did. But it reminded me of what happened after we left Korengal. Same difference. You ever see that movie, *Restrepo?*"

"Heard about it, but didn't see it." Chris knew it was a documentary filmed in the Korengal Valley, the mountainous area where Jed was stationed. "Were you in that flick?"

Jed shook his head no. "But we weren't that far away. We went through the very same things. I knew some of the guys in the movie. Even while we were there, you got the feeling we were just wasting our time." He stopped a moment, rested his elbows on the table. "We were scared out of our minds every day, getting shot at, getting mortared. Guys were getting wounded, some getting killed. Some were good friends. And for what? We were just guarding a bunch of dirt huts on some nowhere mountain for people who still want to live in the Stone Age. And they don't even want you there in the first place."

Chris knew exactly what he was talking about.

Jed straightened up. "In the pep talks they gave us, they kept telling us we had to be there to protect these people from the Taliban. Seemed to us, most of the time they resented us being there more than the Taliban. Most of their sons were off fighting for them. And you know what happened as soon as we pulled out of that area?"

"Everything went back to the way it was?"

"Exactly," Jed said. "Just the way it was before we ever got there. Probably the way it was a hundred years ago, the way it'll be a hundred years from now. And when the president pulls all our guys out of Afghanistan, I wouldn't be a bit surprised to see the whole country go back to the way it was. Like we were never there. Like all those lives we lost never mattered. All those friends we lost. Guys losing their arms and legs, and for what?"

Jed suddenly realized what he'd said. "Hey look, I'm sorry. I didn't mean to say that. I wasn't thinking straight. I was just blabbing away—"

"Don't worry about it," Chris said. "You aren't saying anything I've haven't said or thought about a hundred times. You joked about it this morning, about us guarding the poppy fields. We all knew what was going on. They harvest poppy to make opium and heroin. It's their biggest cash crop. We were told we were there to win hearts and minds and, like you said, to protect the Afghan people from the Taliban. All the guys I fought with felt the same way you do. Most of those people didn't want protection from the Taliban. They wanted us out of there, the sooner the better. They wanted things back the way they were, the way they'd always been."

Both men sat in silence a few moments. Chris spoke up first. "I didn't put my life on the line every day for the Afghan people. And I didn't lose this leg or get half my body all shot up with shrapnel for them, either. I was there to protect my friends. We figured, the government stuck us here. We thought it was for one thing, turned out to be for another. Then you realize, the big picture reasons don't really matter. What matters are the guys I trained with, the guys I'm fighting with. They're what matter."

"And that's why they were there, too," Jed said.

"And when all is said and done," Chris said, "that's the only thing that matters, the only thing that's gonna matter fifty years from now. The rest of it's all pointless. In the overall scheme of things, it doesn't count for a hill-a-beans."

Jed stood up. "And that my friend, is why I'm seeing a shrink."

24

Chris was finally back in his apartment, safe and sound. He closed the door behind him, hating the way he felt. He knew he was no longer in any danger. At least on one level. He could tell that to himself a dozen times, a hundred times. But at some point, this overwhelming feeling of anxiety would come over him.

It didn't happen all the time, but it seemed to be happening more, not less, as time went on. When it did, he seemed powerless to stop it. He knew it was PTSD. He'd already been diagnosed with it. In fact, he was in the middle of being re-evaluated to see if his rating percentage should increase. He'd get more money if it did.

But Chris didn't want his percentage increased. He wanted it to stop. He wanted to be normal again.

So far, his efforts had been entirely unsuccessful. When he was first released from the hospital, he'd started drinking, heavily. But after a month or two, and one seriously close call with a head-on collision, he knew that had to stop. He quit going to bars and stopped bringing booze home from the store. Even beer.

But he needed something. The meds he took helped some. But he hated the way they made him feel.

Carrying the bags of groceries, he stepped away from the front door and brought them out to the kitchen. It didn't take long to put them away. He had planned to stay at the store longer and really stock up on things, but barely a third of the way down his list, the panic attack hit.

Fortunately, he was able to grab a pre-made dish of lasagna first. He read the directions, set the oven to the right temperature, set the timer and shoved it in. He walked over to the living area and plopped down on the sofa.

He thought this recent bout with PTSD may have been triggered by his talk with Jed during lunch. The chat seemed to do Jed some good; Chris wondered if it hadn't come at his expense. For the rest of the afternoon as he mowed, different things they'd discussed played over and over in his head.

Just before the lunch break, Jed mentioned some documentary he'd watched about some aging World War II vets. The interviewer had asked them if they struggled with any PTSD-like symptoms after the war. The men said yes. Some of the men still struggled seventy years later.

That was a depressing thought all by itself. For Jed, and for Chris.

One of the men in his early 90s said he thought the soldiers today had it much worse than they did back in World War II. For one thing, all the bad guys they fought wore uniforms. It was easy to know when you were in danger, and when you weren't. Today's soldiers were in danger from everyone: men, women, kids, even old men. Walking around was dangerous, all by itself.

And the worst part, the old man said, was that they could at least balance out their suffering with the knowledge that they *had* to fight the Nazis and Japanese. Everyone back home fully supported the soldiers and the cause. And the war ended with complete victory; the enemy surrendered unconditionally. Today, returning vets from Iraq and Afghanistan had to sit and watch all the gains won in battle completely erased. All the places they had liberated at such great cost were, one by one, reverting back into the hands of the same enemy. Making it all seemed like it had been for nothing.

Chris certainly didn't need to be reminded of that.

He sat up on the couch and reached for the remote, hoping to find something on TV to reset his mind. The phone rang. He leaned over and picked it up off the end table. It was Kyle, his best friend from Afghanistan.

"Hey Kyle, how are you doing? So good to hear your voice."

After too long a pause, Kyle said, "Hey, Chris."

"You don't sound too good. You're back home now, right?" After the tour Kyle and Chris had shared together, Kyle had signed up for another.

"Yeah, about two months now. This time I'm back for good."

"What happened? You get hurt?"

"I was in a Humvee that overturned a few months back. Got banged up some. But nothing serious."

"Just needed to get away from it all?"

"Something like that," Kyle said. "I wanted to stay in, but you know what's going on. They're wrapping everything up. Besides that, guess I've seen too much and been shot at one too many times."

"Why, what are they saying?" Although Chris thought he knew. He could hear it in Kyle's voice. He was not in a good place. And he sounded drunk.

"Guess I started doing and saying things that were getting me into trouble. So they had me evaluated. Next thing I know, I'm not just going home, I'm being pushed out of the service altogether. Accepting the PTSD diagnosis was the only way for me to avoid being dishonorably discharged."

Chris knew a bit about how this worked. Kyle probably had PTSD for a while and didn't know it. "Are you getting any help? Now that you're home, I mean? Are you seeing anyone?"

"You mean a girl?" Kyle said.

"No, I mean like a shrink. A counselor. I'm supposed to be. Haven't done it yet. But speaking of girls, you seeing anyone?"

"Nope. I don't think I'm sending off the right kind of vibes these days."

Chris laughed.

"How about you?"

"My vibes are probably worse than yours," Chris said. "No girl in her right mind would want anything I'm selling." He heard Kyle sigh on the other end. "What kind of things are you dealing with?"

"I don't know," Kyle said. "Just stuff."

"How are you sleeping?"

"Not good. Too many nightmares. Sometimes I feel like I'm just napping off and on all night long. One nightmare I keep having involves you."

"Me?"

"Yeah," Kyle said. "I keep reliving that day in the poppy field. I keep hearing that click, then you scream, then the explosion. I look and see you flying through the air, then you fall and disappear in the flowers. I scream out your name, but no sound comes out. I run over to you and look down and then—"

He stopped talking. Chris could hear him starting to choke up. Now, it sounded like he was crying. "It was so..."

"Kyle," Chris said softly. "It's okay, bro. It's alright."

Kyle started getting control of himself. "But it's not okay, man. You're not okay. I saw what happened to you. And I keep seeing what happened to you, over and over again. I can't do anything about it. Not then, and I can't do anything now."

"But I'm better, Kyle. Okay, I lost my leg. But I got off easy in some ways. You should've seen the guys around me in the hospital. Some lost both legs. Some lost arms, too. And I've been through all kinds of therapy to learn how to walk again. You should see me…with long pants on, you might not even know the leg is gone. I'm close to not even having a limp."

"So…so you're doing okay?"

What should Chris say? He couldn't lie to his friend.

"Sometimes I am. I've got good days and bad days." Chris couldn't recall too many good days lately. "But it's hard. I'm not gonna kid you. I'm going through probably some of the same things you are, and some extra things because of the leg. I can't stand being in crowds. I feel like I'm always on guard, like I'm back in the war zone. My mind refuses to accept I'm safe now. Some days, I don't feel like I belong anywhere. Like I'm pretending all the time. You know what normal is, so you try to act normal when other people are around. But the whole time, you know that's not how you feel inside. You don't feel normal. You feel off, on edge. It's exhausting."

Kyle didn't answer right away. Then he said, "You're describing my life to a T. I got all that going on."

"There's a lot of us who've got all that going on," Chris said. "I don't know what the percentage is, but it's not small. Read somewhere that twenty-two vets commit suicide every day." He thought a moment. "You ever thought about doing that, Kyle?"

Kyle didn't answer. Wait a minute. "Kyle, is that why you called? Have you been thinking about that now? About killing yourself?"

Another long pause.

126

"Kyle? Tell me you're not. Tell me you're not sitting there with a gun in your hand."

"Not a gun," Kyle said.

"Then what?"

"I'm not gonna do it. That's why I called. See, you talked me out of it." He laughed. "Hearing how messed up you are somehow made me feel better."

Chris laughed. But he knew this wasn't funny. "Now listen Kyle. You did the right thing to call me. But you need to do more than call me. You need to go get some help. Promise me you'll do that."

"I will."

"I mean it."

"I know. Okay, I will."

"You will what?"

"I'll go get help."

"You do it first thing tomorrow," Chris said. "And Kyle, you can't do that to me. You can't leave me down here on my own. You call me anytime you start feeling bad. I got a job now, so leave a voicemail if I don't pick up right away. I see it's you, I'll call you back the first chance I get."

"Alright."

"You promise?"

"Yeah. Good talking with you, Chris."

25

Amy led Finley around the grass area in the yard. Before she'd left, Kim had suggested it might be a good idea considering Finley's car ride followed by all this excitement. After a few minutes of sniffing, Kim's hunch proved right. Fortunately, it wasn't the kind that needed cleaning up.

One thing Amy did notice, though, was all the attention Finley was getting from the other inmates in the yard. He was definitely turning some heads. To her, except for possibly that German Shepherd mix, he was the best looking dog of the lot.

It's not like she had anything to do with it. Her team wound up getting the last set of dogs and she got the last dog available on her team. "And look what I got," she said aloud to Finley. He looked up at her and wagged his tail. She gave him a treat, which he all but inhaled. She rubbed his head. "You ready to go inside? See your new room and new bed?"

She walked him across the yard and stepped inside the main meeting room, the same room where they'd eaten lunch after the graduation ceremony. Rita said this is also where they'd do the bulk of the training, at least the indoor parts.

As she crossed the floor, she had to sidestep around one of the girls holding the leash to a black-and-white pit. Her name was Rafferty. Noticing Finley, she said, "How do you rate getting a dog like that?"

"I don't," Amy said. "I was prepared to take anything. Finley just happened to be the last dog of the day." She looked down at her pit. "But your dog's cute."

Rafferty looked at her dog, who was looking up at her adoringly. "In his own way, I suppose." She bent down and scratched his neck. "But you're not going to win any contests with this face, are you boy? Maybe crack a mirror or two. But that's all. Aren't ya?" She said all this like a mother cooing a baby. Her dog wagged his little rope of a tail, hard enough his whole rear-end shook.

Finley watched the scene with interest until her dog took an interest in him. Then he turned his body sideways and looked away. "Guess he's a little shy," Amy said.

"No," Rafferty said, "that's not being shy for a dog. He's basically telling my dog, hey, I'm cool. I don't want any trouble. Watch, my dog will sniff his butt now."

"I hate it when dogs do that," Amy said. "It's so gross."

"You better get used to it. Dogs do it all the time. It'd be pretty sick if we did that when we greeted each other. But it's not like that for dogs. A dog figures out half the world with its nose. It's, like, a hundred times more powerful than ours. When they sniff each other, it's like you and I small-talking for ten minutes. Supposedly, they find out all kinds of things about each other through a few good sniffs. Andy here, for example, has probably just figured out what kind of napp Finley's been on lately. How his health is doing and even what kind of mood he's in."

"Really?"

"That's right. So we let him do it, at least for a little while."

Amy could see that Finley didn't seem to mind nearly as much as she did. "Well, thanks for explaining. One more thing I learned about dogs that I never knew before."

"You're just getting started. There's a ton more to learn. I remember when I first came into the program, I thought I knew everything about dogs. Had 'em my whole life. But I didn't know nothing. Found out pretty much all my opinions were totally off. But it's a lot of fun when you find out what they're really up to. And it makes it a whole lot easier to train 'em."

"I can't wait till we get started," Amy said. "By the way, know when that is? When we'll start having group classes?"

"First thing tomorrow morning, right after breakfast. You read that booklet they gave you yet?"

"Most of it."

"Well, read all of it. Read it through a couple of times. It helps to know all the terms Miss Brenda will use while she teaches. That way you won't look so stupid, constantly interrupting her with questions during the class."

"All right, I will. Thanks." She turned to Finley. "Okay Finley, let's go check out your new room." She headed toward the doorway in the corner, leading to the dorms.

Through the hallway, several more inmates who hadn't seen Finley yet stopped what they were doing to admire him as he passed. And of course, their dogs took turns "small-talking" with his behind. Finley even returned the favor and sniffed a few himself. It was so hard for Amy not to make him stop.

She was at least relieved to see that all the dogs were getting along. She made it into her room without a single tense moment.

After quickly closing the door, she unlatched Finley's leash and set it on a hook hanging on the wall above his crate. He stood there a moment just looking at her. Then his head swiveled around taking everything in. She sat on the edge of the bed. He came up to her and sat between her legs. With them both sitting this way, his head was just a few inches shorter than hers.

"This is your new room, Finley. You'll be staying with me from now on. Well, a few months anyway." She had no idea if dogs had any sense of time. The dog book said they tended to live in the moment. She wanted to make this moment as pleasant for him as possible. She got up partway and opened his crate door. "See this? This is yours. It's your crate."

He looked at her and at the crate, but she could tell he didn't understand. Then she remembered what Kim said. Pulling out the bag of treats, she unzipped the top. That got his attention.

"You like this smell?" She held the baggy under his nose. He inhaled deeply and began nudging it, like he was trying to get it open. His tail began to thump against the throw rug. "I wonder how they smell." She took a whiff. "Wow, that's not half bad. I expected it to stink. You want one of these?"

She pulled out a couple and walked to his crate. She opened the door and held the treat inside the crate. "Want this? You can have it." She set it down on the pad then set the second one toward the back of the crate. She sat back on the bed to watch.

Finley looked at her, then at the crate.

"Go ahead. You can have it."

His tail still wagging, he took a few steps until his head leaned inside. He looked back at her.

"You can have it, Finley. Go ahead."

He quickly lowered his head to the mat and ate it. Then without hesitating, he stepped in the rest of the way to get the second treat. After he finished, he spun around quickly as if he expected to be locked inside.

But Amy didn't move. "Good boy. You want another one?" She

pulled another treat out of the bag and held it out in her palm.

His tail began to bang back and forth against the crate. It continued to wag as he stepped through the door in her direction. He was liking this, and that made her so happy.

There was a knock on the door. Rita poked her head in. "In about five minutes bring him over to my room. I'll take you over to where we keep the food, so you can give him his first meal. We always have the trainers feed their dogs. Helps the dog sort out who matters. Strengthens the bond."

"Okay, thanks."

Finley came all the way out of the crate and, after eating the treat in her hand, sat next to her. Then he did something wonderful. He got this contented look on his face and leaned against her leg. She had read in the book that dogs did this for three reasons: for affection, to feel secure, or for dominance. Amy could tell Finley wasn't trying to dominate her, which meant he did it either to express affection or to feel more secure. Either one was totally fine with her.

They'd been together for less than thirty minutes but, already, Amy understood why people called them man's best friend.

After enjoying this moment a bit longer, her thoughts drifted to tomorrow morning and her first group training class. She remembered that she was the rookie here. Everyone else knew what they were doing.

She had never even owned a dog before.

26

Finley heard some commotion and woke up. It took him a few moments to realize where he was, and to remember how he'd gotten here. Looking out from behind some bars, he realized the commotion came from a door opening, a woman's voice saying something, then the door closing again. Next, the young woman who began caring for him yesterday, woke up from her sleep and sat up in her bed.

Finley was pretty sure her name was Amy. He'd heard several different people call her that, including the woman who'd just poked her head in the door.

The noise had awakened him from a pleasant dream. He'd been running and playing "fetch the ball" in an open field. Sometimes Kim was throwing the ball, other times Chaz.

"Good morning, Finley. How did you sleep?"

It was Amy. Finley stretched. She reached for him, sticking her fingers through the bars. He licked them, seemed the polite thing to do.

"Hope you were comfortable. I didn't want to put you in that crate, but I was told you wouldn't mind. Hope they were right. But you can get out now, if you want. There's some food in your bowl. Guess you weren't hungry last night. And there's some fresh water, if you want it."

Finley had no idea what she was saying, but he liked the way she talked. So far, she had only used this nice voice. He also liked how much attention she was giving him. He wondered if she'd be somebody he could begin to look to, somebody permanent. Maybe it was too soon to think that way.

She slid the latch over on his crate door and opened it. It was nice to know he could get out, but he wasn't in a terrible hurry. He hoped she had plans to take him outside soon. Those urges were starting to rumble.

"Don't want to come out? That's okay." She reached over, closed his door, slid the latch back over and locked it. "I'm just going to leave you in there for a minute while I go to the bathroom. While I'm out there, I'll find out how much time we have until our first class. Okay? You stay in there, and I'll be right back."

Now what was she doing? Had he done something wrong by not getting out of the crate? She didn't seem upset. He watched her get up and leave, closing the door behind him.

Everything seemed to be fine. Everyone seemed to be fairly happy and positive. Both the humans Finley could see, as well as the other dogs. But he had absolutely no idea what was going on, or what to expect. They were back in the big open room he had walked through yesterday.

A good bit of time had passed since Amy had let Finley out of the crate. When she had returned to the room, she was definitely not upset. She still talked to him in a happy voice. And she'd used that same happy voice all morning. After walking him in the yard long enough to go to the bathroom, she'd put him back in the crate a short while, which he didn't mind, since she had given him two of those yummy treats.

Once again, she'd left the room but wasn't gone long. At least, he didn't think so. He had fallen asleep. When she'd returned, she led him out of the crate on a leash and brought him here. Finley noticed then for the first time that all the women holding dogs on leashes wore the same clothes as Amy. Except for the woman at the front of the room. He remembered her. She had been with Kim.

A few moments later, all the women with dogs, including Amy, spread out on either side the room in two groups. He and Amy were near the end of one line, close to the wall. He wasn't sure what came next, but he didn't really care. All of the dogs seemed friendly, and so did the other women holding their leashes.

And best of all, he could smell the strong aroma of treats. Some were in their hands but even more were in their pockets.

Amy looked down at Finley, standing next to her. Miss Brenda stood in the center against the far wall. All the other inmates along with their dogs were lined up in two rows on opposite sides of the room, facing each other. She was about to experience her first dog training class.

Miss Brenda began to speak again. "Before we start, have you new girls read the manuals we gave you?" Her gaze shifted between two other inmates, then rested on Amy.

Amy had thought she was the only one who was new. The other girls nodded that they had, and Amy said, "I did, too."

"Good," Brenda said. "That'll keep me from having to repeat myself too many times. Most of you girls have been through this a number of times, but for the sake of you newer ones, I'll explain some of the basic things we're going to teach you this morning. Well, that you're going to teach your dogs." She held up one of the treats. "Ladies, what do we call these, besides treats?"

"Lures!" A number of ladies called out.

"That's right, lures. I'll call them both things from time to time. The reason we call them lures is that we use them to lure the dog into performing a behavior we want him to do. As you all know, dogs love treats. Some treats better than others. We make sure to use only treats we know they'll love when we train them. Treats, or lures, along with petting are one of the main ingredients in positive reinforcement methods. Don't even think about training without them."

"Okay," Brenda said. "We're going to start off teaching the dogs to sit. Dogs like to sit, of course. The idea is to get them to sit when we want them to, on command. After that, we're going to teach them to focus. After we get them to sit, we want them to focus on our eyes until we have their undivided attention. Believe it or not, this is a very simple thing to teach a dog. Dogs are one of the only creatures on the planet that will actually look humans straight in the eye. We're going to get them to do that for a treat and, later, get them to do it just because we asked."

Brenda looked around the room, spotted Rita. "Rita, tell these newer gals why it's so important to teach every dog these basic skills."

Rita came to the front with her dog and turned to face the ladies. "Guess I could say it this way. Dogs are not multitasking creatures. Which means, they can only do one thing at a time. Trouble is, sometimes the one thing they're doing is something we don't like or don't want them to do. Instead of yelling at them or telling them to stop, the trick is to get them to do something else instead."

"Re-direct them," Brenda added. "We also call it counter-conditioning."

"Right," Rita said. "Like putting them in a sit, or a sit and focus. When those behaviors become second nature to them, you give those commands and they'll stop the bad thing and do the thing you're telling them. Then you can redirect them into the behavior you want them to do instead."

"Very good," Brenda said. "Did you all get that?" Everyone said yes, or nodded. "Good. So let's get started. I'm going to show you how to put them in a sit, just using a hand signal. You won't even have to say the word."

Amy was really liking this. So far, it all made perfect sense. Of course, she still had a thousand things to learn. She looked down the row at all the other inmates, then down at Finley. She felt like she was standing next to the finest dog in the entire group. Overnight, he had already surpassed the Shepherd.

Part III

Two Months Later

27

Amy

Over the past two months, Amy and Finley had become the closest of friends. Perhaps, too close.

That thought had begun to surface during the past two weeks. Amy had stomped it out every time it did. During that time, the Prison Paws and Pals Program had opened its doors to begin inviting military veterans to come in and observe the dogs and their training.

The real reason for these visits was to begin to let the vets become acquainted with the dogs, and the dogs with them. Almost all these vets suffered from various stages of PTSD. Some significantly so. Miss Bridget had gathered the newer inmate-trainers together before the vets first visit to help them understand what they were about to experience.

She explained they should make no effort to push their dogs toward one vet over another. Instead, let the vets mingle and interact with the dogs at their own pace, and let the selection process happen organically. Don't be overly talkative or try to "sell" your dog to them. Picking out a companion dog is a very personal decision. The veterans need to feel totally confident about the dogs they end up with.

The presence of the vets had even affected the training itself. Since the dogs knew all the basic commands and followed instructions without hesitation, the training had shifted toward getting the dogs ready to care for the "invisible wounds" many of the veterans struggled with. Amy could see several suffered from obvious physical wounds, as well. Some were missing limbs; some were in wheelchairs; some were burn victims.

Quite a few matches had already been made. In fact, after the last interaction with the vets, Rita told Amy the majority of the dogs had been paired with their new owners, including Charlie, her pit-mix. Soon the inmate-trainers would begin teaching the veterans how to train the dogs themselves, so they could do the same things with the dogs when they brought them home.

At the moment, Charlie and Finley were playing in her room. Amy was glad they didn't understand what was coming down the road. Graduation day was less than a month away. After that, these two best friends would be split up and likely never see each other again.

She dreaded the idea. Not just for the confusion and doggie-grief they'd experience. She knew in time, once they had bonded with their new owners, they would adjust fairly well.

The real question was, would she?

When she looked at Finley now, she didn't just see a beautiful dog. Over the last two months, he had become so much more. A knock at the door interrupted her thoughts. She looked up to see Rita popping her head inside. Amy was glad for the distraction.

Finley and Charlie were engaged in a fierce tug-of-war over what had once been a stuffed possum. When they had first begun to play together, it made Amy nervous. Charlie would growl and make so much noise. Finley was bigger, but with Charlie's huge head and broad shoulders he seemed to have a decided advantage. She'd always heard pits were fighting dogs, and she didn't want Finley to get hurt. The whole time, Charlie's tail would wag, but still.

In time Amy's fears disappeared. It soon became clear, Charlie was nothing but a fun-loving dope. He didn't have a mean bone in his body. He loved people, and he absolutely loved Finley.

"Does Finley ever win these tug-of-wars?" Rita said.

"No. But he never gives up easily." Just as Amy said this, Finley dug his feet into the floor and began backing up. Charlie was still on the throw rug, so he slid across the room.

"Hate to break up the fun," Rita said, "but that group of veterans will start showing up here in about twenty minutes. Maybe we should take these two out in the yard, so they can take care of business."

"I forgot they were coming again today." The thought instantly saddened her. "You suppose they'll be any new ones coming?"

Rita came in the rest of the way and closed the door behind her. Charlie and Finley both looked up at her but continued their struggle. Charlie had freed himself from the rug, now bunched up by the desk. "I know what you're going through," she said. "You really need to get over it."

"What am I going through?"

"You don't want anyone to match up with Finley. But you know that's the whole purpose of this program, right? It's not about finding you a forever friend. It's about helping Finley to become someone else's forever friend."

Amy sighed. "I know. But how's that my fault? Nobody's picked him yet."

"You know that's not all that's going on here. Nobody's picked him, because you don't want to let him go. He's the best looking dog in the program, next to that Shepherd."

"He's way better looking than the Shepherd."

Rita smiled. "Maybe so, but that's not the point, is it? I've seen lots of guys look at him these past few weeks. Some even tried to interact with them, but he completely ignores them. He's totally focused on you. That's the only reason he's not with someone yet."

"I don't understand how that's my fault. You know what we were told. We're supposed to let things happen by themselves. Let the vets spend time with the dogs and see what happens. Well, I'm there every time. It just hasn't happened yet."

"I hear you," Rita said. "But I think there's more going on here than that. Finley has chosen you, but it's a fantasy. He doesn't know any better. He thinks you and he are together for good now. I think you need to change the way you interact with him, especially during these meetings. Push him out of the nest a little. What I see is him pulling away when these guys show an interest, and you keep comforting and coddling him. You need to be doing the opposite, start sending Finley the opposite signal."

Amy knew what she was talking about and knew that she was right. But she didn't want to push Finley away. She was right there in the same fantasy.

"Amy," Rita said in a softer tone, "you can't keep him. You know that, right? If one of these vets doesn't take him home, he won't be staying here. He'll be going back to the Humane Society and some family will adopt him. Either way, he won't be here with you. I'm sorry to have to be so blunt, but it's just the truth. That happens, and all this training we've been putting him through was for nothing. And some vet—someone who really could be helped bigtime by a dog like Finley—will lose out."

Amy didn't respond right away. "I know," she finally said. "I know you're right."

"Well, let's get them outside so they'll be ready to go when the vets start showing up."

"Okay." Amy stood.

"Alright Charlie," Rita said in a firm voice, "Leave it."

Both Charlie and Finley stop tugging when they heard her command. Charlie let go of the stuffed animal and walked over to Rita's side. She praised him for it, snapped on his leash. "Let's go."

28

A steady procession of dogs and trainers made their way out of the dorm rooms, down the hall and into the main training room. Finley walked cheerfully beside Amy, totally used to this routine now. As soon as she entered the main room, Amy looked to her left at the guest chairs lined up along the far wall and at the door that opened to the outside.

Many of the vets who'd already picked out their dogs were sitting in the chairs or coming through the door. They smiled and waved at their respective trainers and dogs. Most of the dogs seemed to recognize "their" vets. The inmate-trainers had been given permission to let the dogs spend a few minutes greeting their future owners before the class began.

Those who were still unmatched, like Finley, stood in their usual place in the training line waiting for this little get-together to end. She looked down at Finley, who was looking back at her. He occasionally glanced over at the scene but seemed totally disinterested. His eyes rotated between Amy's face, her hand and the pouch tied at her waist, which contained the bag of treats for today's class.

She reached in the pouch, picked out a treat and handed it to him. Looking back at the scene against the wall, she noticed three or four new faces among the guests. Although not in uniform, she figured they were probably all vets. Each of the men looked to be in their mid-to-late twenties, except for the one with the beard who seemed at least ten years older. Then again, she always had a hard time judging the age of guys with beards. The new vets had that serious look in their eyes she had grown accustomed to. For some, the look came off a little more ominous. Maybe troubled was a better word.

From everything she'd read, they had a right to be.

That look contrasted the countenance on the other vets' faces, the ones petting their future dogs. Their eyes were bright, their faces smiling. They looked mostly…normal.

But she remembered what they'd looked like when they had first arrived. Just like the new guys did. Same firm expressions. What a difference these dogs were already making. She had to remember that, stay focused on that thought. For Finley's sake, and for whichever vet wound up taking him home.

Finley looked at all the commotion across the room. It was something of a familiar scene now but still, when it happened, he never understood it. On most days, things were the same. The same dogs with the same women. They spent some of the time all together, and some of the time with just their trainers.

Finley liked the other dogs for the most part, especially Charlie. But he loved the times with Amy the most. Amy was the best. When he was with her, anyone else could be around, and he was fine. When she was gone, he mostly just waited until she returned, however long it took.

He still remembered Chaz and, when he did, it was a happy

moment. Although he couldn't remember Chaz's scent anymore, and that saddened him a little. The truth was, he liked Amy as much as Chaz, if not more. It wasn't that she treated him better; they both treated him well. But Amy treated him well a lot more often. He wasn't sure of this, but it seemed like Finley had been with Amy longer than anyone.

Maybe it just seemed that way, because they were together all the time. Whatever it was, he didn't remember ever being this happy so often, and for so many days in a row.

Suddenly, the woman named Bridget spoke. All the dogs heard it; some of the people did. A few moments later she spoke again. Now everyone turned and paid attention. Finley could only pick up a few of the words, but he understood she wanted all the dogs and owners to line up like they did every day.

He knew what came next. He was used to it by now. They would go through all the basic commands as they walked back and forth across the room. It was kind of a special time because, for once, he understood everything the humans wanted him to do. Everything made sense. He could tell all the other dogs enjoyed this time, too.

The best part was that he got to do this with Amy.

Well, that and all the treats.

For the next twenty-five minutes, Amy and the other trainers led their dogs through a variety of routines that hit on all the behaviors and commands they had learned. This was mainly just to reinforce things, but it also served to give the new veterans a chance to see the dogs in action.

It never failed to impress them. It still impressed her; not just that the dogs were so well-trained, but that she was right there doing her part. Doing all the dog trainer tasks, understanding it all, and able to teach Finley how to do it all, as well.

The only unnerving thing at the moment was that one of the new veterans clearly had his eye on Finley. And only Finley. It was the guy with the beard. Not that the beard mattered. It was the guy's eyes. They looked so…serious, and penetrating. He never smiled. She looked at the other vets, the newer ones who'd come today. They were all smiling. They weren't when they came in here, but they were now.

But not him.

She tried not to let it distract her. She tried to think of the little talk Rita had given her a little while ago. When Amy came in here today, she was mentally preparing herself to let Finley go. Rita was right. He couldn't stay here with her permanently.

Her sentence would be up in a few months, but that didn't matter. There was no way they would let Finley stay here with her until then. It was too absurd to even bring up. It would be much better for Finley to go home with a vet, not brought back to the Humane Society and adopted later by a total stranger.

But now, looking at the bearded guy, she wasn't so sure.

As she walked Finley back across the room, she glanced at him again. Still staring at Finley. Still giving her the creeps. There was no way she was letting Finley go home with him. She glanced at Rita. Rita wasn't seeing any of this. Surely, after spending all this time training Finley, Amy would have some say in who took him home. How could it be right to let just anyone take him?

So what if a vet wanted to be with the dog. What if the dog didn't want to be with him? Finley was too special. She couldn't let him go to just anyone. The new owner had to be someone equally special. Someone who would love Finley the way he deserved to be loved. The way she loved him.

They came to a stop, back to the place in line where they had begun. Miss Bridget shouted out the command, "Finish your dog."

Amy looked down at Finley and said, "Finish." But of course, he was already obeying the command on his own. He circled around and behind her, then came up by her side and sat perfectly straight. She reached down and gave him a treat.

She looked over at the vet. He wasn't smiling. Still had that stern look on his face. But at least he was nodding.

So you approve, do you? Too bad.

I don't approve of you.

29

Now that he'd finished mowing for the day, Chris did all the things he needed to disengage the mower blades. He raised them up so that he could ride this big monster a little faster as he headed back to the maintenance building. For the last month or so, Tom and Jed had cleared him to pretty much use all the different lawn equipment on all the different grass areas without any restrictions.

Like Tom said, it wasn't rocket science.

During those first few weeks, there were times though when Chris wondered if he would ever master it all. He felt especially bad on one occasion, two weeks in, when Jed had to run him down on a golf cart to get him to stop mowing at the wrong height. Chris had forgotten to raise the blades when he'd moved from the fairway to the rough, and he'd screwed this up for three holes before Jed stopped him.

It was a pretty serious mistake, but Jed didn't ride him too much about it. After all, they were in Florida. In a week it would grow right back. Besides, most of the golfers would probably be happy with the blunder. He'd inadvertently widened the fairways, which would make all their drives roll a few yards further and set things up for an easier shot.

But within a few weeks' time, Chris wasn't making amateur mistakes anymore. In fact, the entire job had slid into a rather easy-going routine. That brought on a new set of challenges.

Boredom.

He didn't have to think about the job all that much anymore, which left his mind unoccupied for large stretches of time, free to drift into all kinds of trouble. Especially on the monster mower he was riding in now. It had a big comfy chair and was enclosed in plexiglass. Between that and the earmuffs, it was almost totally silent inside. It even had air-conditioning, which further added to his nearly zombie-like state.

Sometimes the flashbacks were almost unbearable.

Happened again about an hour ago. He wasn't sure what set it off. But all of a sudden, he was lying flat on his back in the helicopter, just after he'd stepped on the mine. The whole thing was vibrating. Guys worked on him furiously. He saw the look in their eyes, when they looked down at his leg. He could feel everything he felt at that moment. All the fear, all the pain, all the confusion.

He'd only snapped out of it after running over a big tree branch. Thank God it was there. He had been heading right for a retention pond. He'd slammed on the brakes and stopped less than three feet from the water's edge.

Rounding the last cluster of trees, he could see the maintenance building up ahead. There were no worries about being distracted now, with all the golfers and golf carts to navigate around.

After a few minutes, he reached the parking lot, felt a slight bump as he transitioned from grass to pavement. The main garage door was already open. It was a clear shot to ride right in, but since there were nothing to block his way, he carefully spun the mower around and backed into its designated place. He put it in neutral, set the brake and turned it off.

As soon as he opened the plexiglass door, the heat and humidity rushed in. As he stepped down to ground level, Jed came up behind him.

"You're getting to be like an old pro on that thing. I saw how you backed it in. All in one smooth move."

"Yeah, it's pretty much getting like you said it would be when I first started."

"Like driving your car," Jed said. "I'm also noticing how quickly you can get up and down in that thing now compared to when you first started. How's your leg holding up?"

"Fine." Thankfully, that was the truth. "Not really given me any problems at all, especially with this mower. The pedals are way easier than the other mowers. But even they don't bother me much anymore."

"Yeah," Jed said, "this one's definitely the dream machine. Better be, considering how much they paid for it."

Chris nodded. Then he had a thought, wondered if he should bring it up to Jed.

They stood there staring at each other for a moment. Jed finally said, "Something on your mind?"

"How long were you doing this job before they let you start doing…other things?"

"Two years, almost."

That's what Chris remembered.

"Why? Starting to get too easy?"

"Starting to. I just thought it might be nice to mix up the mowing with some other things. Break up the monotony a little. I ride by, see guys planting shrubs and flowers, laying down fertilizer, aerating the greens."

Jed looked at him a moment. "Idleness is the devil's workshop."

"Something like that," Chris said.

"Too much time on your hands opens a door for the PTSD."

Chris sighed. That was it.

"We can talk to Tom about it. I don't know what he'll say. In the meantime you might try something that worked for me. At least some of the time. You got a smartphone, right?"

"Yeah."

"Then you can do this. Start listening to podcasts. There's a ton of them on the internet. Mostly free. Covering all kinds of topics. Anything you're interested in, or even curious about. Another thing I would sometimes do, still do sometimes...listen to books on tape. If you can get deep in thought about something harmless, your mind can't slip into trouble so easy. Listening to books can be fun, the good ones anyway. Kinda like listening to old-time radio shows. They got actors doing the narration. Use different voices for all the different characters. You should try it sometime."

Chris had never done either of these things before. "How much do these books cost?"

"If you don't get the CDs, they don't cost much at all. Go on Amazon and check it out. There's a bunch on there for free, or just a couple of bucks. Some of the big name authors cost more. But you can try it out on the cheaper ones, see if you like the idea. Just remember to check out the reviews first, so you can steer clear of the duds."

"Okay. I'll give it a try."

"Still want to talk to Tom about...doing other things?"

"I think I'll wait on that. Give this a try first." He glanced at his watch. "Better go, time to clock out."

After doing that, he headed toward his car thinking about what Jed had said. He wasn't sure it would solve his problem, but he was willing to try anything that might help.

As he closed the car door and put the key in the ignition, that anxious feeling started coming over him. Almost a claustrophobic thing, like the sides of the car were closing in on him. He quickly opened the door and got out, walked a few steps away from the car.

Take some deep breaths. Slow your heartbeat down. There's nothing going on. Nothing to be afraid of.

After a few minutes pacing around, it started to subside. He walked back to the open car door, deciding if he was ready to climb back inside.

30

The first half of the car ride home went smoothly. Chris listened to a conservative talk radio host and a liberal guest debating climate change. He wasn't sure who was winning the argument and didn't really care. The information that he'd picked up on the issue seemed pretty conflicting, and he rather doubted he could do much to improve the situation if he became a hardliner for either side.

What he mainly liked was that it kept his mind engaged. Listening to music helped sometimes, but he found that too many songs talked about love and romance. That and couples spending the night together. He was in no shape to pursue a romance right now, so why torture himself listening to songs that stirred him in that direction.

Pulling into a 7-Eleven located about midway to his apartment, he turned off the car. He just needed to pick up a few things. Several full-size grocery stores were even closer to home, but he had a problem with the crowds. He paid a little more for things here, but the cost to his peace of mind in the big stores was far greater

Even here, he paused before getting out of the car, sizing up any possible danger zones within his field of vision. This wasn't a bad section of town, even nicer than the area he lived. That fact offered no comfort. He wished it did. He wished he could force himself to accept the likelihood that he was in no danger here, nor anywhere else in this town; that it was a near-certainty he'd never be in the kind of danger he'd experienced in Afghanistan ever again.

Still, he gave the whole place another thorough review. He carefully stepped out of the car, wincing a little as he put his full weight on the leg. A little sore today for some reason. He checked out the parking lot, the area around the gas pumps.

Convinced it was okay to proceed, he closed the car door and headed into the store.

Chris made it home to his apartment safe and sound.

His time in the 7-Eleven had gone fine, right up until he'd gotten in line at the cash register. A short, elderly woman had stood in line in front of him. But then the front door opened, and in walked some dark-skinned Arab-looking guys. Three of them. Totally fit the profile. Mid-to-late twenties. Just guys, no wives or children with them. Sounded like they were speaking Arabic or Pashto, he couldn't tell which.

It certainly wasn't English.

Coming in the door, they were joking and laughing until they saw him in line. Then they straightened up and got serious, quickly looked away after making eye contact. Of course, it might've been the look he had been giving them. His counselor said sometimes when he was struggling like this, he gave a look that was pretty menacing.

Until he paid his bill, he'd kept an eye on them. Even after getting into his car, he sat there watching them. They were just getting hot dogs, burritos, and Big Gulps. He finally decided, they were harmless. They weren't carrying any weapons, not wearing any explosive vests.

Heck, for all he knew, they could be from India. Maybe they were speaking Hindi. The point was, they weren't bad guys. They were just…guys. Stopping at a 7-Eleven for stuff, like he was. Not carrying out some terrorist agenda.

He walked across his living room and set the things he bought on the counter. Now, safe within the confines of his apartment, he started breathing a little easier. A wave of exhaustion suddenly came over him. He rested both hands on the counter. Apparently he was more tired than hungry. Was he more tired out from working all day, or from the workout he'd just been through at the store?

One thing for sure, he'd better get the refrigerated things put away before he gave in and plopped down on the couch.

That only took a few minutes. Somewhere during the task, he got enough energy to heat up his beef-and-cheese burrito and pour himself a glass of Diet Coke. Brought both out to the coffee table and turned on the TV. Had some shows loaded on the DVR, so he turned one on. Picked the show he cared about the least, since he knew after eating this food, he'd be asleep in fifteen minutes.

And that almost happened.

Just after finishing the last bite and swigging down the last sip of Coke, just when the slow blinks began to start, the phone rang. He would've ignored it, accept for the distinctive ring tone.

It was Kyle.

Oh God, he thought, *don't let Kyle be suicidal tonight.*

He picked it up on the third ring. "Hey, Kyle." He tried to sound more chipper than he felt.

"Chris, glad I got you. Tried to leave enough time to make sure you were home from work."

"You got it just right. I'm home and just finished my supper. Just started watching a TV show."

"You want me to call back later, when it's over?"

"You're kidding, right? There's not a show on television I wouldn't put on pause when my buddy Kyle calls."

Kyle laughed. "You sound like you're almost in a good mood. Is that for real?"

Chris sighed. He didn't have the energy to keep this upbeat façade going much longer.

"I didn't think it was," Kyle said. "How you really doing, Chris? Talk to me."

"Not great. Been a tough day for some reason. How about you? You almost sound...I don't know, normal. Is that real, or are you faking it?"

"I'm not faking. Seriously, I'm not. That's really why I'm calling. Not to tell you how good I'm doing—though that's true—but to tell you why. In fact, I'm looking at her right now. She's laying right next to me on the couch."

How about that? Kyle had found himself a girl. "So what did you do, join one of those internet dating sites, make up a bunch of lies about what kind of catch you are?"

"No, nothing like that."

"Then what? This girl know what kind of mess you're in? The struggles you're going through? I mean the PTSD stuff. It wasn't that long ago that—"

"She definitely does. In fact, you could say that's what brought us together."

What was she, a nurse or a therapist? "So what's this girl's name? When did you guys meet? I want to hear the story."

"Her name is Tootsie, but I call her Toots mostly."

Was he kidding? What kind of girl would be named Tootsie, or would put up with being called Toots most of the time? Before he could figure out what to say next, he heard Kyle laughing on the other end. "What are you laughing about?"

"I just realized what you're thinking. And then I realized how well I just set you up, but I didn't even know I was doing it."

"What are you talking about?"

"Tootsie." Kyle paused a moment. "I just thought of a way to string this out a little more."

"String what out?"

"Toots is definitely my girl. You got that part right. And here's something else, she's lying next to me and she's not wearing a thing."

"What? Why are you telling me this? I don't need to hear this."

Now Kyle was laughing out loud. "I'm sorry. I can't do this to you. You just made it so easy."

"Alright, now I'm totally lost. What's going on here?"

"Tootsie's not my girlfriend, you idiot. She's my dog. A hairy, totally lovable dog. A white pit-mix with big gray spots. But she's more than that. She's a specially-trained dog. I can't believe the difference she's making in my life. And I want to tell you the story of how we met. I think I've stumbled onto something that can help you every bit as much as it's helped me."

31

As Chris pulled into the parking lot of the golf course's maintenance building, he was still thinking about his conversation with Kyle last night. Kyle was almost insisting that Chris run right out and sign up for one of these dogs. He went on and on, telling Chris story after story of how Tootsie had changed his life. One fact was unmistakable: Kyle was like a different man.

The last time they had talked Kyle had been borderline suicidal. Now his voice was filled with hope. He talked about the future like a man who planned to be there. He was even thinking about going back to school when the next semester began. Chris had asked him what he'd do with Tootsie while he was in school? Would he have to shut her up in his apartment all day?

Kyle said no. He said if you got the right dog from a certified program the dog could go with you, pretty much anywhere you went. Like how a seeing eye dog goes everywhere with a blind person. That was the idea. You form this special bond with the dog, because the program picks dogs that are especially loyal. The dog is trained to help you better cope with your PTSD stuff. He said "Toots" could instinctively tell when Kyle was slipping into a panic attack. She would intervene and help him pull out before it got too far. When he slept, she'd wake him up whenever he started having a nightmare. Just having her around helped Kyle stay calmer throughout the day.

To Kyle, there was no downside to this situation. It was all good. One downside to Chris was getting stuck with a dog named Tootsie. He wasn't sure he could live with something like that. He closed the car door and walked across the parking lot toward the open garage door. Jed was inside replacing one of the batteries on a golf cart. Chris waved at him then walked over and clocked in.

He'd always liked dogs. Had one for years as a kid, but when it died, his mom and little sister were so sad they decided not to have any more pets. He grabbed the keys to the big mower off the hook and headed there. If he did get one of these service dogs, he didn't see any way he could bring it here to work. Where would he keep it all day?

Halfway across the garage floor, he changed directions and walked over to Jed. "Morning."

Jed looked up. "Morning. Heard it's gonna be a warm one out there today."

"Heard that, too," Chris said. Shouldn't be too much of problem riding the big mower, since it had an air-conditioned cab. "Wanted to ask you a question. I was talking with a friend of mine who served with me in Afghanistan. He's got some PTSD issues, too. He recently got hooked up with…I guess you call it a companion dog, or a service dog. He was telling me how much better he's doing now since getting this dog. You know all the guys that work here better than me. Know if any of them have one of these dogs my friend was talking about?"

Jed wiped some grease off his fingers. "I don't think so. I mean, some of them may have dogs. But you're talking about the kind of dogs people take with them everywhere, right?"

Chris nodded. "My friend said he takes his dog with him most of the time without getting hassled. She wears an official looking vest that identifies her as a service dog. He said sometimes people do give him looks, because he doesn't have any...you know, obvious wounds."

Jed looked down at Chris's leg. "That shouldn't be a problem for you. You thinking of getting one?"

"I don't know. Maybe. Before last night the thought never crossed my mind. But I couldn't believe how much better my friend is doing from the last time we talked. He said he's even been able to cut back on his meds." Chris looked around the garage. "The thing is, if I did get one I don't know what I'd do with it all day. Not like a dog could ride with me on the mower."

He and Jed both looked up at the cab of the big mower. "Then again," Jed said, "you might be able to fit a buddy next to you when you're riding around in that. That's a pretty wide seat."

"Maybe. But I'm only in it half the time. Even if it was all the time, I can't see Tom being okay with me bringing a dog to work every day. And I wouldn't feel right about locking a dog up in my apartment all day by itself."

"You got a point." Jed leaned back on the golf cart. "But I wouldn't give up on the idea completely, not because of Tom. He and the owner have been pretty supportive of all of us guys and our issues. Especially if it's something that would help that much. Maybe you should look into it a little more. Nail down some of the facts. Like the cost, for one. How much this dog set your friend back? Must be pretty expensive training one of these service dogs."

"That's just it," Chris said. "He said they didn't charge him a thing. He just had to agree to go through some training to learn how to work with the dog, and how to take care of it once they gave it to him. But they didn't charge him anything. He said all kinds of people are starting to get behind these programs that help wounded vets. Supposedly, some senators and congressmen are even trying to get a law passed that would release government funding so dogs like this could be available for a lot more vets. Right now, everything is being paid for by donations."

Jed looked like he was thinking about something. "I wonder if they have anything like that around here. Probably have to go to some big city, like Orlando or Jacksonville."

"I don't know. You might be right. Kyle lives near Atlanta."

"Maybe you should go online and check," Jed said.

"Sounds like you're getting interested in this."

"Maybe I am. I love dogs. Never thought of them being able to help me deal with what I'm going through. But if they can...yeah, I think I could be into that."

"Well, I'll look into it then," Chris said. "No harm in looking."

"Let me know what you find out. If there's anything to it, I'll go with you when you pitch it to Tom."

32

Later that afternoon when Chris got off work, he stopped at the apartment complex office. He was wrestling with the idea of parking his car and going inside. Off and on as he mowed throughout the day, he thought through his conversation with Kyle last night, about getting a dog to help with his PTSD issues.

Even before leaving work, right after he'd clocked out, Jed had brought it up again. "You gonna look into this dog thing, right?"

Chris said he would.

Now, sitting there in the apartment parking lot, he tried to work up the nerve to ask the resident manager if they would even allow him to have one. It hadn't dawned on him before, but he hadn't seen any dogs in the apartment complex. Anywhere. He looked around at all the various people out and about. Some were getting in and out of their cars, stopping at the mailbox, jogging along the sidewalk...nobody had a dog.

What if the manager said no? Was it worth the hassle of moving to another place just to have a dog? His first thought was no, it was not. But he couldn't get over how much better Kyle was doing. By the time Chris had hung up, he was almost jealous. Chris hated being on these meds, but he hated even more how helpless he felt during a panic attack or being awakened by a nightmare in the middle of the night in a cold sweat.

What if having a dog meant the difference between getting all your groceries in one place on one trip versus having to stop at convenience stores several times a week because you couldn't stand to be in crowds? Chris pulled the car into a parking place. It wouldn't hurt to ask.

Even though he owned a handicap hang tag, he didn't normally park in handicapped spots. In the beginning, he didn't have a choice. It just hurt too much to walk that far. For the last several months, now that he was walking so much better, he'd kept the tag in the glove compartment.

Then he had a thought. Maybe this time he should use it. He had the right to. Maybe if the management saw him coming out of the handicap spot and noticed the slight limp he still had, they'd feel more inclined to let him have a service dog, even if dogs weren't allowed in the complex. He opened the glove compartment, stared at the blue and white tag, then shut it again.

I'm not going to play the sympathy card. If they said no, they said no. He would deal with that when the time came.

He walked down the sidewalk toward the office door trying even harder to strike a normal-looking stride. A mom pushing a stroller was coming out as he was going in. He smiled and held the door for her. On the other side of the foyer he saw a nice-looking girl with reddish hair at a reception desk typing on a keyboard. Chris didn't know if she was new, because he normally didn't come in here. He paid his rent each month online.

She looked up as he stood by her desk. "Hi, can I help you?"

"Uh, yeah. My name's Chris Seger. I live in apartment 152, Building C. Could I please speak with the manager?"

"She's not in right now."

"Know when she'll be back?"

"In about an hour or two. Is there anything I can help you with?"

Chris didn't want to get into this with her. "Maybe I'll just come back another time."

"That's fine. You want to leave a message? Have her call you when she gets back?"

"Sure. I guess we could do that."

The girl took out a pad and wrote his first name on the top of page. "You said your name was Chris, right? How do you spell your last name?"

Chris told her, then repeated his apartment address again.

"What do you want me to tell her it's about? If you don't want to say, I can leave it blank."

"I just want to talk to her about your dog policies."

"Oh, that's easy. I can tell you that. We don't allow them."

"I thought so. I haven't seen any around. Do they ever make any...exceptions?"

The girl thought a moment. "I don't think so. What kind of dog are you wanting to get?"

"I don't even know yet. I'm not sure what kind of dogs they have, or if I can even get one around here."

"Who are *they*?"

"They?" Chris said. "Oh, I'm talking about getting a service dog. I don't know who *they* is either, at this point. I'm just starting to look into it. A friend of mine called last night. We served in Afghanistan together, and we both have...well, he recently got one, and he was telling me how much it was helping him." He really didn't want to start pouring his heart out to this total stranger, especially one so young.

"First of all...thank you for your service." It looked as if her eyes were welling up with tears. She started blinking fast.

"You're welcome."

"And speaking of service, I didn't know you were talking about a service dog. I don't think we have any in the complex right now, but I'm pretty sure my manager showed me a document about them, in case someone ever asked." She rolled her chair back to another drawer and opened it, then started thumbing through some files. "Yes, here it is." She pulled out a sheet of paper, pulled back to the desk and set it down.

"That's something, that you remembered it," Chris said. "I mean, I'm guessing you've never had anyone ask about it before."

She stopped reading a moment and looked up. "I guess you could say I have a special interest in this." Those eyes, they were welling up with tears again. "Excuse me." She reached for a tissue from a box on the corner of her desk.

"Do you know anything about service dogs?" he asked.

"No, but I wish I did."

Chris had no idea what she was talking about.

She finished dabbing her eyes. "One of my cousins served in Iraq. He came home a few years ago. He was all in one piece, but he was pretty messed up. He never could make the adjustment to living back home. We knew he had PTSD and was on a lot of pills. But nothing ever seemed to help. He killed himself about a year ago." The tears returned.

"I'm so sorry," Chris said.

"Thanks." She held up the piece of paper she had pulled from the drawer. "I remembered seeing a news story about this program that trains dogs to help veterans with PTSD. They were interviewing all these vets who'd gotten one of these dogs, and several of them said they had been suicidal, but these dogs saved their lives. I remember wishing like crazy my cousin could have heard about this before. Maybe he wouldn't have...done what he did."

Chris could hardly believe what she was telling him. First Kyle, and now her. It was almost as if God was shouting at him: *Get one of these dogs.* "Do you remember, was it a local news story, or the national news?"

"It was definitely local. They were training the dogs at a woman's prison just a few miles outside of town. I bet you could find it online pretty easy."

"That's great. I'll definitely check it out." He looked down at the paper she'd pulled out of the drawer. "Does that say anything about whether service dogs are an exception to your no-dog policy?"

"It definitely does. And it's not just our policy, it's the law. You have to get qualified to own a service dog, and the dog has to be certified as a service dog, but if both of those things are true, you can definitely have a service dog here. Really, you can have one anywhere. Have you been diagnosed with PTSD? Oh my gosh, forget I said that. I have no right to ask you that."

"That's all right. Yes, I have. And I've also lost a leg, my left one. Stepped on a mine about two years ago."

"Then you definitely qualify for a service dog. Just the PTSD alone qualifies you. Look what this last line says: '...*calming a person with Post Traumatic Stress Disorder (PTSD) during an anxiety attack.*' Your leg injury only strengthens your case. Look what it says a few bullets above that: '...*providing physical support and assistance with balance and stability to individuals with mobility disabilities.*' A certified service dog can help you with both of those things. I don't remember from the news story if the dogs they train out at the prison are certified, but if they are, you're all set."

This was way better news than Chris had expected coming in

here. He could definitely have a service dog without having to move, and they even trained them locally. Well, he'd still have to verify that point. But this was very encouraging. He reached out his hand, "I can't thank you enough for all your help."

"It was my pleasure. Really, it's an honor to help someone like you. Do you still want to talk to the manager when she gets back?"

"Nope. I've got everything I need. If you wouldn't mind, maybe you could brief her on what we talked about, so it wouldn't be a complete shock if I do wind up getting one of these dogs."

"I'll be happy to do that. Thanks for stopping in."

Chris headed back toward his car with plans to go online as soon as he got to his apartment.

33

Kim finally got to sit at her desk after a half-dozen interruptions had greeted her when she'd walked through the door thirty minutes ago. She turned to face her computer screen and set her just-poured mug of coffee beside her keyboard. Hopefully, no more interruptions while she answered her emails, so she could sip her coffee while it was hot.

Her phone rang.

She was tempted to ignore it, but she couldn't. She picked up the receiver, hoping it would at least be something she could solve in a few moments. A quick question and a quick answer. "Hi, this is Kim."

"Hey Kim, this is Sandy out here at the front desk." Sandy was a volunteer who answered the lobby phone three times a week. "I've got a young man on the phone, a former Marine who says he saw a video online with you in it. Something to do with training dogs out at the prison. Do you have a minute to talk with him?"

"Sure Sandy, put him through."

"Hello. This is Kim Harper, the Animal Behavior Manager at the Humane Society. How can I help you?"

"Hi Kim. Glad I got you. I'm on a ten minute break here at

work. I've only got a few minutes left. My name's Chris, by the way. Chris Seger."

"You must start work pretty early to already be on break." It was just a little past eight-thirty.

"I come in at 6AM. I mow grass out here at the Summerville Golf Course."

"Oh. Well Chris, our receptionist mentioned something about you watching a video that I was in. Something to do with the prison program that trains dogs for veterans?"

"Yeah. I got a phone call from a friend of mine. We both struggle with PTSD issues. He was all excited about a new service dog he'd gotten. He was talking like this dog had completely turned things around for him. I started thinking…maybe I should look into it."

"How long have you been home?" Kim asked.

"Two years. Spent most of that time in and out of hospitals. Mostly surgery and therapy."

"So you've got more than PTSD to deal with?"

"Yeah, but I'm not in a wheelchair. It's a long story. Probably take too long to explain right now. I was talking with someone in my apartment office last night. Went in there to see if I could even have a dog. Found out I can, if it's a certified service dog. The gal I was talking to mentioned this news story she had seen. I found the video on YouTube. That's how I got your name."

"Well, I'm glad you did. And you're right, there is a program out at the prison that trains dogs to help veterans. And I'm very involved with it. In fact, I'm one of the people who selects the dogs that get trained for the program. Some of these programs just train dogs to be companion dogs, meaning dogs who just provide emotional support and friendship. Our dogs do that, but It also trains dogs to help veterans with PTSD."

"So, the dogs out there are service dogs?"

"They are."

"That's great. Do you know if there are any dogs available now? Or how much something like this would cost?"

Kim looked down at the date in the corner of her computer screen, did some figuring in her head. "The program going on right now has reached the place where they're matching up dogs with interested veterans. It's actually been going on for a couple of weeks. I'll have to call out there and see if there are any left. There might be. But I don't know off the top of my head. As for cost, there's no charge to veterans. You just have to show that you're capable of providing a stable home for the dogs. And obviously to take care of their practical needs. Would you like me to call and see?"

"Definitely." He gave her his cell phone number. "I get a break for lunch in a couple of hours, then I get off at three. If it's better for you to call me back in between those times, just leave a message. I can't take calls while I'm mowing, but I'll definitely listen to them. Just let me know if there are any dogs available, and what I need to do to make this happen."

"Then that's what I'll do," Kim said. "And Chris, if all the dogs have been spoken for, it's not the end of the world. In about a month or so this class of dogs will graduate, and we'll start another class almost right away."

"That's good to know. Well, I better get. My break's over. Thanks so much for your time."

"You're welcome. And thanks for serving our country. I hope we'll get to meet real soon."

Kim set the receiver down and released a contented sigh. That interruption didn't hurt one bit.

Kim had planned to call Captain Bridget out at the prison as soon as she'd hung up with Chris. But his phone call had been followed by two others; the second call involved her getting up and meeting someone in the lobby. She was back at her desk and took a sip of her now-lukewarm coffee. She dialed the prison's number, then Bridget's extension.

Getting hold of Bridget was a fifty-fifty proposition, at best. This time, it worked. She recognized Bridget's voice on the other end. "Hey Bridget, it's Kim."

"Hi Kim. Nice to hear from you. What's up?"

"I had an interesting phone call about twenty minutes ago from a Marine, named Chris Seger. He was discharged a couple of years ago. He's got PTSD and some kind of other injuries. He didn't specify, and I didn't ask. I only know he's not in a wheelchair. But he's interested in getting a service dog."

"And he called you?"

"Yeah. He saw a video of that news story they filmed last year, where we talked all about the program. He got my name off that." Kim told Bridget everything else she remembered about the phone call with Chris. And then added, "He seems pretty intent on getting a dog, even talked to his apartment people about it, to make sure it was okay. I said I'd call and find out if there are any dogs left. I know you've been inviting vets to the training sessions for a couple of weeks now. How's it looking?"

"Hmmm," Bridget said. "Actually, I believe there are still two. But only two. We have a couple other vets coming out tomorrow to look at them. Is there any chance he can get out here tomorrow? Say around 9:30? If not, he might just have to wait until the next round."

"I don't know. I know he works during the day. He called me on his break. All I can do is call and let him know what's going on.

Can I give him your number?"

"Sure."

"Then that's what I'll do. He said to leave a message, so I'm not sure when he'll call back. But I'm pretty certain he will get back with you."

Bridget sighed. "Sounds like we'll be playing phone tag for a while. Maybe you should leave more in the message than simply my name and number. Why don't you tell him that if he'd like to get a dog from this current batch, he better be out here tomorrow at 9:30. What's his name again?"

Kim repeated it.

"I leave his name out at the guard desk. Could you also tell him the security procedures in your message? I'm not saying he shouldn't try to call me, just trying to think of a way to make this happen, since I'll only be at my desk about half the time today."

"No, I can do that," Kim said. "I'm sure if he can make it out there some way, he will. By the way, which two dogs are still left?"

"You're never going to believe who one of them is. Finley."

"Finley? No one has picked him yet? How is that possible? He's beautiful."

"I know. For one thing, a lot of these guys are into pits. But I think the real reason is Amy, the girl who's been training him. The two of them are joined at the hip."

"That's good, and not good," Kim said.

"I know," Bridget said. "At this stage of the game, mostly not good. But I've talked to Amy, and so has Rita. Amy admitted she's been living in something of a fantasy. She says she's ready now to do the right thing and help let him go."

"She's the new girl, right?"

"Yeah. This is her first training session. And it looks like it might be her last."

"She's not working out?"

"No, just the opposite. She's fantastic. I haven't told her yet, but I've picked her and Finley to be in the Top Five contest."

Kim remembered; it was a competition they always did toward the end of each class. Five dogs and their trainers were picked for a performance evaluation. The winner was announced on graduation day and selected to do a live obedience display for all the attendees.

"If she's doing so well, why is this Amy's last training session?"

"Because there's something else she doesn't know yet. I just found out they've given her some extra gain time. She'll be getting out of here about two months after graduation day. She won't be here long enough to train another dog."

34

Chris just finished mowing the fairway on the tenth hole. He glanced down at his watch. A good time to break for lunch. He turned off the mower blades and set them in place, so he could ride a little faster. There was a nice row of shady trees in between the tenth and eleventh holes. He headed there, figuring there'd be less chance of someone hitting the mower with their golf ball.

He was in the big mower, but he didn't want to leave it running all through lunch. As he lowered the windows, he was thankful for a nice cross breeze blowing through. Between that and the shade he should be just fine for the next thirty minutes. Reaching back into the cooler, he pulled out a cold can of Diet Coke and a turkey-and-swiss sandwich.

He pulled out his smartphone thinking about which podcast he might listen to, when he noticed he had a voicemail. *Oh man, it could be about the dog.* He tapped the app, entered his password and listened to the message:

> *Hi Chris, this is Kim Harper getting back with you about the prison dog situation. I spoke with the director of the program. Her name is Captain Bridget Cummings. She told*

me there are only two dogs left in the current class. But also, there are a couple other veterans attending tomorrow morning's training class for the first time. She said if you hoped to get one of the two remaining dogs you should plan to be there at tomorrow's class. It meets out at the prison. I'm sure you can get the address info online. Be there no later than 9:30am. At the end of this message, I'll give you her phone number. If you don't reach her, she said to just leave a message saying whether or not you can come. I gave her your name. She said she would leave it with the security personnel at the front gate just in case you can make it. Call me if you have any other questions. Her phone number is....

Chris repeated the phone number out loud, over and over until he could write it down. He wanted to call the lady at the prison right away, but he knew there were two important details he needed to check on first.

Would his boss even be open to the idea of him getting a dog and bringing it to work? And second, would he let him have the time off tomorrow morning to attend the training class?

Ten minutes later, Chris arrived back at the maintenance building. He wolfed down his sandwich on the ride here. He was glad to see Tom's car still in the parking lot. Sometimes Tom went home for lunch. He pulled the mower into the shade of the garage and turned it off.

Where was Jed? He didn't see him anywhere. Jed said when Chris was ready to pitch this idea to Tom, he'd go with him. He walked all around the garage area, then out by the picnic table where Jed usually ate lunch. Still no sign of him.

Chris walked toward Tom's office. There was a big interior window that faced the maintenance area. Although the blinds were down, they were cracked enough to see Tom sitting at his desk eating a sub. Chris started to tense up. He hadn't enough time to think through what he was gonna say.

Then it was too late. Tom looked in his direction. He had seen Chris. He even waved for him to come in. Chris nodded, took a deep breath and opened the door.

Tom set what was left of his sub on the desk. "Hey Chris. Something I can help you with?"

Chris stepped inside, moved forward a little.

"Have a seat."

The air-conditioning felt great. Chris sat in the chair. "I guess there is."

After Chris hesitated, Tom said, "Okay, what is it?"

Chris thought a moment. "It's kind of hard to explain. Guess I'll just say it. Have you ever heard anything about vets with PTSD getting service dogs?"

Tom got a surprised look on his face. He clearly didn't expect the question. "Uh, well...I guess I have. I don't know anyone with a dog like that. I mean, I know some of the guys have dogs, but not service dogs. Why?"

"I'm seriously thinking about getting one."

"Really."

"I talked with my best friend from Afghanistan. He got discharged a few months ago. His PTSD situation, I think, is even worse than mine." Chris immediately regretted saying that. He hadn't talked about this kind of stuff with Tom since he was first hired. "I mean, I was actually pretty worried about him, you know, whether he'd make it or not. Well anyway, he just got one of these service dogs, the kind especially trained to help guys with PTSD.

It's amazing, the difference this dog has made. In a pretty short amount of time."

"That's what I've heard," Tom said. "Supposedly, they've even helped some guys pull back from being suicidal."

"Like my friend," Chris said. "That's what I'm talking about."

Tom leaned forward in his chair. "Have you ever felt...like that, Chris?"

"What? No, not really. Well, maybe in those first few months after I got home. I've had some pretty low moments since then, but I haven't gone that far. But I'm not gonna lie to you. I still do struggle most days. Sometimes several times a day. Not usually when I'm here at work, but—"

"So how can I help? I don't really know any organizations that work with these kind of dogs."

"No, it's not that. I do know of one. Just outside of town. They train them out at the prison. I've been talking to a lady at the Humane Society, the one who picks the dogs for the program. She called out there for me. They're doing a class right now. They have two dogs left, but she says I have to get out there tomorrow morning if I hope to get one. After that, they'll probably be gone."

"So, you're asking for time off tomorrow?"

"Yes, but I think it'll only be a couple hours. I was thinking, if you're okay with it, I could just make up the time after three. You know, I could work till five or something."

Tom sat back in his chair. "I suppose we can do that. But you know it's a lot hotter in the late afternoon here than it is in the morning."

"I know. But the big mower has an air-conditioned cab. I figure I can structure my day so I'm riding it in the hottest part of the day."

"Sounds like you're talking about more than just tomorrow."

"I guess I am. I don't know what the schedule is, but I'm guessing they're going to have to train me how to work with this dog. Sounds like they do their training in the mornings."

"I see. Well, I think I'm okay with this, Chris. You've been totally trustworthy since you started. I know you'll follow through on keeping your hours straight."

Chris sat there, trying to think of how to bring up the next thing. A much bigger thing.

"Is there something else?"

He nodded. "If I wind up getting this dog, the idea is you're supposed to be with each other the whole time. You know, not just at home. Even in the car, in the store, at restaurants…"

"At work?" Tom said.

Chris nodded.

"You want him to ride with you on the mower?"

"No, I'm not thinking that. He'd only fit on the biggest one anyway. Besides that, I wouldn't want him to fall off and get hurt."

"So what are you suggesting?"

Chris didn't like the new look on Tom's face. "I can't see shutting him up in my apartment all day every day, from when I leave at five-thirty till I get home at three-thirty. I was kind of hoping we could keep him here." Chris's eyes shifted toward the wall facing the outside.

"Keep him here? Where would he be all day?"

"I could make a pen for him outside. It's shady all day under that live oak out back. I could visit him on my breaks. I'd pay for the materials myself. Put it together after work."

"Gee Chris, I don't know about that."

"He wouldn't bother a soul. I've already looked into it some. These dogs are super well-behaved. Very calm. Obedient."

"If that's the case," Tom said, "maybe we could build him a

pen in here. I don't think the outside idea will work. It can get pretty hot even in the shade in Florida."

"We could do that?"

"I'd be open to it, if he's as well behaved as you say. I like dogs. Maybe he'll become something of a mascot."

"That would be great, Tom. And look, if it didn't work out for some reason, I could bring him to a doggy day care somewhere."

"That could get expensive," Tom said.

"Well, I'm hoping it won't come to that. Point is, I wouldn't want this to give you any trouble at all. If it does, I promise I'll make it right."

Tom sat forward again, put his elbows on the desk. "I appreciate that. I can't give a final yes on something like this by myself. I'll run it by Colonel Banks, see what he says. If he's okay with it, then I'm willing to give it a try." Banks was the golf course owner.

"Thanks, Tom. Means a lot to me. Know when you'll be able to speak with him? Any chance it can happen today?"

"I'll try and get with him this afternoon. But look, either way, you can go ahead attend that class tomorrow. Give you a chance to see if this is something you really want to do. I'm sure I can have an answer for you by the time you get back."

"Thanks so much." Chris reached his hand across the desk. Tom shook it. "I better get back to work." He headed back toward his mower. As he walked, he pulled out his phone to call the lady out at the prison, let her know he'd be there tomorrow.

35

Chris had showed up to work the next morning at the usual time, 6am. He'd already mowed the rough along three holes on the golf course. Now he was back in the maintenance building putting the mower up. It was time to head over to the prison for the dog training class.

After washing up, he hung the mower key on the hook where it belonged. As he did, he heard footsteps behind him. It was Jed.

"Heard you had a talk with Tom already about the dog idea."

"I did. Yesterday afternoon. Looked all over for you to see if you wanted to go with me."

"Sorry. I had an appointment with my shrink. I guess your chat went okay, though. Tom said he gave you permission to go to some kind class out at the prison."

"That's where I'm headed now. Starts at 9:30. Are you still interested in getting one of these dogs?"

"I think so. Talked to my shrink a little about it. He said he thought it would be a good idea."

"Want to see if Tom will let you go with me? I'm not really losing any hours. Just making the time up after three. I'm sure he'd be fine about you doing that too."

"I don't think so. I'm definitely interested. But that's moving a little too quick for me."

"I really wasn't planning on doing anything this fast. But when I talked to the lady at the Humane Society, it turned out there's a class going on right now. She said there were only two dogs left, and they'd probably be spoken for after today. So I figured, what the heck. Why not just go there and check it out? If it doesn't work out with one of these two, I can just slow it down and sign up for the next round."

"Makes sense," Jed said. "You go on and scout out things for the both of us."

"Alright. Well, I better get going. I'll tell you all about it when I get back."

Amy and Finley had already gone through their now familiar morning routine. She loved how Finley faced the day. So full of enthusiasm and joy. Tail constantly wagging, facial expression set on his playful doggy-smile. He looked up at her as if to say, "Isn't it all just so wonderful?" She wondered if part of his optimism came from not knowing what the future might bring. It must be nice to have no idea what lies ahead.

She knew, for example, that this morning there'd be another training session. She thought Finley might actually know that. If so, he'd consider it just part of a delightful routine. One more chance to be out and about, to do all kinds of drills together; he'd get to be with his doggy friends and get a steady dose of meaty treats.

But Amy's heart was filled with dread.

Yesterday afternoon Miss Bridget told her that two more military vets would be attending today's session. She reminded

Amy that there were only two dogs left who hadn't been paired with anyone yet. Amy had gotten the hint. Don't do anything to jeopardize Finley's chances to find a new home today.

Finley walked over to the hook by his cage, grabbed his leash in his mouth, came back and handed it to her. She took it and patted his head. "You don't get it, do you boy? We only get to do this for another month. That means, I only get to see you for another month..." She thought about it a moment. It was even less than a month. Closer to three weeks now. She started choking up and blinking back tears.

She really loved it here, getting to be in this part of the prison, working in this program. But right now she wondered if she was really cut out for this. If she could really do this all over again with another dog.

Because she didn't want another dog. She wanted Finley.

Uh-oh. Amy was upset. Finley didn't understand why. Everything seemed to be going fine. He stopped a moment. He looked up at her then looked around the room, trying to think if there was anything he had done wrong. Nothing came to mind.

He took a step closer to her, nudged her with the leash. Maybe that would help, get her mind on the leash, on taking him for a walk. She reached down and grabbed it. He immediately let go and headed for the door. It seemed to work. She wiped her eyes and stood. Now she smiled.

"Okay Finn, you win. I'll take you out before the class starts, so you can go the bathroom. Might do me some good to get some fresh air."

She came toward him and clipped on his leash. They walked down the hall, through the main room, then outside. Finley saw

Charlie all the way on the other side of the yard. He strained at the end of his leash, trying to give Amy a signal. She gently pulled back and went in a different direction, off toward the side.

"I see him," she said. "We don't have time to play this morning. Class starts in a few minutes. I'll let you and Charlie hang out after we're through."

Finley didn't know what she said. He heard Charlie's name, but the direction she was leading him made it clear she was saying no to his request. He put his nose to the grass and decided to focus on what he'd come out here to do.

At least she seemed to be in a better mood.

Fifteen minutes later, all the inmate-trainers and their dogs were in the main classroom. All the extra chairs along the walls had been filled by the veterans who'd come to take part in the training. One by one, they linked up with the dogs they had already been paired with; all except for Amy and Finley and one other trainer and her dog.

There were still two veterans present who Amy didn't recognize. These must be the new guys Miss Bridget had mentioned. Sure enough, both of the men were eyeing Finley and the other dog. They seemed nice enough. Neither one of them gave her the creeps. But neither of them stood out to her in a good way, either.

She wondered if she should walk over and introduce herself, and Finley. The other girl already had. Amy looked down at Finley. He hadn't even noticed them. Not exactly the beginnings of something wonderful.

But then the front door opened. Another guy walked in wearing a denim long sleeve shirt like a light jacket, over a burgundy-colored T-shirt. Definitely a new guy. He wore jeans that were a slightly darker shade of denim. He had blondish-brown hair. Amy guessed he was about her age, give or take a few years.

He looked around the room, taking everything in. The door closed behind him. He stood in the doorway a few moments, then Miss Bridget saw him and walked over to him. She extended her hand and introduced herself. Amy stepped a few feet closer to listen. Finley sat beside her.

"Hi, Captain Cummings. My name's Chris Seger. I believe Kim Harper at the Humane Society talked to you about me. I left a voicemail on your phone last night."

"Hi Chris. I remember you and your phone message. And you're right, Kim did talk to me about you. I'm so glad you could make it."

"Me, too. I was told there are still two dogs left. That still the case?"

"It is right now," Bridget said softly.

"So, what do I do?" Chris said. "From here, I mean."

"Well, why don't you have a seat? We're about to get started. You might have heard, there are two other veterans here, who are also interested in getting a dog."

"Are they here?" Chris said, softly.

Miss Bridget nodded.

"How's that work?" Chris said. "I mean, if all three of us want a dog, but there are only two left?"

"If that happens, then all three of you will get a dog. One of you will just have to wait till the next round. But we start the classes up almost immediately after one closes, on graduation day. That's less than a month from now."

"I see. How will you decide which one has to wait? Do you flip a coin or something?"

"No, nothing like that. The most important thing is that the dog and the vet are a really good fit. Sometimes they just click, and the decision becomes obvious. Sometimes a dog will pick out a person, like they instinctively know they're supposed to be together. We don't try to force those things. But don't worry, there's no hurry. Let's just take it slow. In a minute, I'll call the class together. But before that, I'll point out the two dogs to you, so you know which ones are still available."

"Great," Chris said. "I really appreciate your help." He looked at the row of chairs and spotted an empty one at the end.

He hadn't noticed Amy yet. As he and Miss Bridget talked, she'd stood a few feet away. There were a couple of dogs and trainers between them.

But she had definitely noticed him.

She looked down at Finley. Finley had noticed him, too. His eyes were still glued on this newcomer, following him as he walked past the others and sat down. Finley looked up at her, then back at this vet. His tail began to wag. He was even leaning a little bit towards the man, as if he wanted Amy to take him over there.

She had never seen him act this way before, about anyone.

36

As Amy stood there holding Finley's leash, Miss Bridget turned and saw her. "Oh, Amy. I was just talking about you. See that young man who just sat down there on the end? Could you go introduce yourself and Finley? And while you're there, point Benny out to him. I'll go make sure the other two vets know who Finley and Benny are.

"Sure, Miss Bridget. I can do that." Amy started walking toward Chris. As soon as she did, Finley began tugging her in his direction. When she was standing in front of him, Finley sat beside her.

"Well, hello there," Chris said to Finley. "Aren't you a handsome boy?" He looked up at Amy. "Or is he a girl?"

"No, he's definitely a boy. His name's Finley." Finley's tail instantly began to wag. "Finley, greet."

Finley walked up to Chris. He patted his head and scratched behind his ears. "He's a beautiful dog." Finley yielded happily to his touch, even began to lick Chris's hand.

"He really seems to like you," she said.

"Looks like a friendly dog."

"He is," she said, "but he's normally not this friendly to

strangers. He's definitely giving you some special treatment."

"Really? Don't tell me he's one of the dogs still available?"

"He is." She turned and pointed toward Benny. "The other one's over there, the brindle pit mix. His name is Benny."

Chris looked for a moment, then fixed his gaze back on Finley. "How is it even possible that a dog this beautiful could still be available? I'd have thought he'd be the first one to go."

"There were definitely some guys interested in him." How could she say this next part?

"But it didn't work out?"

"No, he just wasn't interested in them." She decided not to add, *and neither was I.* "Like I said, I've never seen him react this way to anyone before."

Now Chris was massaging Finley's shoulders. Finley was actually leaning against his leg, wearing his favorite contented look. Still looking at Finley, Chris said, "Well, I'm honored then, Finley. It's very nice to meet you." He looked up at Amy, extended his hand. "I'm Chris, by the way. Chris Seger."

She shook it. It was strong, and calloused. "I'm Amy. Amy Wallace. I'm Finley's trainer."

"Nice to meet you, Amy. Have you trained many dogs?"

"Finley's my first."

"Well, you'd never know. He's so well behaved, and you seem very comfortable with him."

"That's more him than me. He's super easy to work with. Super smart and obedient, and so loving. We're like best friends."

"Okay everyone, let's get started." Miss Bridget called out. "Ladies, line up with your dogs."

"I've got to go," she said to Chris. "It was nice meeting you."

"You too. And you, Finley. Will I get to see you again before I have to leave?"

"Sure, if you'd like. I mean, if you can stay until the end. During the last part of the class, she'll invite the vets who are already paired up with dogs to work with them and their trainer. She'll probably let us, and Benny and his trainer go outside by the picnic tables. You can come out with the other two veterans over there and have sort of a get-more-acquainted time. Think you can stay for that?"

"Definitely," Chris said.

Chris watched as Amy and Finley took their place in the line of dogs and trainers. Over the next thirty minutes, he watched as a series of commands were called out. The trainers directed the dogs to respond to each one with almost military precision. It was a most impressive display. He had never seen one dog so well-trained, let alone a whole roomful.

The entire time, Chris was totally preoccupied with Finley. He was by far, the best looking dog in the room. But Chris thought it was more than that. Of all the dogs, he seemed the most attentive to his trainer, and the quickest to respond to the commands, often starting to obey as soon as the words came out of Captain Bridget's mouth.

But there was something more. It took a little while for Chris to realize what it was.

From the first moment Finley had begun to interact with him, an almost overwhelming sense of peace and calm had come over Chris. Driving here, Chris had worried about how he would handle this new situation. Being around all of these people, all of them strangers, and in a confined space no bigger than a classroom. What if he got ambushed by a sudden panic attack? What if he wound up making a scene as he fled the premises? He might ruin his chances of ever getting a service dog.

But instead, he met Finley. And Amy. There was something also very calming about her. He'd watched a few TV shows about women in prison. She was nothing like he'd expected. There was a kindness in her eyes, a softness in her smile. Chris looked at her now as she led Finley through a sit and stay drill. She wore an orange jumpsuit, just like the women on the TV shows. Her hair wasn't styled, and she wore no makeup. But she was pretty in her own way. She could be downright beautiful if given half a chance.

Just then, she looked right at him. He was embarrassed and quickly shifted his gaze to another dog and trainer. What was he thinking? She wouldn't be interested in someone like him, and he certainly was in no condition to start a relationship. Besides that, where could it go? She was in prison.

He wondered, then, what she had done. It had to be a felony of some kind. This wasn't the county jail.

After what felt like a safe amount of time, he looked back at Amy and Finley. This time, he focused more on Finley. Chris loved the way he held his head up high as he walked. Such confidence and dignity. Looking at the wall clock, he wondered how much longer before these drills would be over? Before he'd get an opportunity to spend some more time with them outside.

He looked down the row of chairs against the wall, all of them occupied by other veterans. Many were around his same age, some were younger and some much older. Which two were his competition? He was certain they would want Finley, too. How could they not? But there was no way they wanted him more than Chris did.

Chris heard all the trainers say the word, "Finish" firmly. He watched as Finley walked behind Amy, then come around to the other side and sit beside her. She reached down and scratched beneath his chin. He licked her fingers.

He liked Finley. A lot. He had to find a way to make this happen.

37

Finley could tell, the training class was over. His eyes focused on Amy. She always seemed to know what came next. The other dogs and trainers mingled in the center of the room with the men who'd been sitting in the chairs along the wall. He didn't recognize all the men but some were becoming familiar. If not by sight, then by scent.

He looked up at the new man, the one who'd come in just before the class began. He liked this man instantly, although he didn't know why. Finley had looked at him off and on as they trained. Every time he did, the man was looking at either him or Amy. And he was always smiling.

When he and Amy had talked before, Finley enjoyed listening to his voice. It was deeper than Chaz's, and they didn't look anything alike, but something in the way he looked at Finley felt very familiar.

Finley detected something else in the man's mood that reminded him of Chaz. Not the way Chaz had been in the beginning, before he'd gone away. But how he was when he'd occasionally come home from those long trips. Chaz was different then. When he'd hug Finley, especially during those last few trips,

Finley could tell something was different about Chaz.

Something seemed broken.

Chaz seemed to need Finley's comfort more than anything, and Finley was happy to help him. Chaz was everything then. Now Amy was. She loved him more than he'd ever been loved before.

"Okay Finley, let's go outside," Amy said. "We'll spend some time with that nice man. And those...two other men."

She said that last part in her quiet voice. The only word Finley totally understood was *outside*. It was obvious that's where they were headed. As they neared the front door, that nice man stood and walked toward them.

"Is this the time you talked about?" he said. "When we can spend a few minutes together getting acquainted?"

"Yes," Amy said. "I'm glad you could stay. We'll just head outside to those picnic tables you walked by on your way in here." She looked around the room a moment. "We'll probably be joined by Benny, that brindle pit I pointed out to you before, and his trainer. Those two guys talking to her are the other two vets who came here today to check out the two remaining dogs."

Chris opened the door for her and Finley, then followed them as they walked to the picnic tables.

Chris didn't like the sound of that, but he liked what he saw just before they'd left the room. The other two vets—his competition—were both talking with the trainer and the pit. Maybe he'd get lucky, and they'd battle it out for him instead of Finley.

Chris sat on the bench seat. "I gotta say, that was pretty impressive. Watching you and Finley the last thirty minutes. Really, watching all the dogs. But especially you guys. I've never seen so many dogs so well-trained."

Amy sat on the tabletop. Finley sat in front of her. "Thanks. Sometimes I can't believe it myself, that I'm actually doing this. A couple of months ago, when I got here, I couldn't imagine ever being able to get it all down."

Chris reached over and pet Finley's neck and back. "You've only been in here two months?"

"Not in the prison, I mean in this program. I've been in here a little over two years."

"You've only been training dogs for two months?" Chris was curious about what had gotten her sent to prison, but he'd never ask something like that.

Amy nodded. "Some of the other trainers have been doing it for years. They really helped me out a lot. And I've had some books to read and watched some videos. And of course, Miss Bridget and the other trainers who run the program, they're really great teachers."

"Well, whatever they're doing, it's obviously working."

"Thanks. But I've gotta give most of the credit to Finley. He makes me look good."

"Do you mind if I ask...how much longer will you be in here?"

"This is my third and final year. They're refiguring my gain time. That's the time they shave off your sentence for good behavior and other positive things. Like being in this program. I'm supposed to hear back something pretty soon. I'm hoping they'll say it's closer to six months."

"That won't be too long," Chris said. "Have any plans for...after?"

"Not really. Obviously, I'm going to need to start my life over. I won't really have any friends or family waiting for me when I get out. That's probably a good thing. At least the friends part.

Hanging around them is what got me put in here."

He was interested in hearing more but didn't want to cross the line. He knew what it was like to be on the receiving end of someone's overactive curiosity.

"So, are you thinking you might like to have Finley?"

Chris looked right at Finley's eyes. Finley returned the gaze, then licked him on the nose.

"Finley," Amy said.

"I don't mind. To answer your question, I'm definitely interested in Finley. I've been having a pretty hard time since I got out. It's not just the leg, but more so the PTSD issue."

"The leg?"

Chris was surprised she didn't know. He reached down and pulled up his pant leg, revealing the prosthetic limb, then tapped on it. "Stepped on a mine in Afghanistan."

"I'd never have guessed the way you walk."

"I'm glad to hear that," he said. "That's been my goal, trying to get to a place where I'm not limping anymore."

"I'd say you've arrived."

"Thanks. But if you hung around me often, you'd see how far I still have to go. But I am making progress, and I'm grateful for that. Have you ever met anyone struggling with PTSD?"

"Not personally," she said. "You're probably the first active-duty soldier I've ever talked with. Thanks for your service, by the way. I should've said that right up front."

"That's okay. But you're welcome."

"I did study up on it a little, as part of our training. We know many of the dogs are probably going to guys with PTSD. I watched a few videos of guys talking about what it's like. It sounds pretty awful. I can't even imagine. I'm sorry. I shouldn't have said that. If you hung around me more often, you'd see how often I put my foot in my mouth."

Chris laughed. "I'm not offended. You're right, it is pretty awful. When it flares up anyway. It doesn't affect me all the time. Seems like it's been getting worse as time goes on, though, not better. I hate taking the drugs they give you. They help some, but I don't like the side effects." He was petting Finley the whole time he talked. Just now, Finley rested his head on Chris's lap.

"Would you look at that?" Amy said. "I've never seen him do that with anyone else but me."

"Really?" Chris said.

"Nope. And he didn't start doing that with me until we were friends for almost a week."

"He's an amazing animal," Chris said. "I thought for sure I'd get in some trouble coming here, with my PTSD I mean. Usually do when I get with a lot of strangers in confined places. But I don't know, somehow with Finley here, I'm feeling just the opposite. As calm as can be."

He thought of something else, how easy it was to talk to Amy. She didn't make him nervous at all.

Amy slid off the tabletop, down to the bench and sat beside Chris.

"What's the next step from here?" he asked. "Because I definitely want to find out. I would absolutely love to have this dog."

"You'll interview with Miss Bridget. She'll give you some forms to fill out to make sure you're able to provide a good home for a dog. Not just for Finley, but any dog in the program."

"I've got my own place. It's only a twenty minute drive from here."

"That's good. Then, of course, there's matching you up with the right dog. It's not totally my call, and the other two vets might need to spend some time with him. If they want to, that is. But I'd say things are looking pretty good with you and Finley. He certainly seems to have made up his mind."

Hearing that made Chris feel even better than he already did.

"Uh-oh," Amy said. "Looks like we've got company."

Chris looked up, then tensed up a little. The two veterans who were looking at the brindle pit were headed this way.

38

Amy stood. It was her job to be polite and friendly. But she didn't really want to be. Chris was the guy. If she had to let go of Finley to anyone, it would be him. And look, Finley had already chosen him.

The taller of the two men spoke first. "You Amy? Captain Bridget said we were supposed to talk with you. Guess you're the trainer of this handsome animal."

"That's me." She reached out her hand. Both men shook it. "And this is Finley."

"Fidley?" the shorter man said.

"No, Finley," Chris said. "With an *N*."

"Sorry. Don't hear so good. Used to work a tank."

"Finley, greet," Amy said. Finley instantly obeyed. He walked up between the two men and sat. Looked up with his friendliest face and wagged his tail.

"Aren't you something?" the taller man said. "I'm Rich, and this here is Matt. We're actually roommates, but our counselor thinks we should both get our own dog."

"He's a golden retriever, right?" Matt said.

"Mostly," Amy said. "But he's part something else. We just

don't know what. But it's obvious, he's got mostly retriever genes. Have you two met Chris yet?"

"Don't believe so," Rich said. The men shook hands.

"You interested in Finley?" Rich said to Chris.

"I am. What did you two think of the other dog you were just with, the brindle colored pit?"

"Loved him," Rich said. "We had ourselves a nice visit."

"We're both interested in him," Matt said, "but obviously, we can't both have him. But he's the only pit left."

"You like pits?" Amy asked.

"I do," Matt said. "Had one before I went into the service. Had him for a long time, as a matter fact. He died while I was over there. Sure would like to get me another one. Especially one as smart as these, one that can help me with my…with my struggles. But I'm gonna let Rich have him."

"You are?" Rich said. "We hadn't decided on anything, yet."

"Well I have. You're hurtin' worse than me. We both know that. And that dog took to you like butter on bread."

Rich had a stunned look on his face. "That's mighty nice-a-you, Matt."

"Think nothing of it. It's a done deal." He turned his attention to Amy and Chris. "We're just coming over here, mainly because Finley is the last dog left. He is the last one, right?"

"After Benny, he is," Amy said. "But I thought you loved pits."

"I do," Matt said. "But it appears we got here too late to get one. And this dog is certainly a fine looking specimen." He looked at his friend. "I'd be a chick magnet walking this dog down the street, don't ya think?"

"I don't know if you want to get started with a dog that's way better looking than you are," Rich said.

These two guys were nice, in a rough-sawn sort of way, but

there was no way Amy wanted Finley going home with either one of them.

"So, what do we do?" Matt said. "How do we decide who gets Finley?" He looked at Chris. "Want to flip a coin for him?"

"I don't think that would be a good idea," Amy said. "Besides, that kind of leaves Finley out of the process." Suddenly, she had a thought. There was a slight risk involved, but Amy was almost certain things would end up the right way if they did this.

"You want to let Finley choose?" Rich said.

"That's the idea. How about I stand here with Finley? Matt and Chris, you stand over there about fifteen feet in front of me." They did. "Now move to the side till you are about fifteen feet apart." They did that, too.

"Do you want us to do anything?" Chris said.

Amy could tell by the look on his face, he wasn't liking this. But she was certain he had nothing to worry about. "Yes, when I count to three, both of you say gently, and in a happy voice, 'Here, Finley.' We'll see which one he goes to."

"That seems fair enough," Rich said. He looked at Amy. "But dogs don't choose like people do, right? He won't care about how homely my friend Matt is here, right? He won't choose Chris cause he's the better looking fella."

They all laughed. "No," Amy said. "Dogs will love anyone, no matter what they look like."

"Good," Rich said. He looked at Matt. "You still got a chance. Don't give up hope."

"This how you gonna treat me. After I been so nice to you?"

"I am being nice. I'm looking out for your interests." He pronounced it *inner-rists*.

"Okay," Amy said, "are we ready to do this?"

Matt nodded.

"I guess so," Chris said.

"Okay, call him...now."

"Here Finley," both men said just the way Amy asked. Matt added, "Come here, boy."

Finley looked at both men, slightly confused for a moment. Then he instantly ran right where Amy expected him to...right to Chris's side. He even performed the finish command all on his own, walked behind Chris then sat beside him on the opposite side. To top it off, he leaned his head against Chris's leg.

No one said anything for a moment.

"I thought you said he didn't care about Matt being ugly," Rich said. That sufficiently broke the tension and everyone laughed. "He walked up to Chris like he was his daddy."

Matt stuck out his hand to Chris. "I know when I'm beat. You won fair and square."

"Thanks," Chris said. "And just for the record...I think you're way better looking than Rich." Everyone laughed again.

This turned out even better than Amy hoped.

"Probably just as well," Matt said. "I really had my heart set on getting a pit anyway."

"Then you won't have long to wait," Amy said. "This class graduates in less than a month. Then we start up another one right away. As you can see looking around, almost half the class are pits or pit mixes. You sign up now, and you'll have your pick of the next class."

"Sounds good to me," Matt said. "C'mon, Rich. Let's go over and have a chat with that Miss Bridget, see if we can get you signed up. You all have a fine afternoon." They waved and walked away.

Amy walked Finley back to the picnic table. She sat on the bench; he sat beside her.

Chris rejoined her. "That was kind of unexpected. Gotta be

honest, I was a little nervous. Is that how you usually settle these matters?"

"I don't know. This is my first training class, remember?"

"What if Finley chose Matt?"

"I knew that wouldn't happen. He's already chosen you, Chris." She thought it, but didn't say it: *And so have I.*

39

Chris waited for the other two vets to be far enough away to speak freely, then asked Amy, "So, does that mean…I get Finley? He's my dog? I mean, *going* to be my dog. There's no other chance I could lose him to someone else?"

"I'm pretty sure that's how it is. You've already been preapproved. Finley is available. You want him, and he clearly wants you."

"You said *pretty sure*. Is there any—"

"I'm real sure. It's just, I've never done this before. But I've seen matches happen all the time the last few weeks. It goes just like this. The next step is just to talk to Miss Bridget and make it official. She'll probably have a few more things for you to sign, maybe have a few more questions. But before all of you came, she had a little talk with me. She wanted me to be ready to let go of Finley today. So I'm pretty sure she'll be all for this."

Chris picked up something in what she just said. Not just the words, but her tone, the slight change of expression on her face. "I can imagine it's pretty hard for you."

"What is?"

"Letting go of Finley." He reached over and scratched behind his ear. "He's not even mine yet, and I was struggling bigtime during that little contest a few minutes ago. I couldn't imagine seeing him go home with Matt. Nothing on him, just the idea of losing him."

"He certainly has a way of growing on you," Amy said. "I've never had a dog before. Wanted one my whole childhood, but…well, that's a long story. Since I went out on my own, my life's been too unstable to have a dog."

"You look like someone who's been around dogs your whole life."

"No, just Finley. But having him makes me want to be around dogs the rest of my life. I mean, when I get out of here."

"Well, that shouldn't be too long from now. You said six months, right?"

"I said I hope it's six months. I'm waiting to hear back something on that any day."

"Will you be training other dogs between now and then? I mean after Finley graduates?"

"That was the plan."

"But not anymore?"

Amy patted Finley on the head, then looked away. It looked to Chris that she was getting teary-eyed. "I'm not sure I'm cut out for this."

"Training dogs?" Chris said. "Amy, I'm only here this one day, but I have been watching everything. You're one of the best trainers in here."

She sighed, seemed to regain her composure. "Nice of you to say. But it's not the training part I'm struggling with. It's the letting go part. My friend, Rita, says you get used to it. She's been doing this for three years. But I can't see how." She leaned over and kissed Finley on the forehead. "We've only been together for a couple of months, but it's like he's a part of me now. Closer than any friend I've ever had."

Chris could easily imagine this. He already felt a significant bond forming between him and this dog, and they'd only just met. "Guess that's why they call them, man's best friend." It was a stupid thing to say. He wished he could take it back. She didn't seem to notice. He had to think of something else to say. "Why do you think these dogs are so effective at helping veterans with PTSD?"

Amy leaned back, like she was thinking. "I don't have any official-sounding answer. We didn't really cover this in our training. But I've been doing a lot of thinking about it on my own. Not so much from a veteran's point of view, since I've never served. But I think there might be some parallels to the kind of help they provide, even to people like me. I've definitely had some trauma in my life. Nothing like what you went through. You and guys like you in the military. Your trauma came from being heroic. Mine came from making a complete mess of my life. Getting addicted to drugs. Totally destroying family life. Constantly feeling hopeless and out of control. Stealing to try to keep from becoming homeless. Then I end up here."

She paused and looked over the grounds in front of them. "I don't mean this part of the prison. It actually hasn't been too bad since I got here. I'm talking about the main prison, in the general population. I think I was scared the whole time I was in there. Every minute of every day. My faith certainly helped me some, but I still felt like I was barely keeping my head above water. Until you came into my life, Mr. Finley." She gently took his face in her hands. He seemed to smile at her and wagged his tail.

"It was like God knew I needed him, at just the right moment. I know this part'll sound kind of crazy. But I think God made dogs different than other animals and gave them a special gift. Some days, I swear I feel God's love coming right through Finley, straight into my heart. For the first time in my life—just being around him—I think I understand what unconditional love and acceptance feels like, or something very close to it. Finley likes me regardless of my problems. He gives his love away for free, every day, without judgment, without prejudice or a moment's hesitation. One look in his eyes and you can tell, he doesn't care about anything you've done, or any of the stupid mistakes you've made. Whatever's wrong with you, even whatever you think is wrong with you, Finley doesn't care."

"Wow. You've given this a lot of thought."

"I'm sorry. That was probably way too much information."

"No need to apologize. I like what you said. And you might be onto something. Dogs really do seem to have a special gift. I actually came here today because a good friend of mine, really my best friend, was in seriously bad shape not that long ago. He was suicidal. I didn't think he would make it. He called me a few days ago, and it was like he was a different person. We didn't talk about it in depth, not the way you and I are doing here. But my guess is, he could relate to everything you just said about Finley."

"I bet he could," she said. "Now you know why I'm having a hard time letting go."

Chris did. He absolutely did, but he didn't know what to say. How to comfort her. He knew she didn't mean it this way, but he almost felt guilty being the one taking Finley away from her. "Well, you still have him for a month, right?"

"Closer to three weeks now."

"Well, I don't live that far from here. After graduation, I could bring him by to visit."

"Oh no, Chris. I'm sorry. I don't want you to feel bad. I'm

really glad you came today. And I'm really glad Finley likes you so much. This is what's supposed to happen. All of this training and all this time I spent with Finley was to get him ready to be with you. There were a bunch of guys who wanted Finley before you came here today. But he didn't want any of them."

"You could tell?"

She nodded. "I could definitely tell. I could also tell, I didn't want any of them to take him home. You're the first guy he's reacted to this way, and the first guy I've felt comfortable about releasing him to. Seeing him here with you, I'm actually relieved."

Chris liked the sound of that. A lot.

But if that was true, why were tears now welling up in her eyes?

40

Amy looked up from her cot in response to a quick knock on the door.

Rita peeked her head inside. "You okay? Can I come in?"

It was amazing to see how much softer and gentler Rita had begun to treat Amy in the last month or so. It was fair to say they were friends now. The age difference put Rita in something of a big-sister role. "Sure," Amy said.

Finley had been napping inside his pen. He lifted his head briefly, then laid it down again when he saw Charlie wasn't with her.

"Charlie's napping, too. Thought I'd get caught up on how things went with those vets you were talking to. Miss Bridget said you got Finley paired up with one of them."

Amy sat up. "I did. After we talked, he met with her, got everything all squared away. It's official now."

"Which one was it? One of the two guys who came here together or the good looking one?"

Amy smiled. "The good looking one. His name's Chris. Chris Seger."

"I'm glad. A dog as nice looking as Finley deserves an owner in the same league. You've seen the guy Charlie's paired up with, right? Short and stocky, minus a neck. Just like Charlie."

Amy laughed. So, Rita thought Chris was nice looking, too. She'd thought he was but wondered if he was the kind of good looking that might seem that way to one woman, but not another. Knowing Rita thought it, too, meant Chris actually *was* good looking; which probably also meant he wasn't in her league. What was she thinking? Chris wasn't in her league, either way.

She wasn't in anyone's league. She was in prison.

"So, what was he like? I looked over a few times, seemed like Finley really liked him."

"I barely know him," Amy said. "But I like what I know. He's the kind of person you almost can't help but like right off the bat. Know what I mean? Easy to talk to, easy to listen to."

Rita just nodded and smiled. "Easy to look at."

"It's not like that, Rita."

"Of course it's like that. It might not be all it's like, but I'm just saying…he's a handsome man. A far sight better looking than any of the other guys we've had in this latest group."

Hearing Rita go on like this about Chris made Amy feel even more certain she had no chance with someone like him. Not that she ever did.

"What's the matter? I thought you liked him."

"I do, and he's the first guy Finley's taken to."

"So, you only like him because he's a good fit for Finley?"

"No. He also seems like a genuinely nice guy. But what difference does that make? I don't have a chance with a guy like him. Even if I wasn't stuck in here and looking like…*this*." She held out the side of her orange jump suit.

"Don't be so hard on yourself, girlie. You're a beautiful young woman. All you need is one of those—what do they call 'em—

overhauls."

"Makeovers?"

"Yeah. Get you all fixed up, your hair done, the right outfit, I think you'd be just as good a fit for him as Finley."

Rita was just being nice. Ridiculous, but nice. None of it was true, of course, but it made her feel a little better. "He's missing a leg, did you know that?"

"He is? I couldn't tell. I didn't notice him limping."

"He said it was kind of a goal he had been shooting for, to get his stride to where people couldn't even tell."

"Is he ashamed of it? The leg being gone? Seems like nowadays with so many vets missing limbs, people are pretty used to it."

"No, I don't think so. He talked about it pretty easily. He didn't say why, and I didn't ask. Maybe he just doesn't want people feeling sorry for him all the time."

"That could be. He tell you what happened?"

"A little. We talked some more after he met with Miss Bridget, just before he left. He stepped on a mine in Afghanistan. I think it was two years ago. But I'd say he's been struggling more with the PTSD thing than his leg. That's why he was so excited about Finley. He said he could already see Finley making a difference in him."

"In what way?"

"He said he felt totally calm when Finley was near. He was certain when he drove in here that he wouldn't last twenty minutes, but he was here over an hour. And there at the end, you could tell he didn't want to leave."

"I'm sure some of that was Finley," Rita said. "Maybe even most of it. But I'll bet you some of it was being there with you."

Amy sighed. "You're delusional, Rita. A girl can tell when a guy is interested, and he wasn't sending me any of those signals. All his signals were going Finley's way."

"We'll see," Rita said. "We'll see. When's he coming back again?"

"He said tomorrow, if he can make it work. He asked how often he could come back between now and graduation. I told him as often as he wanted. The more time we can spend together, the better."

"I'll say."

"I mean, for training. You're just being silly. You know how this goes. Miss Bridget's been saying to the other vets, the more time they can be here bonding with their dogs and learning all we've taught them, the smoother the transition will be after they graduate. So, that's what I told Chris."

Rita just smiled.

"I don't know why you're going on like this, as if there was even a chance for something romantic between us. He'll be gone with Finley in a few weeks. I'm stuck in here at least six months, maybe more. He'll forget all about me long before then."

Rita's smile grew wider. "Maybe. Maybe not."

"What are you talking about?"

"Let's just say, I know something you don't. And maybe you should have a talk with Miss Bridget. Like, right now."

"What? What do you know?"

"I'm not supposed to say. You need to talk to her. But I was in her office just before lunch, saw something on her desk. That's all I can say." She got up, waved, and slipped out the door.

41

After Chris got back to the golf course, he got right to work on the mower. He didn't want to give anyone the impression that this new development would become a distraction to his job. He couldn't let that happen. But one thing was clear: that sense of calm he felt back at the prison with Finley and Amy lingered the whole drive back and for the first hour or so as he mowed.

And he was aware of something else he hadn't felt in quite a while: Hope. That and something in his life to look forward to.

He was mowing the ninth hole now, which led him back toward the clubhouse and maintenance building. It was also time for his lunch break. It felt odd taking it so late in the day, but he'd better get used to it. He had been thinking through a plan that would allow him to be out at the prison for training every weekday until Finley's graduation.

It was still daylight savings time. Didn't get dark until eight p.m. He could come in early, like he did today, take two hours off and head out to the prison, then work two hours later in the afternoon. It took some time, but he came up with a plan where he could do all the mowing in the big mower during the hottest part of the day, since it was air-conditioned. He was certain Tom would okay the plan once he understood it.

He rode down the last section of grass that ran between the fairway and a row of trees, which finished up this hole. He disengaged the mower and lifted the carriage up to a setting that let him travel at a higher speed. Up ahead at the maintenance building, he saw Tom's car in the parking lot. Jed was just riding a golf cart from around the side of the building into the garage. Chris waited for a foursome of golfers to pass, then rode the mower into the parking lot and parked under a shady tree.

As he got down from the mower and walked across the lot toward Jed, he rehearsed his spiel for Tom. Fortunately, Jed was facing the other way, hooking up a battery for recharge. It wasn't that he minded talking to Jed, just not now. He quietly walked past him toward Tom's office.

"There you are, Chris," Jed said over his shoulder. "How'd it go at the prison?"

Chris stopped and turned around. "It really went great. I got the perfect dog."

"You already got a dog?"

"Well, I got paired with one."

"What's that mean?"

"He's going to be mine, in a few weeks when he graduates. He's got to stay there until then. But he's perfect, Jed. You really should sign up for this thing. I can already see this is going to be a good thing for me."

"Yeah?"

Chris nodded.

"What kind of dog is it?"

"He looks like a golden retriever. Amy said he was part that and part something else, but I couldn't see any other kind of dog in him."

"Who's Amy?"

"She's the girl who's been training him."

"She's a prisoner though, right?"

"They call them inmates."

"Okay, inmates. But that's what she is, right? You know, *Orange Is the New Black*?"

"Yeah. She was even wearing an orange jumpsuit."

"You said girl. So she wasn't an old lady?"

"No. I didn't ask her age obviously, but I say it's close to mine."

"You sense any desperation in her? You know...those ladies all shut up in prison with no men around? For years?"

Chris smiled. "No Jed. She wasn't desperate. Not even a little. She seemed like a really nice girl."

"Maybe she's not into dudes. Happens in a place like that."

"This wasn't that kind of thing. What she's into is training dogs, and she's amazing at it. All of them were. I've never seen so many dogs so well behaved. And Finley seemed like the smartest one of them all."

"That's the dog's name?"

Chris nodded.

"What other kind of dogs they have?"

"I'd say about half of them were pits."

"That's what I'd want."

"The rest were all different. Couple of hounds. Saw one that looked mostly like a German shepherd. But I'm sure you can find one you like, especially if you sign up early. This class ends in less than a month, but I asked the main lady in charge and she said you could sign up anytime, online. They'll email you when the new class starts. But hey look, I gotta get in there and talk with Tom before my breaks over."

"He needs to approve it?"

"Mainly, I'm hoping he'll let me change my schedule for the rest of this month to be more like today. They train the dogs every morning, and I want to be there for it."

"Well, that's great, man. I can tell this dog is already doing you some good."

"You can? How?"

"You're smiling. You've been smiling, off and on, the whole time we've been talking. I've never seen you smile before. Hope this thing works out for you, bro."

"Thanks." Chris turned and headed for Tom's office.

Amy knocked on Miss Bridget's office door.

"Come in."

Amy did. "It's just me. Can I talk to you for a few minutes?"

"You certainly can. Actually, you're saving me the trouble. I was planning to come find you. Something I need to talk to you about."

So, Rita was right. Amy wondered what it could be.

"But first, congratulations on getting Finley matched up with his new owner today. That's a very big step."

"Thanks, I guess. No, I'm sorry. I'm really happy it happened. For him and for Chris."

"Chris seems like a really nice guy. He was so excited when I talked to him. It sounded like he's going to try to get here to be part of Finley's training every day until graduation."

"That's what he told me, if he could get his boss to agree to it."

"Well, that's a very good sign," Bridget said, "for the new owner to be willing to get that involved. That's gotta give you good feeling about what kind of home Finley will have when he leaves here."

"It does," she said, with absolutely no joy.

"I know it's hard. It's especially hard letting go the first time. But unfortunately for you, or maybe I should say, fortunately for you...Finley will be the first and last dog you train here with us."

"What? Why? Aren't I doing a good enough job?"

"You're doing a great job. As a matter fact, keep this to yourself until I announce it at the graduation ceremony, but you and Finley have made the Top Five competition."

"We have? Really? But I don't understand. If that's true, why can't I train any more dogs?"

"Simple," Bridget said, "because you won't be here that long. They refigured your gain time, adding in all the extra time you get for being part of this program, and you're going to be out of here, girl, less than three months from now. Two months after Finley's graduation. There's not enough time for you to train another dog. But I've got it worked out that you can stay in the program, as an assistant trainer."

Amy couldn't believe it. Three months. Less than three months, she would be free. "That's wonderful."

No one said anything for an awkward moment.

"You don't seem as happy as I'd expect you to be."

"No, I am happy. This is wonderful news. It's just I wish...I wish there was some way I could've kept Finley. Someplace he could go for those two months after he graduates where he could wait until I got out."

"Amy, I know how attached you are to him. But you've got to know, this whole program is set up to train dogs like Finley to help guys like Chris. And you've done a wonderful job with him. I can already tell, Finley is going to change Chris's life. And you've played a major role in that."

"I know. I know. I'm just being selfish. It's just Finley's

changed my life, too. I can't imagine not having him around."

"I'm sure it'll be hard at first. But here's the good news, you can take the skills you've learned with you. I can talk with Kim Harper at the Humane Society. She'll help you pick out a dog that would be a perfect fit. You can train him, or her, just the same way. And I'm sure you'll bond with that dog just as strongly when the time comes."

"I'm sure you're right." Amy stood. "Well, thanks Miss Bridget. Not just for the good news, but for helping me think this thing through. I'm sure I'll be fine in a few days, once I get used to everything."

"I'm sure you will."

Amy took a few steps toward the door then turned. "Can I ask you something?"

"Sure."

"Since I will be getting out two months after Finley graduates, do you think it would be okay if I mentioned that to Chris? I could just mention that I'd be okay if he wanted to call me…if he had any follow up questions about Finley's training."

Miss Bridget made a face. She clearly was against the idea.

"Never mind. It's a bad idea. I can see how it would come off as kind of pushy. I don't want to be like that."

"I won't forbid you from telling him. But you're right, I don't think it's a good idea. We never mention that as an option to the new owners because, let's face it, all the women who've trained their dogs are still in prison. Plus, we really want the vets to move forward, not stay in a long-term relationship with us. Usually, we give them a short list of certified dog trainers in the area, if they want to do any follow up training."

"That makes sense," Amy said. "Just forget I ever mentioned it. Thanks again for the good news, and for putting Finley and me in the Top Five. That's such an honor. I'll see you later."

"Remember, now. Don't say a word about that."

"I won't." She opened the door, stepped into the hall and closed it behind her. She just heard two bits of wonderful news. She should be absolutely elated. But all she felt was confused. Even a little bit sad.

42

Two Weeks Later

Finley was getting excited. Since waking up, he and Amy had been going through their normal morning routine. As best he could tell, everything they'd done so far meant this was another training day. He hoped so. He'd get to see Chris again. Finley knew his name now.

He could tell, Amy was just as excited to see him. Her mood completely changed when he arrived. Finley was beginning to recognize an in-between mood change in her that began even before Chris arrived.

It was happening now.

She had just put him on the leash. They were heading out to the hallway. All the other dogs with their trainers were coming down the hallway with them. They headed toward the main room up ahead. It *was* training day.

When they came into the big room, Finley's eyes instantly focused on the chair where Chris always sat. It was empty. Most of the other chairs were filled with the other men who'd been coming also. Not all of them as faithfully as Chris, but Finley was getting used to seeing their faces.

But where was Chris?

He looked up at Amy, as she led them both into their normal place in the lineup. She was looking at the same empty chair. Her mood had already changed; she was sad. She missed seeing Chris, too. A few moments later Miss Bridget said what she always said to get everyone's attention.

Soon they were going through the first sets of commands, the ones they always started with. Finley was so used to them by now, he'd often begin to obey before Amy even spoke. Every few seconds, he'd glance at the door hoping to spot Chris. In just a few more minutes, they'd finish the preliminary routines and Miss Bridget would invite the men to come up to start their part of the training. They did that all the time now.

Finley actually loved this part. Chris would take the leash with Amy right beside him. But Chris would be the one telling him what to do. At first, Chris made mistakes that confused Finley. Amy would gently correct him and make everything clear again. Now he seemed to understand everything, and Finley enjoyed following his direction. He especially enjoyed the way Chris rewarded him. The treats were nice, but Finley enjoyed the words Chris said and the way he said them even more.

They walked across the room; Finley expected it to be the last time in this routine. Sure enough, Amy gave the command, "Finish." He walked around her to the other side and sat. Just then, the front door opened. Chris walked in. Finley couldn't help it. His tail began to thud on the floor and his front paws marched in place. Chris saw them, smiled and waved. He seemed to be mouthing some words but no sound came out. Finley looked up at Amy, who was smiling back. She nodded to Chris as if she understood.

It didn't matter. What mattered was, Chris was here. He loved it when the three of them were together.

For the last half of the training session, Chris handled Finley. Amy felt he was really getting the hang of it. She could also see how eagerly Finley responded to his voice now. There really wasn't any difference anymore. He treated them the same. A few minutes ago, Miss Bridget ended the class.

"You want to go outside for a little while before you have to go?" Amy said.

"Definitely," Chris said. "I've got some questions to ask you anyway."

"Really? What about?"

"Nothing too serious. Let's wait till we can sit at the picnic table."

Amy watched as Chris walked Finley around the perimeter of the fence, giving Finley a chance to go the bathroom. After, he joined her on the picnic table where they usually sat. She sat on the bench, Chris on the tabletop; Finley sat between them.

"So, what's up?"

"Sorry about being late. I didn't plan my work very well this morning. Wound up getting stuck mowing on the opposite side of the golf course from the clubhouse. Then it seemed like I hit every light between here and there."

"That's okay. You know you don't have to come every day."

"I want to. It's the highlight of my day."

It was hers, too. But she wasn't going to say it.

"But that's not really what I wanted to talk to you about."

"Okay…"

"It has to do with Finley and the whole PTSD thing. Last

night, I was talking with my friend Kyle on the phone. I told you about him before. He's the one that told me all about getting a service dog. His dog, Tootsie, really turned his life around."

Amy laughed. "You did tell me about Kyle. I guess I never heard his dog's name before."

"Yeah, it's Tootsie. Or Toots for short. Anyway, he was asking me about the training, and I was telling him everything we were doing. He asked me one question I didn't have an answer to."

"What is it?"

"He said Tootsie instinctively knows when he's starting to lose it. You know, when the PTSD thing is kicking in. She'll stop whatever she's doing and totally focus on him. He said she'll kind-of get in his face in a nice way. Do whatever she has to do to get his attention. She'll poke him. Lick him in the nose. If he's standing and starts zoning out, she'll even jump up at him. And she'll keep doing it until he comes out of it and refocuses on her."

"And you're wondering if Finley will do that for you?"

He nodded. "I realized as he was talking, Finley's never done that with me when we're together."

"Have you ever had one of those attacks when you're here? I've never seen it."

"I haven't. Which is kind of amazing in itself. Somehow, just being around him...and you, it's like the switches all get turned off."

He just said...*and you.* That's the first time Chris had ever mentioned her in that way. He had talked about the effect Finley had on him several times before.

"I haven't had a single panic attack out here. Not one. Which is great. But it doesn't give me a chance to see how Finley would act when we're out there." Chris pointed past the barbed wire fence.

She could see his point.

"Do you know what he would do? With graduation a week away, how would we find out? Have you guys trained the dogs for that kind of thing before I started coming?"

"We have. I don't think you have anything to worry about, Chris." How could she explain this? "On the one hand, you know this good feeling you get in general, just being around Finley? That's real. Same thing happens to me. We learned a little bit about why. It's partly because dogs are just so lovable, and they love us so unconditionally. We just don't get that kind of positive input from people. Not most of the time anyway. But another thing dogs do, just by being with us, is keep us from being self-absorbed, from constantly focusing on ourselves. When our minds go drifting off in unhealthy directions, they pull us back. Keep us grounded."

She reached down and scratched under Finley's jaw, then behind his ears. He rewarded her with a lick. "Even besides all that, I've experienced what Kyle was talking about with his dog. I don't have PTSD, like you guys. But believe me, it can get pretty depressing in here at times. I do have some friends, but they're not close ones. I've got some family, but…well, let's just say we're not close at all. So I'm pretty much alone, and I feel alone. A lot. And then I start thinking about why I'm here, and that I only have myself to blame. Guys like you and Kyle, you're suffering because you were serving your country. You're real-life heroes. Not me. I'm alone because I let myself get hooked on meth, then I ruined every relationship in my life, one by one. I even stole from my own family." She started choking up. Tears began to form in her eyes.

Instantly, Finley moved in. He gently brought his face right up to hers and licked her under the chin. Then he nudged his nose in that same place and leaned on her, almost like giving her a hug. Amy couldn't help but respond to his affection. She hugged him back and started patting his head. "See what I mean?"

"I do," Chris said. "That looks exactly like what Kyle said Tootsie does."

"And he'll stay close to me like this until I've totally pulled out of my dark mood. He'll even intervene when I have nightmares. Do you ever have nightmares?"

"Sometimes," Chris said.

"I don't really have them much anymore, either," Amy said. "But I used to, the first few weeks I was here in this program. Life in the main prison can be pretty terrifying. At least for someone like me. I used to get these horrible dreams of being cornered or bullied by a bunch of big angry ladies, and Finley would wake me up. He sleeps in his crate. But he'd whine and make noise in his crate till I'd wake up. I'd reach over and open his door, and he'd jump right up on the bed with me, kind of like he just did now. And he would just stay with me, comforting me until I calmed down."

"I'm sorry you've had it so rough in here. But it's great to hear how much he helped you." Chris reached over and patted Finley on the shoulder. "He is an amazing dog. But I feel kinda bad taking him from you. Seems like you still need him."

"I don't want you to feel that way, Chris. I'm doing a lot better now. Besides, they wouldn't let me keep him. If you weren't taking him, they'd just bring him back to the Humane Society, and he'd get adopted by some family. And all this training would go to waste."

Chris thought a moment. "You think he'll ever treat me that way? The way he treats you?"

"I know he will. He already loves you as much as he loves me."

"You think so?"

"I know so."

They sat together in silence a moment. Then Chris said, "I'm glad you've had Finley, at least the last few months. Will they give you another dog to train after graduation?"

Amy shook her head no. "They can't. But it's really for a good reason."

"What's that?"

"They're letting me out early. My release date now is set for two months after...graduation." She was about to say, two months after you and Finley leave, but she couldn't say it.

"Two months?" Chris said. "Really, that's all? Just two months?"

She nodded.

"That's not very long." He smiled, looked as if he had more to say but didn't say it.

She wondered what he was thinking.

It was probably nothing.

43

Later that day, Chris decided to use his lunch break to pick up a large crate they could use in the maintenance building and some other supplies for Finley. Tom had already gotten permission from Colonel Banks to keep Finley in his office during the day. As Chris pulled into the parking lot, he looked down at the digital clock. He only got thirty minutes for lunch, so he really only had time to unload everything before his break was over. He'd have to wolf down his sandwich when he was back on the mower.

He backed the car near the garage door opening. After carting a load of supplies inside, he came back to find Jed pulling out the big box containing the crate.

"Thought you could use a hand," Jed said. "Guessing this is for that dog?"

"Thanks. Yeah. Thought I'd put it together after work."

"How much longer till you bring Finley home?"

"Graduation's just one week away." Chris grabbed the other side of the crate box. "It's really getting harder and harder to leave him there every day."

"And harder to leave that girl whose training him? Amy, right?"

Chris looked at Jed. "What? Why do you say that?"

"Lately, you talk about her just about as much as the dog."

"I do?"

Jed nodded. "Something brewing there between you two?"

"I don't think so," Chris said.

"You don't think so? What kind of answer is that? Either there is, or there isn't. All I'm saying is, when you first started going out there, you'd come back talking all about Finley. I'd say for at least the last week, that's changed. You spend at least half the time talking about Amy."

They brought the box inside and set it down near Tom's office. Chris had no idea he'd been talking so much about Amy. He definitely did like her. But did he like her *that way*? "She's an amazing girl, especially the things she's done with Finley."

"Yeah," Jed said, "I've heard that, too. But the look you get when you talk about her lately...I just figured there was more going on than that."

"I don't think there is. I'm not ready for a relationship anyway. Not in the condition I'm in."

"Okay. Maybe I'm reading you wrong. But from the way you talk about her, she doesn't seem like the kind of girl you'd have to worry that much about."

Chris didn't follow.

"You know, the kind you have to keep trying to impress. I mean, you're already talking with her about all your biggest struggles. I ain't going home to nobody these days, but I know if I was, I'd want her to be somebody real, somebody I could talk to. You know what I'm saying, somebody who gets me."

Jed was right about that. Amy was somebody Chris could really talk to, about anything.

"How long she in for? What did she do, anyway? She ever tell you?"

"She gets out in two months. She told me a couple days ago she got arrested for shoplifting."

"Shoplifting. People go to prison for that?"

"That's what I thought. Apparently, it has to do with how many times you've done it and the cost of the stuff you stole. She was with some friends and they were stealing a diamond ring. She got caught. They got away. The judge gave her three years. She also said she used to be a meth addict."

"That's why she was shoplifting?"

"No. I guess she had stopped using sometime before that and was trying to stay clean, but then she lost her job and was running out of money. She was stealing to get rent money, so she wouldn't wind up back on the street."

"And start using again," Jed said.

"Guess so."

"So instead, she winds up in prison. Sometimes you just can't win."

"Nope," Chris said.

"But see, that goes back to why things could work out for the two of you. You're both broken, just in a different way. So all the tension's off. You already know what's wrong with her. She already knows what's wrong with you. You're already talking about things with her most guys don't get to with a regular girlfriend for the first six months."

That was probably true.

"You think she likes you?" Jed asked.

"I don't know. She likes me fine, I guess. As a friend."

"I don't mean as a friend."

"I know." They were back at the car. Chris needed to move it to a regular parking space. "I don't know if she likes me any other kind of way. I don't even know if I could tell anymore if she did."

"Maybe you should start paying attention. See if she's giving out any signs."

"Signs? What are you talking about?"

"I'm no expert, but I know a few things. When I decided I was ready to get back in the game, I was pretty rusty like you. So I looked up some things online. For an example, has she ever asked you if you have a girlfriend, or if you're dating someone?"

Chris thought a moment. "No, I don't think so. Does that mean something?"

"Could be," Jed said. "Usually a girl asks that, she's definitely interested."

"So if she hasn't, she's not?"

"Not necessarily. There are other things. How close do you guys sit together?"

"I don't know. A regular distance, I guess. When we're sitting together, we're usually sitting on one of the picnic benches they have outside. Sometimes I sit on top of the table, she sits on the bench. Sometimes we're both sitting on the same level, next to each other. But we're mostly focused on Finley. He's usually sitting between us."

"Okay. Why not try an experiment next time? Just scoot a little closer, see what she does. Not to where you're touching. Just a couple of inches. See if she stays put, or scoots away about the same amount."

"If she stays put, that could mean something?"

"That's the idea," Jed said. "Here's another one...when you guys are together, is her body facing you? Is she looking right at you? Or is she facing sideways, sometimes looking away while she talks?"

"I don't know, Jed. I've never paid attention."

"Well, think about it. You were just with her this morning.

You've been with her almost every day since this training thing started."

Chris thought about it. Pictured Amy in his mind. Thought about what they had talked about this morning. "I guess she was facing me. Her body was kind of turned in my direction. She was definitely looking at me while she talked. But mine was, too."

"See?"

"See what?"

"That shows interest. If a girl's not interested, her body will usually face away from you. And she'll look away when she's talking, like she's got better things to do. But here both of you are facing each other, and looking right at each other while you're talking. It's a sign. She's probably is interested in you, at least on some level. And I know you're interested in her."

Chris remembered a conversation he'd had that morning with his elderly neighbor by the mailbox. She was facing him as they talked. Looked right at him, too. Was he supposed to think she was interested? He looked around, to make sure no one was close enough to hear what they were saying. "This conversation is getting kind of weird, Jed."

"No, it's not. I'm just trying to help you. Just like I'm helping you carry this crate here. Same difference."

Chris looked at his watch. "Maybe we better wrap this up anyway. I've only got a few minutes till I have to clock in."

"Alright. I hear you. Just one more thing and I'll shut up. You ever catch her looking at you?"

"No. I mean we have to look at each other, we're the only two people in the conversation."

"This is something else," Jed said. "Try to pay attention next time. Like, if you're doing something with Finley, look up at her, quick-like. See if she's looking at the dog, or at you. Do it several times. If every time you do it, she's looking at you, it's almost a slamdunk she's interested."

This was just crazy. Like a conversation two girls would be having. "Okay."

"Okay, you'll do it? Or okay, now shut up?"

Chris smiled. "The second one."

44

It was Saturday, a regular workday for Kim Harper. Saturday was the day she scheduled her group dog training classes. She had two today, both before lunch. Then one private training class this afternoon. The dogs and owners for the first class should start showing up in about twenty minutes. She was back at her desk getting some things together when the phone rang. She was going to let it go to voicemail when she noticed it was Captain Bridget out at the prison calling. She rarely called Kim on Saturdays.

"Good morning, Bridget. How are you doing this fine Saturday morning?"

"I'm doing very well," Bridget said. "You probably already have this on your calendar, but I thought I should call just to make sure. You remember that next Friday morning is our graduation ceremony for the Prison Paws and Pals Program."

Kim looked up at her wall calendar. She wasn't thinking of it at this moment, but there it was. "I definitely have it down."

"Does that mean you're planning to be here?" Bridget said.

"I wouldn't miss it. I love the graduation ceremonies."

"Good. So glad to hear it. But there's a special reason I'm calling. Two reasons, really. The first is to let you know—now this is top secret; I haven't even told her yet—but we've selected Amy and Finley as the winners of the Top Five Contest. That means Finley will be named the Top Dog."

"Really? That's so wonderful. Especially when I remember the condition Finley was in the day I picked him to be part of the program."

"I remember you telling me about it," Bridget said. "Although, I never saw him like that. He seemed pretty lively from the moment you brought him out here. And, of course, he and Amy bonded right away. They got so tight, I thought she'd never get him matched to a vet."

"I was glad to play small role in that. Remember he called me first? His name's Chris, right?"

"Yes, and he's been a wonderful addition to the program. You can tell, he's mad about Finley. I think he's been out here every single day since he started training with us."

"Doesn't he have a job?" Kim asked.

"He does. But somehow he was able to get his schedule changed."

"That shows some serious devotion. How does Amy seem to be handling the idea of letting Finley go? I know that was something of a challenge."

"I think she's doing okay. It certainly helps knowing he's going to someone like Chris. And I also think it helps knowing she'll be getting out of here just two months after that."

"Really? I hadn't heard that. I don't know her all that well, but she seems like someone who likely won't be getting into any more trouble when she gets out."

"I definitely don't expect to see her back here," Bridget said. "By the way, she might be calling you sometime soon, or maybe she'll just talk to you at the graduation."

"About what?"

"Let's just say after her time with Finley, Amy is definitely a dog person. To help her get over the idea of letting him go, I suggested after she gets out she should talk to you, let you help her pick out a dog that would be a perfect fit for her."

"I'd be happy to do that," Kim said. "But I think there's something more I can do for Amy than that."

"Like what?" Bridget said.

"You know from time to time, when we can, we like to hire inmates when they come out of prison. Especially ones like Amy. We just got approval to add one more employee to my department. The money won't be there to hire them for about a month. But I'd be willing to wait another month to get someone as skillful with dogs as Amy."

"Really? That would be wonderful. I don't know Amy's plans yet, whether she's staying in the area. But I'll definitely mention this to her. If she is planning to stay, she'll be thrilled."

"Let me know if you find out that Amy doesn't want this position," Kim said, "so I can hire someone else."

"I definitely will."

Kim remembered something else Bridget had said at the start of this call. "Didn't you say you had two things to talk to me about?"

"You're right. This is kind of short notice, so don't feel any pressure. But I was wondering if you wouldn't mind getting up to say a few words at the graduation? About Finley, I mean. You know, since he and Amy are the winners of the Top Five Contest, they're the ones I'll be calling on to do an obedience demonstration during the ceremony. I was thinking about what you told me about Finley's original owner. Didn't you say he was a young soldier killed in Afghanistan? I thought it might be kind of a touching story for people to hear how well Finley's life has turned out, going from that tragedy, to becoming a shelter dog and now to becoming a service dog to another Afghan war veteran."

"You're right," Kim said. "That would be a wonderful story. Have you talked to any of the news people?"

"You know, I always invite them to these things. Sometimes they come, sometimes they don't."

"Well, they should definitely come to this one. But to answer your question, I'd be happy to give the background of Finley's story. Just let me know when I need to get up to speak."

"I will," Bridget said. "And thanks so much."

After they hung up, Kim sat back in her chair and remembered the first time she met Finley, the day he was brought in by that soldier's mother. She had forgotten her name. Kim remembered how sad the woman was and how confused and sad Finley was when she walked down the hall and out the door. Then the terrible depression Finley went through in the days that followed.

Thinking of these things, she couldn't help but smile. For all the ups and downs and challenges this job presented, stories like these somehow made it all worthwhile.

She sat up and finished gathering her things together for the training class. Just then, an idea popped into her head. She thought about it some more. It was a great idea. She wasn't sure it could work. If it did, it would make the graduation ceremony even more special.

She quickly created a To Do item on her task list so she wouldn't forget. Then she had another thought. Was there any way to pull this thing off and make it a surprise?

45

Off and on over the weekend, Chris involuntarily found himself mentally reviewing the various signals Jed had shared with him on Friday, the ways a guy can tell if a woman was interested in him. He'd think of one—like if a woman's body is facing you while she speaks—then start trying to recall different conversations he'd had with Amy recently.

He didn't want to put too much stock in it because it came, after all, from Jed. But that didn't necessarily mean it was bad info; Jed said he got it from Google. The thing was, with each signal he could remember he could also remember Amy doing that very thing when they were together.

Was it possible? Was she interested in him, as more than just a guy who'd soon become Finley's new owner? And if she was, how did he feel about that? He wasn't sure. He certainly liked her, and really enjoyed being around her. And Jed had a point about the fact that she already knew all about Chris's missing leg and his PTSD issues. It didn't seem to bother her even a little bit. The problem was, Chris had completely written off the idea about ever being romantically involved with anyone until he got straightened out somehow.

But that was kind of what was going on now, wasn't it? Ever since he'd begun to pursue getting Finley, his life really had begun a new direction. He still had panic attacks sometimes when he was on his own, and occasionally still had nightmares. But there it was...*sometimes*...*occasionally*. They weren't happening as often as before. They didn't last as long. And they didn't seem as intense. Or maybe they didn't seem as intense because he had something new going on in his life. Something positive. Something that gave him hope.

That something was Finley, pure and simple.

Chris couldn't wait to bring him home for good. Not seeing him all weekend felt almost unbearable. But he had to admit, this past weekend he had been thinking about Amy almost as much. And thinking about her also made him feel good.

Maybe he was ready then. Maybe Jed was right.

He was thinking about all this as he drove the now familiar route off the main road and around the prison property. Out the window to his right were the various prison buildings all enclosed behind that ominous triple-barbed-wire fence. Up ahead, he saw the separate section of the prison where the Prison Paws and Pals Program was housed. Where Amy and Finley lived. Amy said they called them dorm rooms, and these buildings really did resemble an educational facility more than a prison.

It was Monday. Friday was graduation day. As happy as he was that he'd finally get to bring Finley home for good, it also made him happy to know Amy would be released from this place two months from now. He wondered what her plans were once that happened. They had never really talked about it before. All he knew was she said she'd need to start over. And that she didn't expect to have anyone from her family there to meet her.

Maybe he'd work up the nerve to ask her about it today.

The training session that morning had gone smoothly. Amy tried to keep her mind on the things at hand, not on the fact that this was the last week she would be with Finley...and with Chris. It was less than a week; really, after today they were only four days left.

They were headed outside now, which was how they usually spent their remaining time together before Chris had to go back to work.

"You want me to take him?" Chris asked. "Let him have a chance to go the bathroom?"

"Sure. I'll go stake a claim on our picnic table." As she handed the leash to Chris, their hands overlapped a few moments. Was that...did he just...? No, it couldn't be. She was certainly reading more into it than it was. But it felt like Chris's hand had lingered in hers a little longer than usual, longer than necessary.

She watched him lead Finley around the border of the fence. Finley was so happy whenever Chris was around. And why shouldn't he be? That had been the goal for all her efforts. As much as she hated the thought of losing Finley, she was glad he would be in such good hands. It was abundantly clear, Chris loved Finley as much as she did.

After he walked a few yards, Chris looked back at her. Was that unusual? Did he always do that? He probably did. She was just becoming desperate, hoping to see something she wanted to see. She had known for a couple of weeks now, her feelings for Chris were taking on a life of their own. At first, she figured it was simply the fact that Chris and Finley were connected now. Her interest in him, as well as any desire to stay connected with them after this was over, was linked to her desire to stay connected with Finley.

But that wasn't true anymore. And she knew it. She didn't want to lose either one of them.

After Finley had finished, Chris walked him back to the table. Today, she was sitting on top of the table. Chris sat up there with her. Finley sat on the ground between them. She pulled a treat out of her pocket and handed it to him. The look on his face seem to say thank you. He continued looking at her for a moment then at Chris, then back at her. Now he wore that contented look that resembled a smile.

"I missed you guys over the weekend," Chris said. "I used my spare time to get Tom's office ready for Finley's arrival. That helped some. It's all ready for him now."

Did he just say, *you guys*? "Tom's office? Isn't that your boss?"

"He is. But he's been totally supportive. Turns out, he's a dog lover. I set up a crate for Finley in Tom's office, but Tom's even hinted he'll probably let him out whenever he's there." After he said this, he scooted a little closer to her.

She wasn't sure why, but she certainly wasn't going to move further away. "That's amazing how much support you're getting at work."

"I know," Chris said. "It's not just from Tom. Even the owner of the golf course. He's a retired colonel. Most of the guys I work with are vets, and several of them have PTSD issues." Chris reached down and patted Finley's head. "This guy here will probably steal their hearts inside of a week."

"It's really great how this has worked out," she said. "I couldn't have wished for a better situation for Finley. And if I have to let him go, I'm glad it's to you." Suddenly and without warning, tears welled up in her eyes. She tried blinking them back, but she could tell it wasn't going to work. A few tears slipped down her left cheek. Finley instantly moved close to her, as close as he could without jumping into her lap. She was about to apologize and wipe her face with her sleeve.

But Chris beat her to it. He put his hand on that side of her face and gently wiped the tears away with his thumb. "That's okay, Amy. I know how much you love him. You've had him so much longer than me, but I totally get what you're feeling right now."

"I'm sorry. I appreciate how kind you're being about this, but I don't want to make you feel bad. This is a good thing, and Friday's gonna be a great day. I wish I could say these are happy tears. Maybe half of them are."

"I understand. But let's change the subject for a minute, if you don't mind."

"Yeah, let's."

"You're getting out of here in two months, right?"

"From Friday," she said.

"Maybe you told me this before, but I was wondering if you've made any plans yet? You know, what you're going to do after you get out?"

"Not really. Some people have family or loved ones waiting for them when they get out, and they're the ones who help the inmates transition. But from what Miss Bridget told me, half of them are like me. Kind of burned their family bridges, so to speak. She said there's a bunch of different programs I can look into for help, some of them run by churches. And some halfway houses I can stay at. Apparently, there's some government programs that might help me for a little while, too. I haven't really looked into everything yet. Guess I better start getting on that pretty soon."

"So, it sounds like you're not planning on leaving the area then?"

"No. At least not for a while."

Chris didn't say anything back for a moment. But he was smiling, and he had this look in his eye. Then he said, "I'm glad."

46

After Chris had said goodbye, Amy headed back inside with Finley. She saw Miss Bridget just inside the door. She was looking right at Amy, like she had something to say. Amy might have worried except the expression on her face seemed pleasant. Amy stepped closer to her. "Did you want to see me?"

Miss Bridget looked around as if making sure no one else was nearby. "Not here. Why don't you put Finley back in his crate then come by my office.

"Alright," Amy said. "He's probably ready for a nap anyway."

Miss Bridget turned and walked down the hall. Amy headed toward her dorm room. What in the world was going on? It didn't seem like she was in any trouble. Once inside her room, Amy opened Finley's crate door, and he happily walked inside, circled once and laid down. Amy handed him a treat through the bars. "You get a head start on your nap, and I'll be back in a few minutes."

His tail thumped on the floor in reply.

Amy slipped out into the hallway and turned toward Miss Bridget's office. When she got there, the door was closed. She knocked.

"Come in."

Amy peeked her head inside. "It's me."

"I hoped it was. Come on in, close the door and have a seat."

Whatever it was, Miss Bridget had a big smile on her face now. Amy did as she was told.

"How are things going with Chris? He seems like he's really catching on."

"They're going great. I don't see how they could be going any better." Well, Amy could think of one way.

"And how are you doing about the idea of releasing Finley to Chris? Now that we're getting so close?"

Amy inhaled deeply. "I know. It's SO close. I guess I'm doing okay. To be honest, I'm trying not to think about it."

"Well, you've got to be happy about where Finley's going."

"I am. Chris is a perfect fit. Finley loves him, and he adores Finley. And it's already clear, Finley's making a huge difference in Chris's life. He talks about it every day."

"I can tell. It shows on his face."

Could we please change the subject? Amy thought.

"Well," Miss Bridget said, "Let's get to why I asked you here."

Yes, let's.

She held up a sheet of paper. "You know what this is?"

Amy shook her head no.

"These are the final scores for the Top Five Contest. All the girls did a great job, especially the trainers who made it into the Top Five. But after all the results were added up, guess which dog and which trainer came out on top?"

What was she talking about?

"It's you, Amy! You and Finley! You guys won!"

"What?"

"You won the Top Five contest. You and Finley. And that

means you two will be the ones giving the big demonstration at the graduation ceremony Friday."

She said this second part like it was a big deal. But Amy had never even been to a graduation ceremony before. This was the first time she'd ever even trained a dog. "I don't know what to say."

"You don't have to say anything. But let me say, we have all been so impressed with how well you've done in this class. It's hard to believe you've never trained dogs before."

"I've never even owned a dog before."

"That just proves our point. You're a natural."

"Isn't that going to cause some...*tension* with the other girls in the program? I mean, if we win? Especially since I'm so new."

"I don't think so. The way you've handled yourself since joining the program has definitely helped with that issue. You're the opposite of a know-it-all. And the girls look up to Rita. She's clearly taken you under her wing. Having her as a friend has helped. Besides that, word will get around that you're being released in two months, so it's not like you're going to be an ongoing threat to the more competitive ones."

Hearing this helped.

"But there's more good news," Miss Bridget said. "At least I think it will be good news. It depends on whether or not you plan to stay in this area after your release."

"I'd like to stay, if it's possible. But that kind of depends on whether or not I can find a job. Summerville's kind of a small town. I'm sure what few jobs are available will probably first go to the—"

"Then I do have good news for you," Miss Bridget interjected.

"What is it? Some kind of job?"

Miss Bridget nodded. "I was talking with Kim Harper on the phone, asking her if she could speak at our graduation ceremony, which she can. I also mentioned to her about you and Finley winning the Top Five Contest, which she was thrilled to hear. Then she told me the board at the Humane Society had just given her permission to add one more employee to her team."

Amy couldn't believe what she was hearing.

"She told me, she wants to hire you. And she's even willing to hold the position until you get out of here."

Amy couldn't help it. Tears began rolling down her face. This was even better news than winning the Top Five Contest. "I would totally love working with Kim. It would be like a dream job to me."

"I thought you'd like it." Miss Bridget handed her a box of tissues from the credenza behind her desk.

Amy dabbed her tears away with a tissue. "Do you know what I'd be doing? Not that it matters. I'd do anything they ask if I could work in a place like that."

"I don't. But you can ask Kim yourself in a few days, at the graduation ceremony."

"That's right. That's what I'll do. Oh thank you, Miss Bridget. This is such exciting news. Both things are." She stood up. "About the demonstration you want us to do during the ceremony…I've never actually done one before. What do we do?"

"It's very simple. It's the same routine you do at the beginning of every training day. I will even call out the commands like I do every day. But instead of everyone responding, it'll just be you and Finley."

"That sounds easy enough."

"I'm sure you'll do great."

"Would you mind if I involved Chris?"

"Well, we've never really done that before."

"I just thought it might highlight the program even more if I do the first half of the demonstration, then invite Chris up to do the second half. It would show how effectively the training transitions from the trainer to the new owner."

Miss Bridget smiled. "Amy, that's a great idea. Do you think Chris would do it?"

"I think he would. I'll ask him and let you know."

"Great. I hope he says yes."

Amy stood there a moment. "Guess I'll head back to my dorm."

As she closed the door behind her, she instantly thought of another reason why this news was so exciting, besides just the chance of getting to work with Kim and caring for animals. She would get to stay in the area, which meant maybe she'd get to see Chris and Finley every now and then.

That thought made her the happiest of all.

47

Later that evening, after Chris had arrived home from work and taken a shower, he sat down at the dinette table in his apartment, a hot tray of *Michelangelo's* chicken parmesan in front of him. Since the day he'd bring Finley home was rapidly approaching, he'd stopped at one of the big franchise pet stores and picked up a few things. Right now, he was looking down at the matching stainless steel food and water bowls sitting in a slightly elevated ornamental iron stand.

The clerk said these were the right size for a golden retriever. He'd also purchased two matching dog beds, one for the living room and one for his bedroom. Although he was starting to think he'd better hold on to the receipt. Chances were better than average Finley would soon be up on the couch with him, and he'd probably let him up on the bed if he wanted, at least down by his feet.

Only four more days.

Although lately, such hopeful thoughts were instantly paired with pangs of regret at the pain this would cause Amy. But maybe her pain would be short-lived. He started rehearsing in his mind some of the signals Jed had mentioned. Hoping he wasn't obvious, he'd tried to see how many were in play in his time with Amy today.

He picked up a big forkful of food, smiling as he thought on it. She seemed to pass the test on every one. Of course, all this could be bogus. But then again, what if it wasn't? He wasn't about to make a fool of himself and rush into anything, but the signs were certainly encouraging. And she said she was interested in staying here if she could find a job. If that worked out, there'd be plenty of time to get to know each other better.

Since her release was still two months away, it was too soon to do anything yet. Maybe he could at least ask what kind of job she was hoping to get. He could start checking around town when it got a little closer to the date.

The following day after the group part of the training class was over, they walked outside and Amy handed Finley's leash to Chris. Normally, Chris would then lead Finley around the perimeter fence to go to the bathroom while Amy headed toward their picnic table. Today, she continued to follow Chris toward the fence. He wasn't sure why, but the look on her face said she had something to say. He could also tell during the class, she was in an unusually happy mood.

"Is something going on?" he asked.

She looked behind her then back at him, her smile even wider. "You could say that."

"So, what is it? What's up?"

"We need to get a little further away from everyone."

Now he was really curious. Finley suddenly stopped their forward motion, deciding this was the place and the moment he had to go. After bagging things up, they continued on to the far corner.

They stopped walking. Finley continued to sniff around. "Okay," Chris said, "what's going on?"

Amy took one more quick look back. "I guess this is far enough." She turned her back toward everyone else in the yard.

Chris looked over her shoulder. As far as he could tell, no one was paying any attention to them.

"I heard some exciting news yesterday. Well really, two things."

"And I guess whatever it is, it's a secret?"

"Part of it is. At least until Friday."

"Graduation day?"

She nodded. "Did I ever tell you about the Top Five Contest?"

"I don't think so."

"Apparently, during the last month of the class they start keeping score on all the dogs and trainers. Then they pick the top five—I guess the top five highest scores—as the finalists for this contest."

"And you made the top five?"

Amy suddenly looked nervous and glanced over her shoulder.

"Did I say it too loud?"

"Doesn't look like it. I don't know why Miss Bridget told me in advance. Rita said they don't announce the finalists till graduation day. After that, they pick one of the five dogs as the Top Dog. Yesterday afternoon, Miss Bridget said we not only made the Top Five, but Finley's going to be named the Top Dog. He's won the whole thing."

"Really? Amy, that's great!" Without even thinking, Chris hugged her. Not in a romantic way. It just seemed the right thing to do. She definitely hugged back. He enjoyed feeling her so close and felt if he didn't let go right away, things could get awkward. When they parted, their eyes stayed locked on each other. That didn't feel awkward at all.

It felt very nice.

Then she said, "This news actually involves you. That is, if you're okay with it."

"Me? How?"

"After they announce Finley as the Top Dog—"

"Which means you are the top trainer."

"—Yes," she said, smiling. "...they'll ask me and Finley to do an obedience demonstration. I thought I'd do the first half, then invite you up as his new owner and let you do the second half."

"What would I have to do?"

"The same thing you've been doing every day. She wants us to do the very same routine."

Chris hesitated a moment. He wasn't sure how he'd handle being in the spotlight."

"So, will you do it?"

Look at her face. How could he turn her down? "Sure. How badly can I blow it?"

"You're going to do fine. And Finley will be as perfect as ever."

Chris bent down so that his face was at Finley's level. "Did you hear that, boy?" he said in a loud whisper. "You're not just in the top five around here. You are the Top Dog." Finley licked his chin.

"Chris," she scolded gently, then put her index finger to her mouth.

"Nobody heard me." He stood back up.

"I've got another piece of good news," she said. "This part's not so secret. We can start walking back to our picnic table." As they did, she continued. "This news is almost more exciting than the first news. For me, anyway."

"Are they going to let you out even sooner than two months?"

"Would that be good news to you?"

"That would be great news." He wondered if she knew what he meant by that, or how she would take it. "I was thinking about what you said before, about wanting to stay here if you could find a job. I thought maybe if you told me the kind of jobs you'd like to get, or what work experience you've already had, maybe I could start seeing what's available around here."

"That's sweet of you, but totally unnecessary."

"Why?"

"That's my news." They reached their picnic table. "I've got a job waiting for me when I get out. A job I will absolutely love."

"Really? Doing what?"

"Working at the Humane Society with Kim Harper. I don't know if you've met her, but she's the Animal Behavior Manager there. She's also the one who introduced me to Finley. She told Miss Bridget they just created an opening in her department, and she's willing to hold the job for me."

"Amy, that is so great. I'm so happy for you." And for me, he thought. He almost said it.

"Isn't it? I could hardly believe it when she told me. And you know what the best part of it is?"

Chris nodded. "I do. Now you can stay. Right here in Summerville, near me and Finley."

48

It was finally here, Graduation Day.

As she made her way through the morning, Amy was experiencing a number of differing emotions. She was nervous about doing the demonstration with Finley and Chris. It wasn't the demonstration itself; something by now she could do in her sleep. It was doing it in front of a whole crowd of strangers. And she was a little worried about how all the girls would react to the news that she had not only made the Top Five, but Finley had been named Top Dog. She had to live with these girls for two more months after today.

Thankfully, the news she'd received about a job waiting for her with Kim Harper at the Humane Society had erased some of the dread she'd expected to feel today. Finley was still going home with Chris today, but now she at least would get a chance to see him from time to time. She had no idea how often. That depended on how often Chris would want to see her once she got out.

Back on Tuesday, she'd been feeling pretty good about this. But that was the last time she had seen Chris. He'd called Miss Bridget Wednesday morning and asked her to deliver the message to Amy. They were doing some special project at the golf course and needed everyone to work overtime for a few days. But his boss promised he would still have this morning off.

In the time gap between then and now, she had begun to wonder if she'd simply been imagining that Chris cared for her on some level beyond friendship. After he'd left on Tuesday, she was almost certain there was something there. The way he'd talked to her, some of the things he'd said. She could still remember his gentle touch on her face when he'd wiped the tear from her cheek. And feel the warmth of his hug when he'd congratulated her about the contest. Then there was that moment when they pulled away, the way he had looked at her and how long he had looked at her.

On Tuesday after he'd gone, she replayed these things in her mind over and over. They seemed to really matter then. Now, she wasn't so sure. Two days of not seeing him, not hearing anything but that brief phone message...maybe there really wasn't anything there. Maybe it was all in her head. She'd taken a handful of innocent, unrelated things and stitched them together into some kind of romantic dream.

She looked down at Finley. He was lying on the rug near her feet. She reached out her hand. He lifted his head to meet it, and she stroked the silky hair on his forehead. "You really don't know what's about to happen, Finley. Do you boy? Your whole life's about to change again." He licked her hand. "And so is mine." But at least this change wouldn't be a traumatic one for him. She was sure of that. Finley was as comfortable with Chris now as he was with her.

And he had brought so much hope into Chris's life. That's what Amy needed to focus on. Not on her loss.

There was a knock on her door. Rita peeked her head in. "Hey Amy, can you give us a hand. I'm supposed to round up a dozen of us to set up a bunch of extra chairs outside for the ceremony. Miss

Bridget just said we're supposed to have a bunch more guests coming than usual. And supposed to be some local news stations coming out to do a story about it."

Amy sighed. That's just what she needed...more strangers at her demo. She hoped Chris would be okay with this.

Chris had been sitting in his car in the prison parking lot with the A/C turned on for the last fifteen minutes. The graduation ceremony was due to start in ten minutes. He was working up the nerve to get out of the car and get in line for the security check.

That was part of his problem. There was a line to get in. That had never happened before.

There were so many more people coming for the graduation than he'd expected. Even worse, a television news crew had shown up. He had no idea this was such a big affair. He wished Amy had prepared him better, but then he remembered she had never been to one herself before.

He was also a little jumpy, because he hadn't been with Finley or Amy since Tuesday. He didn't struggle that much at work, because they had worked so hard and put in four extra hours a day. For the most part, he just came home and collapsed on the sofa. He started off this morning in great spirits, so excited to be bringing Finley home today.

And excited to see Amy again.

He was pretty sure now the interest was mutual, especially after a conversation with Jed yesterday afternoon. He hadn't planned on involving Jed any further in his personal life, but they had worked four hours together on a project yesterday, so there was no escaping it. Jed kept pressing him about how his last visit with Amy had gone, and whether Chris had paid attention to all the signs Jed taught him. Chris finally told him how the conversation went. Even before Chris had finished, Jed's face lit up and he held out his fist for a bump, saying, "Man, you are there, my friend. That's proof positive."

Sitting in the car now, Chris wasn't so sure. He wanted it to be true, hoped it was true. But an endorsement from a guy like Jed—however enthusiastic—still didn't count for much.

Chris glanced at his watch. He'd better just get out and do it. He reminded himself that once he made it through the line, he'd be with Amy and Finley again. It would be a good test, he decided. A chance to see how Finley could help him with his PTSD challenges in the real world.

He took a deep breath and opened the car door.

49

Finley sat in his crate, his eyes fixed on the doorknob. He tried to lay down, but he wasn't tired. If anything, he was on edge. Amy left a few minutes ago. After she'd asked him to get in the crate and gave him a treat, she had uttered the words, "I'll be right back." Finley understood. Whenever she'd said it, she was never gone for long.

Something big seemed to be going on. There were so many extra noises, especially outside. He could detect a totally unfamiliar mood going on inside Amy. It seemed almost equal parts happy and sad. Sometimes she was one, sometimes the other. One thing was clear: this wasn't going to be a typical training day. He wondered if that meant he wouldn't see Chris again. He hoped not. He hadn't seen Chris for several days now.

Finley hoped this wasn't the start of some new trend. That's how things began to go with Chaz, his first owner. He started to go away for days at a time. Then Finley wouldn't see him for months. Then he went away for good.

Finley stopped thinking about this, because it made him sad. Things were much better now with Amy, and with Chris.

I'll be right back. That's what he needed to focus on, Amy. She was here, now, and she would return through that door any minute. He spun around once in his crate then found another, more comfortable spot to sit. The doorknob turned. The door opened. It was Amy.

See, she did come back. It wasn't that long.

"Finley!" She was smiling. "You ready to get out of there, boy? Today's the big day." She unhooked his leash from the wall then walked over and looked out the window. "So many people are here. You're not gonna believe it." He didn't understand most of what she said, but he heard, *get out of there.* That usually meant she was going to let him out of the crate. He looked at her eyes; they seemed to be searching through the window for something.

She gasped and her smile got bigger. "There he is." She hurried around Finley's crate and unlatched the door. "He's here, Finley. Chris is here. He didn't chicken out."

Finley couldn't help but catch her excitement. She must have seen Chris. She had to tell him to sit still, so she could connect the leash. "Are you ready? It's time to go." He wagged his tail in reply. As they stepped into the hallway, Finley saw that most of the other dogs and trainers were all heading the same way, toward the big room.

Once there, it became obvious…this was definitely not a training day. It looked totally different. So many wonderful smells coming from tables set against the wall in the far corner. All the dogs noticed, their noses jabbing the air. A few began to pull on their leashes toward the food and had to be corrected. Miss Bridget said something and everyone lined up in single file.

All the trainers put their dogs in a sit, but instead of facing the door they were all facing the center of the room. Miss Bridget walked to that spot and began to speak. Finley didn't understand. Were they going outside or not?

Chris wasn't in here. He was out there.

Amy was almost certain about what came next.

Miss Bridget had everyone's attention. "You old-timers know what we're about to do. For you newbies, we're going to go outside in a few moments and take our places for the ceremony. I've already shown you the separate section of seats off to the side that we set up for the dogs and trainers. We do this so everyone in the audience can see the dogs throughout the ceremony. And you, of course. You might have noticed the first row has only five chairs. Right now, before we go out, I'm about to announce the finalists for the Top Five Contest. After I announce the names, in just a moment, I want those five trainers and their dogs to move to the front of the line. Once we go outside, you five will sit in the first row. And at some point during the ceremony, I will announce from these five finalists which dog has been named Top Dog. That dog and that trainer will do a live demonstration for the audience."

Hearing these words sent a chill through Amy. Miss Bridget began to name the finalists, prefacing her statement with: "In no particular order…" All the girls clapped and cheered as each name was read. Some of the dogs couldn't help but jump and bark in all the excitement.

There were only two names left. Amy was so excited to hear Rita's name spoken, followed by Charlie's. More cheering and applause. Of course, Charlie was a perfect gentleman and walked right beside Rita toward the front of the line. As she passed by Amy, Amy said, "Congratulations, I'm so happy for you."

Miss Bridget allowed for a longer pause before reading off the last name. A sense of anticipation filled the room. Amy felt something else. She wasn't sure if she was thrilled or terrified.

"Amy Wallace and Finley," Miss Bridget proclaimed.

To Amy's shock and surprise, the cheers and applause for her seemed twice as loud as for the others. She looked at Rita, who was cheering the loudest. Amy couldn't help it. Her eyes began to tear up. She quickly blinked them back as she led Finley to the fifth place in line.

"There you have it, ladies. Our Top Five finalists for class Number Twenty-Three." Another round of applause. "With that settled, I believe we're ready to go. Let's go out and take our places. After you've all gotten your seats, I'm going to allow a few minutes for all the new veteran-owners to connect with you and their dogs. Then I'll call everyone together, and we'll get started."

50

For two reasons, Kim Harper was a little nervous as she and her special guest made their way into the seating area for the graduation ceremony. First, she was always nervous when she spoke in front of a crowd. And second, she was supposed to be here fifteen minutes ago to coordinate things with Bridget; her guest had been running late.

But she was here now. They found two seats toward the back near the main aisle. "I'll be right back," Kim said. "I'll leave my purse here next to you. I need to see that lady officer up front there by the podium for a minute, let her know I'm here." Kim hurried down the main aisle toward Bridget.

As she cleared the front row, Bridget saw her and waved. She was talking with someone but finished the conversation right as Kim arrived. They hugged and Kim said, "So sorry I'm late."

"You're not late. We haven't started yet. We're just about to, though."

"That's what I mean. You asked me to come fifteen minutes early."

"Don't worry about it. I'm just glad you made it. Are you all set?"

"Ready as I'll ever be. When do you want me to come up?"

"I'll start to introduce you when the time comes. You'll have enough time to make your way up here." Bridget looked over her shoulder. "I saw that woman you came in with. Is that her?"

"It is," Kim said. "She's part of the reason I was late. I'm so glad she came. I think it'll make a special moment even more so."

"Me, too. Do you think she'll come up with you?"

"She said she would. As long as she doesn't have to give a speech."

"That's great. I can't wait." Bridget looked around at all the crowd. "Looks like everything's in place. I better get things started."

Kim was just about to head back to her seat when she noticed Amy and Finley sitting on the front row. Finley had already seen her. His tail began wagging and his front feet pranced in place. "There you are, Finley." She bent down as she reached him.

"Greet, Finley," Amy said firmly.

Finley rushed up to Kim but did as he was told and sat like a perfect gentleman. His whole body was shaking with happiness. Kim reached down and put her arms around him, gave him a big squeeze. "Look at you. So behaved." She stood but continued to pat his head.

Amy stood as well. "I was hoping to get to talk to you before you leave."

"We definitely will," Kim said. "I'm guessing it's about the job?"

Amy nodded. "Is it still…for real?"

"Definitely. I'll tell you all about it after the ceremony. But I better get back to my seat. It's about to begin."

"I can't wait to hear about it," Amy said. "I'm so excited."

Kim leaned close and whispered, "And I can't wait to see you and Finley do the obedience demonstration. Congratulations."

Amy smiled. "Chris is going to help us, to show how well the dogs respond to their new owners."

"That's a great idea. Well, I better get back to my seat."

As Kim neared the back row, she was glad to see a television cameraman next to a young woman holding a microphone. They were standing a little further back. She decided to go up and introduce yourself. "Hi, my name's Kim Harper, the Animal Behavior Manager at the Humane Society. I see you guys are with Channel 7. I'm the one who called you about the special story we're going to share during the ceremony."

The young woman, a pretty redhead, smiled and held out her hand. "I recognize you, Miss Harper, from your picture on Facebook. My name's Angela Morrow. Did everything work out like you planned?"

Kim nodded yes. "But please, call me Kim. I don't know how much of this you can show. But they're going to call me up to introduce Finley and his trainer at some point. He's the dog I told you about. I'm also going to share a little bit of Finley's back story. Make sure you don't miss that part. And I've just learned an added bonus just got added to the story. Chris Seger, the Afghan war veteran who's going to become Finley's new owner, will be coming up and to help Amy with the obedience demonstration."

"That'll be perfect," Angela said. "And that woman you came in with, she's part of the story, right?"

"Definitely. Don't forget to include her. I'll introduce you later."

"Can we interview you all afterwards? It'll only take a few minutes."

"You can interview me, but I'm not sure how the others will feel. It won't hurt to ask."

"Great, I'll do that," Angela said.

Bridget's voice came over the microphone. "Good morning everyone. Thanks so much for coming. If you're all get to your seats, we're about to begin."

Chris heard her, but what she said didn't sink in. He was starting to feel hemmed in by the crowd. It hadn't become a full-on panic attack. Not yet. He prayed a quick prayer. *Please God, not here. Not now.* Amy was counting on him. He had to get past this, hold it together.

He had been doing okay at first. Better than he expected. He'd picked a seat on an outside aisle, thinking it would help. And it had...for a while. An aisle seat would make it easier to get up and help with Finley's demonstration. But there were empty seats to the left of him. A big group had come in and stood right beside him. The first one in the bunch, a big guy, asked him politely to move in so they could sit in the same row.

Chris should have stepped out into the aisle, let them all slide in past. It wouldn't have taken but a second. But he didn't. Instead, he started moving into the center. They filled in behind him. Now he was completely surrounded by strangers.

He closed his eyes, tried to control his breathing. Mercifully, Finley's face appeared in his mind. That peaceful, smiling face. One image after the other came; Finley reaching out to him, reassuring him, loving him without measure, resting his head on Chris's lap. Chris opened his eyes and looked toward the row where Finley and Amy sat.

He could just see Finley's head leaning against Amy's leg. He looked up at her adoringly. Seeing him had a calming effect on Chris. He looked at Amy's face; she was looking toward the podium. They hadn't talked yet, just exchanged smiles and a wave.

She turned her gaze toward him now, to the aisle seat he had been sitting in before. She looked confused. Her eyes scanned the crowd for him. Chris lifted his right hand slightly to catch her attention. It worked. She smiled, made a face like she was relieved. They continued to look at each other a little longer. Her expression changed to concern. She mouthed the words, "Are you okay?"

Could she tell he was struggling? She must. It felt very nice, though, this new feeling. Having someone who cared about you. He smiled and mouthed back the words, "I'm fine."

It wasn't a lie. Not anymore.

51

Amy sat patiently listening to Miss Bridget speak. She spent the first several minutes welcoming everyone, singling out all the various officials and dignitaries in attendance. Polite applause followed. The superintendent of the prison then got up and spoke for a few minutes also. Mainly commending Miss Bridget and her staff for the wonderful job they were doing with the program. He also congratulated the inmate-trainers for successfully graduating another class of service dogs, talked about how pleased he was that their prison could make such a vital contribution to improving the lives of our returning war vets.

Several times as they spoke, Amy looked at Chris. He was paying attention for the most part, but twice she found him looking right at her. Maybe it just seemed like he was. Maybe he was really looking at Finley.

When the superintendent sat down, Miss Bridget came back to the podium. "Now it's time for our big moment. Time to pass out the graduation certificates to all our trainers and their dogs." She turned her attention to them. "The trainers and dogs will form a line to my left."

The inmates began to stand, so Amy did, too.

Rita gently stopped her and motioned for her to sit back down. "The Top Five stay put to the end," she said. "Miss Bridget will introduce us separately."

"As I call out your name," Miss Bridget continued, "you can come up with your dog and get your certificate. If you want to share a few words, feel free. But you don't have to. As I hand out the certificates, those of you in the audience, feel free to take pictures if you'd like. The only thing I ask is that you either do it from your seats or, if you do come up, please don't block the view of the other guests."

In a few moments, all the other inmate-trainers had formed a line. Their dogs stood by their side, almost at attention. Finley started to whine and squirm a little. "It's okay, boy." She patted his head. "You'll get your turn in just a minute."

Miss Bridget began to call the trainers and dogs, one by one. As she did, people applauded. Some dogs received louder applause than others. Amy guessed some had more guests attending the ceremony. She wondered if there'd be any applause for her and Finley.

Well, she could count on at least one, Chris.

As they came up, almost all the trainers said something to the crowd, even if only to introduce their dog, say a few things about how special they were, and thank everyone for coming. A few of the more outgoing ones talked for several minutes. Finally, everyone had received their certificates except the front row.

"Now we stand," Rita whispered to Amy.

"You may have noticed we have five trainers and dogs who haven't received their certificates yet," Miss Bridget said. "They haven't done anything wrong. Actually, it's just the opposite. We started doing this last year, something we call the Top Five contest. My team and I pay especially close attention to the trainers and dogs in the last month of the class, giving various scores on a number of different training assignments. The trainers and dogs receiving the top highest scores receive special honor at the graduation ceremony. Please hold your applause until I read out all five names, and hand them their graduation certificates. Then you can let them have it."

She read aloud the names of each trainer and their dog. Amy and Finley were the last to be announced. One by one they went up, were handed their graduation certificate, shook Bridget's hand, and stood off to the left. She then came back to the mic and said: "Ladies and gentlemen, I present to you Prison Paws and Pals Program's Top Five winners for Class Number Twenty-Three!" The applause was strong; this time it included all the other inmates. Several people in the audience stood. Amy guessed they were friends and family of the four ladies beside her. Then she noticed Chris standing with them. He smiled and pointed at her, then Finley. Then made the number one sign with his index finger and a gesture with his eyes that seemed to say, *Guess what comes next?*

The applause died down and everyone returned to their seats, including the Top Five winners. "We have one more special event in our program this morning," Miss Bridget announced. "Well, really two. I just introduced the Top Five trainers and dogs, but I haven't yet the named who earned the prestigious title of Top Dog. All five trainers did a wonderful job with their dogs this time around, but one dog has edged out the rest. In just a sec I'll name our Top Dog, then that dog and his trainer will put on a special obedience demonstration, so all of you can see many of the commands and behaviors all the dogs have learned over the past few months."

Miss Bridget paused. It seemed to Amy it was just to build

suspense. She could almost imagine hearing a drumroll. She looked to her right and noticed the other four ladies, Rita included, sitting up straight in their seats, eyes set on the podium.

"The Top Dog of Class number Twenty-Three is…FINLEY!" Finley's ears perked right up when he heard his name. "Finley's trainer, Miss Amy Wallace, is the youngest and newest trainer in our program."

Amy quickly stood. Before taking a step she heard, then saw, Chris stand in the middle of the audience and shout out, "Yay Finley! Woo-hoo, Amy!" Everyone else in the audience joined in with their applause. She couldn't believe it. By the time she reached the podium, a new round of applause came from behind her. She turned to see all the other inmates, including the other Top Five finalists on their feet, clapping and cheering.

After a few moments, things quieted down. Miss Bridget handed Amy a second certificate that showed Finley as the Top Dog for Class #23, and named her as his trainer. She asked Amy to remain standing there a few more moments.

Looking back to the crowd, she said, "We have a special surprise for you all. I've asked someone who knows a little bit about Finley's story to come up and share it with us. Kim Harper is the Animal Behavior Manager for the Humane Society. She's also the one who helps pick out all of our shelter dogs for this program. And she's the one who hand-picked Finley and introduced her to Amy, which was obviously a perfect match. Kim? Would you join me and tell us all a little about Finley's story?"

Amy watched Kim Harper stand to light applause and make her way down the center aisle.

52

Kim had spoken publicly many times during the course of her job. She had even spoken at a number of these graduation ceremonies before. But this one was unusually crowded, and it was being covered by the local TV news. The only times she had appeared on the news before was answering questions in a scheduled interview, and it was usually just her, the reporter and a cameraman.

As she stepped up to the podium, she took a deep breath and tried to remember just to be herself. She wasn't here to impress anyone. Just the opposite; she was here to honor some precious people and one well-deserved dog.

"Thank you Bridget—I mean, Captain Cummings." She looked back to the crowd. "We're good friends."

"You can call me Bridget," she called out from her seat.

Kim smiled at her then at the crowd. "I love it whenever I get a chance to talk about this wonderful program. To all you veterans here—those of you who'll be taking home these precious dogs today—your lives are about to improve dramatically. Although, I probably don't have to tell you that. I'm sure you've already begun to experience the benefits these dogs have to offer. I've lost count of the emails I've gotten from vets struggling with PTSD—some who said they were on the verge of calling it quits—who now tell me their lives have totally turned around. And it's because of these dogs. When I get a chance to talk to them in person, they can hardly get a few sentences out before they start to choke up. They love their dogs so much and, Chris?" Kim looked through the crowd until she made eye contact with him. "I know you're going to absolutely love Finley."

She looked over at Finley and Amy, then back to her audience. "So let me tell you a little about Finley's story. Amy, I don't think you've heard some of these details, either. Finley came to our shelter one day, brought to us by his original owner's mother. She was entrusting him to our care for two reasons. First, at the time he was absolutely out of control. Hard to imagine it looking at him now. He was just a big lovable dog who didn't know a single command and jumped up on everyone he met. He was too much dog for her to handle. But the main reason she brought him to our shelter was, his original owner, her son, Corporal Charles— Chaz—Perez had been recently killed in Afghanistan."

A collective gasp arose from the audience.

Something in Kim's peripheral vision caught her attention. She looked over at Finley. His ears were at full attention, and he shifted his position from laying down to sitting up. "Those of you sitting in the front might have noticed Finley's reaction to hearing his first owner's name. He heard me speak of Chaz."

Now Finley stood and looked around. Kim noticed many of the people in the audience were standing, trying to see him. Amy instantly began to comfort him and try to get him back into a sit. "I'm not going to say his first owner's name anymore," Kim said, "because I don't want to frustrate Finley. But you can clearly see Finley remembers him. He hasn't seen his first owner for a very long time, but dogs don't forget their owners, especially those who loved them dearly. And Finley was dearly loved."

Kim started to feel her emotions rise. She paused and took a breath. "Another way I knew how much Finley loved his owner, and how much his owner loved him was the deep depression Finley sank into after he was brought into our shelter. He wouldn't eat for days. He was no longer the lovable dog who jumped up on everyone. He would just lay there in the back of his pen, barely move all day. Some of our staff wondered if he was sick. But he wasn't sick. He was just confused and missed his owner terribly. I knew he would be a perfect candidate for this program, and that as soon as he began to receive the love, affection and attention of his trainer, Finley would snap out of his depression and start the transformation into the dog he was capable of becoming. You'll see exactly what I mean in a few moments, when Amy and Finley do their demonstration."

Kim looked over at Chris, then at Alicia Perez, Chaz's mom. Alicia was dabbing her eyes with a tissue. But she was looking right at Kim. Kim gave her a nod, to let her know she was about to introduce her. "Before Amy and Finley come up to do their demonstration, we have a very special guest here in the audience. I've asked Alicia Perez, the mother of Finley's original owner—the young man who gave his life in Afghanistan—if she would like to come to the ceremony and observe the transformation that's taken place in Finley's life. And she said yes, she would. Alicia, would you come up and join me now? I think you're really going to enjoy seeing this."

Alicia stood, carrying her tissues and began making her way down the aisle. As she did everyone began to applaud. Some began to stand. Then everyone stood. Then their applause got stronger and more sustained. It became clear to Kim and, she thought, to everyone else that this applause was no longer just for this woman, but for her son Chaz as well, who'd given his final breath in service to his country.

By the time she reached Kim, tears were flowing down Alicia's face. She did her best to wipe them away, but they kept coming. And so did the applause…for a full minute or two, once she turned to face them. Several people throughout the audience were crying, and not just women. Some of the men, even some veterans were. Kim reached for a box of tissues Bridget had wisely placed on a little shelf inside the podium. She handed some fresh ones to Alicia and used a couple for herself.

After a few moments, things began to settle down and people returned to their seats. Kim regained her composure and returned to the mike. "As you can see, Alicia, everyone is grateful you came here today, and grateful for your son's sacrifice for his country." She looked over at Bridget. "I guess now is a good time for Amy and Finley to do their demonstration?"

Bridget nodded, indicating Kim could go ahead and set it up.

"Amy and Finley, are you ready?"

Amy stood and gave Finley a hand signal. He instantly stood by her side. "We are."

Kim had seen these demonstrations a number of times before, so she explained to everyone what to expect. As she did, Amy brought Finley to an open grassy area close by.

Once there, Amy said loudly, "I'm going to take Finley through a series of commands that he knows very well. For your sakes, I will give him verbal commands, but we've also taught him hand signals for each of these commands, and he responds to them equally well. And we have another special treat today, one which I think you will especially appreciate, Mrs. Perez. Halfway through my demonstration, I will invite Chris Seger to come up and do the second half. Chris is a Marine Corps veteran, who also served in

Afghanistan. He will become Finley's permanent owner today. You will see that Finley responds to Chris just as well as he responds to me. They have already become the best of friends."

53

They had just finished the demonstration.

Chris had been a little nervous at first, but he'd calmed down as he watched Amy working with Finley. Amy had handled herself like a real pro, calling out one command after another. Finley kept his eyes totally locked on her, instantly obeying everything she had asked of him. He never once became distracted, even with the applause of the crowd, which grew steadily as the routine unfolded.

The one-time Finley did lose focus, Chris didn't mind at all. It was just after Amy had finished her part. She had re-introduced Chris and invited him to take Finley's leash. Finley got all excited when he saw Chris coming. He didn't jump on him but his tail wagged furiously and his front feet pranced in place. When Chris got right next to him, Finley sat and leaned against him, and rubbed his head against his leg as Chris patted it.

"As you can see," Amy had said, "I wasn't kidding about how Finley feels about Chris."

She turned her attention from the crowd back to Chris as she handed him the leash. Chris kept her in his gaze for several moments. For one thing, she was much nicer to look at, but it also helped him keep his mind off of the crowd. When their fingers had touched in the exchange, Chris squeezed them gently and whispered, "You did a great job."

She had whispered back, "and so will you."

And Chris did.

He went through his entire routine without missing a beat. And of course, Finley did everything asked of him without a moment's hesitation.

Now they were standing together with Finley on the left side of the podium. Kim and Mrs. Perez were standing a few steps back. Two things happened then. Finley started to get fidgety. He was even pulling a little bit against the leash. Amy gave him a hand signal, and he stopped. But Chris realized, this was all about Mrs. Perez. Finley was looking right at her and only at her.

Next, Chris saw Mrs. Perez whisper something to Kim. Kim smiled and nodded yes to whatever she had said. Then Kim came back to the mike. Mrs. Perez followed and stood just behind her.

"Didn't they do an amazing job?" Kim asked the crowd, who responded with strong applause. "And really, all the dogs who received graduation certificates this morning can do everything you saw Finley do. The truth is, they can all do much more than this. Finley demonstrated only a fraction of the commands and behaviors they've learned in our Prison Paws and Pals Program."

After this, Kim stood off to the side near Chris and Amy to allow Bridget to come up and finish out the program. Mrs. Perez followed Kim and stood beside her. Before Bridget began to speak, Kim whispered to Chris and Amy, "Right after this is over, before everyone heads over to the luncheon, Mrs. Perez asked if she could say something to both of you. Would that be okay?"

"Sure," Chris said. Amy agreed, too.

"Okay," Kim said. "We'll meet back here right after."

After Miss Bridget officially ended the ceremony, Amy congratulated then thanked Rita and the other four trainers in the first row. She was thanking them for being so supportive; it was not the reaction she'd expected. She noticed Chris coming back up the aisle. Kim and Mrs. Perez left their seats and walked with him toward the front. Amy finished up with the ladies and headed toward the spot Kim had asked them to meet.

As soon as they were together, once again, Finley began pressing against his leash, in the direction of Mrs. Perez. It was obvious he remembered her. That's what this was about. He wanted to see her. Amy repeated the hand signal, and he calmed down.

Mrs. Perez looked at Amy, then at Chris, then down at Finley. "I can't believe I am looking at the same dog," she said. "He looks the same, physically, but I never would have imagined he could do any of this. I've never seen any dog do so many things before. Whatever you call them, I know they're not tricks. But he was amazing. My Chaz would have been so proud to have a dog so obedient and so will behaved. And yet you can still see, he's just as fun and loving as he always was." Her eyes started welling up with tears.

"When I say that, I mean the way Finley was with Chaz. Chaz was the one who really took care of him, who really loved him. I'm sad to say, I'm not really a dog person. I tried my best to take care of him after Chaz...had gone. But I couldn't keep up. I felt so guilty bringing him down to the shelter, but Kim assured me they could find him a good home. But I never expected anything like this. He is like, it is like he has become...a super-dog."

The three of them laughed. The remark broke some of the emotional tension that had been building since she began to speak.

Kim said, "Alicia, you have nothing to feel guilty about. And you need to know, Finley holds no grudge toward you. I've been watching him, ever since he noticed you were here. He remembers you, and he wants to see you."

"He does?" Alicia asked.

"Oh yes," Amy said. "Believe me, he does. Are you okay with that?"

Alicia nodded. "If you're sure it will be okay."

Amy let go of his leash. Finley rushed to her. Amy could tell he wanted to jump up on her, he was so happy. "Greet, Finley," she said. Finley instantly obeyed, but he got as close to her as he could, the whole time wagging his tail, and rubbing his head against her thigh. She reached down to pet him, and he licked her hand. She bent down to hug him, and he licked her chin then her neck. Then he nestled his head on her shoulder as she hugged.

Chris began to cry. So did Amy. Kim's eyes started to tear up. She began passing around the tissue box.

"See Alicia," Kim said, "he not only remembers you but he's so happy to see you again."

Alicia looked up with tears in her eyes. "But how can he? I wasn't very nice to him. And I...I gave him away?"

"That's the amazing capacity dogs have to love, and to forgive. As you can see, he's not upset with you. Not even a little. You're the closest thing he has to Chaz."

After a few moments, Alicia stood, wiped her tears away. Amy gave a gentle tug on the leash and called Finley back. He instantly obeyed and sat beside her. Alicia took a step toward Chris. "I have one last thing to say, if I can get it out." She took a deep breath. "I just want to tell you, Chris, how happy I am that Finley will be living the rest of his life with you. When I brought Finley to the shelter, I had no idea that his life would make a difference in the life of another soldier, especially one who has given so much to serve his country. Whenever I've thought of my son, ever since I let Finley go, the memory always came with an added dose of pain, because I knew how much Chaz loved this dog. But I didn't know where Finley was, or how he was doing."

"But now I know." She looked at Amy. "He's been with you, Amy. And you've been teaching him all these amazing things. And now he will be going home with you, Chris. I can see how much you love him, and how much he loves you. It is like he is going back home with Chaz." Tears filled her eyes again. "And that makes me so happy." She reached for the tissue box. "Now, when I think of Chaz, there will still be some pain, but now I will also think of Finley and how happy he is, and I will also be able to smile. I thank you for that."

Chris reached out for her. It seemed the only thing to do. She stepped into his arms, and they hugged.

Amy noticed two more people coming toward them down the aisle. It was the woman reporter from Channel 7 and her cameraman.

Kim saw them, too, and said, "Would you guys be open to answering a few questions from this TV news reporter? She's been here covering the whole event. This kind of publicity can really help the program, help us get the word out about everything that's going on here."

"Sure," Amy said.

"I guess I can do that," Chris said.

"Would they want to talk to me, too?" Alicia asked.

"Definitely," Kim said. "If you're okay with that."

54

They were back in the main room, the place where they normally trained, which today had been reset for the luncheon. Because of the television interview, Chris and Amy were the last ones to go through the food line. Kim had already said goodbye and left to take Mrs. Perez home.

Chris and Amy had already eaten lunch and were now sitting in two of the chairs that lined the perimeter of the room. Well, Chris had eaten his lunch. Amy had forced down part of a sandwich and a few chips. Apparently, suppressing the thoughts about Chris and Finley leaving shortly had also suppressed her appetite.

More than half the vets had already left with their new dogs. Amy could barely watch these goodbye moments. But she did watch a few. The ones she did hardly made any sense to her. Everyone was acting so normal, so happy and upbeat. None of the inmates cried as they parted with their dogs. How was that possible? How did they pull it off?

Finley discerned her decreasing mood. He moved closer to her and began nudging her hand with his nose.

"Are you okay?" Chris asked.

She took a bite of sandwich then pointed to her mouth, as if to say it wouldn't be polite to talk with your mouth full.

"No fair. You took a bite after I asked. Besides, the way Finley is acting I already know the answer."

She kept chewing.

"We didn't talk much while we ate, because I was raised the same way. But I watched you the entire time. Every time one of the dogs left, I saw pain in your eyes. And it got deeper with each one."

She swallowed, hard.

"I'm all done," he said, "and obviously you aren't going to eat anymore." He looked around. "It's too crowded in here anyway. I don't want to say goodbye with all these people. Can we go out to our picnic table?"

He was saying goodbye already? "Okay, we can do that."

He stood. "Besides, I have something I need to ask you. I'd rather do it out there."

She handed Finley's leash to him. "Why don't you take him out, and I'll throw out these plates?"

He took the leash. "But cheer up, Amy. I hate to see you so down."

She smiled as she took his plate, but there was nothing behind it. Cheering up wasn't an option. The best she could manage was trying not to look as terrible as she felt inside. She was willing to try that, for Chris's sake. She didn't want him to feel bad or guilty for taking Finley away. This was the right ending to this story. Finley had found a forever home with a wonderful man who loved him, and who dearly needed the love Finley could give him in return. God had allowed her to play a role in that. Not many people got to do something as rewarding as this. Besides, look how far she had come from the meth-addict-turned-shoplifter she had been just two years ago.

She had no reason to wallow in self-pity. Today was a good day. She looked up. He was just about to go through the door. She smiled. "I'll be right there."

After walking Finley near the bushes, Chris headed back to their favorite table. He sat on the tabletop, then on the bench. Now he was standing. Finley had a confused look on his face. "I'm nervous, Finn. That's all. I'm fine."

He sat on the bench again, then pushed himself back up to the tabletop. This is where he should be. He glanced at the doorway. She was coming. What's the worst that could happen? She would say no. And it would mean he had read this all wrong, and she wasn't interested in him *that* way. He could live with that. They would still be friends, right?

But could he, could he live with that?

As she neared, he took a deep breath. Finley rushed to greet her.

"What did you want to talk about?" she said.

She was standing too far away. "Could you stand here?" He pointed right in front of him. "I don't want anyone to hear me."

She looked around. "No one's even close." But she did what he asked.

Look her right in the eyes, he reminded himself. It needed to be emphasized.

"I think you're going to like what I want to say. I'm not totally sure of it. But I think you might. I hope so anyway."

"Okay…what is it?"

He paused. Looking at her now, he'd forgotten the lines he'd rehearsed. A deep inhale and exhale.

"What is it, Chris?"

"Amy, as you know I am leaving today, with Finley. But…I

want…I want to see you again."

"I'm glad. I was hoping you would. That's probably the main reason I was so excited to get the job with Kim at the Humane Society. So I could see you and Finley again."

"No. I don't mean that. Well, I mean that, but not *only* that." *Just do it.*

He reached for her hand. She didn't pull away. He squeezed her fingers gently. "I want to see you…like this." He squeezed her fingers a little more firmly. "I want to see you…as more than a friend. As more than just Finley's trainer."

"You do?"

"Yes. And not just every now and then, but as often as possible."

"You do?" Tears instantly welled up in her eyes.

"Yes, I do. I don't know exactly when it happened, but I started to realize whenever I thought about coming out here, Finley wasn't the only reason why. I also wanted to see you. When I'd leave this place, I wouldn't just miss seeing him, I missed seeing you. And when I heard you were getting out in a couple of months, I got real excited. And it wasn't because you'd get to see Finley more often. It was because, well, I might get to see you more often."

She stood there, just staring at him with a big smile on her face. She blinked away her tears.

"So what do you say?"

She nodded her head.

"Yes, you're okay with all this?"

She nodded again. Now she looked behind them, to see if anyone was watching.

Chris didn't see anyone looking their way.

She hugged him around the neck. Quickly, then pulled away. "I can't believe you're saying this."

Still looking in her eyes, he said, "Can I kiss you?"

"I think it might be against the rules."

He leaned forward and kissed her lips. "I don't care," he said, as their lips parted. Then he kissed her again. He could tell she was nervous, so he didn't make it a long one. "I've been wanting to do that for weeks," he said, now looking at her face.

"So have I," she said.

He looked at his watch. "My time is almost up. But I looked into it and talked with Miss Bridget about it already."

"Looked into what?"

"Visiting hours. She said because they've already cleared me to be out here, and I've been out here so much, I don't have to wait the customary thirty days to get on the visitors' list. I can't be out here every day like I've been, but I'll be out here every weekend during regular visitor hours. And because Finley's my service dog, he'll be coming with me."

"Really?"

"Really. So see, that's why I said to cheer up in there. Today's not the end for you and Finley. Or for you and me. It's just the beginning. And once you get out in two months, the three of us can see each other every day if we want."

Amy didn't care about the rules. She was happier than she'd ever been in her life. She wrapped her arms around Chris and gave him a passionate kiss. And he kissed her back just as eagerly. The kiss ended because Finley began to bark. They both pulled away before anyone looked.

Amy looked at Finley. His face looked confused, but his tail was wagging away.

"I better go, Amy. It's a few minutes past the time."

"I know." She bent down to Finley's level. "Okay boy, you're going to go with Chris now." She held his face in the palm of her hand. "I know you won't understand a thing I'm about to say, but I know you can read my heart, even better than I can. I love you, Finley. You've been like a gift from God to me, and the best friend I've ever had. So this isn't really goodbye. I'm going to see you real soon. Okay?" The tears came back. "Before you know it, Chris'll bring you right back for a visit. Okay?" She hugged him as tight as she dared. He didn't pull away. Instead, he leaned into her hug and rested his head on her shoulder.

Chris reached down and touched her hand. She let go of Finley and stood but still kept hold of his hand.

He stood there a moment. "I've got something I need to say to you. You and Finley have given me two things I thought were gone from my life for good."

"What are they?"

"Hope," he said. "And love. I know I've still got a ways to go, but you've both made my load so much lighter. I'm not all that afraid of what's up ahead. Not anymore. And I've got the two of you to thank for that."

She didn't know what to say. She felt like she was the one who should be thanking him.

"I really better go," Chris said. "Don't want to get you in any trouble."

"I know." She patted Finley on the head, and stepped back. "Now you go with Chris, Finley. You're going to be with him now."

Chris stepped back and let go of her hand. He held Finley's leash in the other. "But we are going to see you very soon, Amy Wallace. This weekend, in fact. And every other weekend till you get out of this place."

He walked a few more steps, turned and said, "Me and Finley both. We're going to come back just to see you, every chance we get."

55

The day had finally come.

Amy couldn't believe it. Thanks to the regular visits each weekend by Chris and Finley, the last two months had flown by. She was so excited. Yesterday evening, she had said her final goodbyes to Miss Bridget, Rita and some of the other girls she counted as friends. And now, she was going through the final release procedures. She was already wearing her street clothes, the first time she had worn blue jeans in three years. The doorway to the outside world and total freedom was just down the hall.

If things had gone according to plan, Chris and Finley should be waiting there for her in the parking lot. It was clear from their weekend visits that she and Chris were officially a couple now. They still had never been on a first date. Chris said he had plans to change that this evening.

She couldn't wait.

"Just one more paper to sign," the female guard said, "and I can give you the rest of your things."

Amy signed it and watched as the guard brought out a box.

From it, she pulled Amy's old black purse and a big envelope that contained everything left in the purse from three years ago. Amy quickly opened the envelope and set everything back in her purse, exactly where they belonged. Then she slung the purse around her shoulder. "Is there anything else?"

"Nope, that's it," the guard said.

"I'm free?"

"Free as a bird. Have a good life. And stay out of trouble."

"I will. Thanks." Amy turned and headed down the hallway.

She opened the metal door into the bright sunlight. The first thing she noticed as her eyes adjusted to the light was the absence of a barbed wire fence around the parking lot. One second later, she heard the most wonderful sound.

Finley barking.

She quickly found him by a dark blue sedan, standing next to Chris who waved his arm to get her attention. Finley's tail was wagging, and he was prancing his front feet. She waved to Chris and headed that way. "Hey Finley. I see you. I'll be right there."

"I don't think he can wait," Chris yelled, then let go of Finley's leash.

Finley ran toward her, his blue leash flapping behind him. She bent down and braced herself for an over-the-top greeting. Which is exactly what she got. You'd think Finley hadn't seen her for ages. He was jumping all over, licking her face and hands, totally out of control.

And she was perfectly fine with that.

Chris walked up and joined them a few moments later. By then, Finley had begun to settle down. He picked up Finley's leash, then he gave her a big hug and kiss.

Their longest kiss to date.

"Not breaking any rules now," Chris said as they parted lips.

"I can't believe it. I'm free."

He took her hand, and the three of them walked toward his car. "You definitely are. Have you eaten breakfast yet?"

"No, I was too excited."

"Hungry now? I didn't eat thinking maybe we could get some breakfast together."

They reached the car. "I'd like that."

He opened the back door and Finley hopped in. Then he opened her door, "Hope you're okay with this. I'm kind of old-fashioned."

"I like old-fashioned," she said as she got in.

He walked around the front of the car then sat behind the wheel. He put the keys in the ignition and sat back in his seat.

"Aren't you going to turn the car on?"

"I am, but I need to talk with you about something first. It'll just take a minute."

Amy could tell, it was something serious. She hoped it wasn't something that would spoil this wonderful moment. "Okay..."

"It's kind of a surprise. A pretty big surprise actually. I hope it's something you'll like. But before I tell you what it is, if you're not okay with it, it doesn't have to happen. Not today anyway."

What in the world? She had no idea what it could be. "Okay, I guess I'm ready."

"Do you remember about three visits ago, I asked you about your family. I know it was a difficult subject for you and, at the time, I asked if you'd be open to talk about it, just so that I could get to know you better. That's really all I had in mind at the time. But then as I got home, I started to think about it. It just seemed wrong to me that the reason they haven't stayed in touch with you all this time is because of the things you did to them back when you were on drugs."

"They were some pretty bad things, Chris. I lied to them constantly and stole money from them more times than I can count. I even stole some of my mother's jewelry and sold it at a pawn shop."

"I know that and I get why they had to cut you off. But Amy, that was, what, almost four years ago? You're a totally different person now. In every way. You said you were raised in the church, that your folks are church people. Well, Christians —church people—are supposed to forgive, especially when the other person's totally sorry for what they did."

"They don't know I'm sorry. I've never been able to tell them. I sent a letter to Cassie over a year ago but it came back as the wrong address."

"Well, that's kind of my surprise. They do now."

"Do now...what?"

"They know you're sorry. I did some snooping on the internet, and I found out where your brother, Peter, lives now. He and Cassie. I found out the place he works, and I was able to email him. Told him all about you, what you're like now, about us, about Finley about you getting out today...so much earlier for good behavior. And remember that TV interview we did with Channel 7 after the graduation? That reporter did a whole feature story on it. I found the link on YouTube and included it in the email to your brother."

Amy couldn't believe what she was hearing. She couldn't believe Chris would do all this, all on his own. "Did you hear anything back?"

"I did. Later that night. We exchanged cell phone numbers, and then we talked on the phone a good while."

"You talked with...Peter? My brother Peter?"

"I did, Amy. And with Cassie. They only live three hours away from here, near Clearwater. A few days later I got a call from your mom. She lives there, too. Just about a half-mile away from them."

"You spoke with my mom?" She couldn't help it. Tears began to fill her eyes.

"She read my email to Peter and watched the video. Amy, they want to connect with you. They want you guys to be a family again."

Amy couldn't even speak. She started to cry. Chris leaned over and hugged her. And of course, Finley got in on it, too.

As he held her, he said, "There's more. I told them maybe they should wait a day or two, but they didn't want to do that."

"Do what?" she said, pulling back.

"Your brother Peter, and Cassie. They wanted to be here when you got out."

"They're here?"

"Yes, but not here…in the parking lot. I thought that might be too much for you. They're at a Starbucks in downtown Summerville. I called them on the way here. They really want to see you, but I said you might need a little bit of time. They're okay with that. They got a motel room for the night. They said they can wait until tomorrow morning, if you'd—"

"—No, I don't want to."

"You don't want to see them?"

"No, I don't want to wait. Can we go see them now?"

Chris turned the car on. "Sure, we can."

"You don't mind? Isn't this going to spoil your plans? For our date night tonight?"

He put the car in reverse and pulled out of the parking spot. "Not at all. We can go on our first date tomorrow night, or the night after that, or the night after that. I'm not going anywhere, Amy. You, me and Finley? We've got all the time in the world."

Author's Note

I've been a dog lover for as long as I can remember. Growing up, we had two dogs. Six weeks after we got married, my wife and I picked out a dog from our local Humane Society. We've had at least one dog in our home ever since (we've been married for thirty-nine years). Right now, we have two.

It's fair to say my wife, Cindi, loves dogs even more than I do. Five years ago, we officially became empty-nesters. After homeschooling our children and working as a bookkeeper at our church, I told her I thought she should spend our latter years together doing something for herself, something she enjoyed. When asked what she'd like to do, she didn't hesitate. "I want to go back to school and become a certified dog trainer."

She did just that, earning a 4.0 GPA and, for the last 3 years, she's been the Animal Behavior Manager at our local Humane Society. Since then, she's trained hundreds of dogs, both privately and in group classes. This year she was voted the "best dog trainer in town" in the greater Daytona Beach area. She's amazing to watch, and I've learned so much about dogs and dog behavior from her. I've done a lot of additional research, but Cindi has been a primary consultant throughout this book, and she's agreed to help me with the rest of the books in this series.

Although not totally based on Cindi, many aspects of my character, Kim Harper, have come from conversations with her. I should also mention that in *Rescuing Finley*, I depict a local Humane Society and a prison training program where female

293

inmates train shelter dogs to be used as service dogs for military veterans. Such shelters and prison programs like this do exist (I'll say a little more about them in a moment), but it would be wrong to conclude the ones depicted in my novel are based on actual places or programs.

They are not. Both are fictitious.

In my research, I studied about numerous animal shelters and prison programs that train shelter dogs. I decided to create something of a composite situation that better served the needs of my story. But I do want to say how much I greatly admire all those who work in animal shelters—both the paid staff and volunteers. If you enjoyed this story, please do all you can to support their ongoing efforts.

The idea for *Rescuing Finley* came from spending time listening to Cindi's stories and volunteering some of my time at Halifax Humane Society, our local non-profit shelter serving the Daytona Beach area. They support a local prison program that trains dogs; many who are adopted by veterans struggling with PTSD.

I began to look further into this and read numerous stories on the news about other programs across the country doing similar things (matching trained shelter dogs with military vets). I researched them online and watched dozens of video testimonies. The sad reality is that tens of thousands of our young men and women, who've served us so heroically in Iraq and Afghanistan, come home suffering the debilitating and life-dominating effects of PTSD. The VA provides some help, but it is clearly not enough. Tragically, even now, 22 veterans commit suicide every day in the United States.

This is a national tragedy.

A significant part of my motivation to write *Rescuing Finely* was to draw attention to this issue, and to one very solid solution that offers veterans dramatic and positive results. I've listened to veterans who've received one of these trained service dogs, and they were all saying the same thing: "*This dog saved my life.*" Many of them have also struggled with suicidal thoughts, some had even tried.

But they aren't thinking that way anymore. They've experienced a complete turn-around in their situation and our coping with their PTSD symptoms far more effectively.

It is also my hope that *Rescuing Finley* will open the eyes of thousands of storekeepers, restaurant owners and ordinary citizens to the great value these service dogs provide our veterans. Veterans shouldn't feel like anyone is looking down on them or judging them because of their dog. When we see them, we should do everything we can to make them feel welcome.

Some veterans don't bare any obvious physical battle scars. I think people are more naturally sympathetic when they see a veteran with a service dog if they're in a wheelchair or wearing a prosthetic limb. But PTSD, all by itself, is a very real and very serious consequence of living in mortal danger for months or years at a time.

Every veteran who struggles with PTSD deserves our compassion and deep respect.

Thanks for listening,
Dan Walsh

Want to Read More?

Rescuing Finley is Book 1 of the Forever Home series. Dan is already working on Book 2, *Saving Parker*, and Book 3, *Finding Riley*. We plan to release both in 2016 (likely 4-5 months apart). If you'd like to receive an email letting you know when, visit Dan's website at the link below and sign up for his newsletter (just scroll down the left sidebar a few inches). He always gives his readers the inside scoop on book specials and new release dates.

In the meantime, why not check out some of Dan's other novels? Since 2009, he has written more than fifteen, mostly for the inspirational or Christian fiction market. All of them are written in a similar genre and style as *Rescuing Finley*, with character-driven storylines, page-turning suspense and a strong romantic thread. All are available on Amazon and other online stores, in print or ebook editions. Some are still available in retail stores.

To sign up for Dan's newsletter or get a sneak peek at Dan's other novels, visit this link (click on any book cover to go to that book's page):

http://www.danwalshbooks.com/books/

Want to Help the Author?

If you enjoyed reading this book, the best thing you can do to help Dan is very simple—*tell others about it*. Word-of-mouth is the most powerful marketing tool there is. Better than expensive TV commercials or full-page ads in magazines.

Dan would greatly appreciate it if you would rate his book and leave a brief review on Amazon, Facebook or any other social media site.

About The Author

Dan Walsh was born in Philadelphia in 1957. His family moved down to Daytona Beach, Florida in 1965, when his dad began to work with GE on the Apollo space program. That's where Dan grew up.

He married, Cindi, the love of his life in 1976. They have two grown children and two grandchildren. Dan served as a pastor for 25 years, then began writing fiction full-time in 2010. His bestselling novels have won many awards, including 3 ACFW Carol Awards (Book-of-the-Year) and 3 Selah Awards. Three of Dan's novels were finalists for RT Reviews Inspirational Book of the Year.

If you'd like to get an email alert whenever Dan has a new book coming out, or a special deal on one of Dan's books, you can click on his website below and sign up for his newsletter. From his homepage, you can also contact Dan or follow him on Facebook or Twitter.

http://danwalshbooks.com

Acknowledgments

Writing a novel is mostly a solitary effort.

A picture comes to mind of an author hammering away on a laptop all by themselves as days, weeks and months go by. It's an accurate picture for the most part. But for some very good reasons, every writer depends on the help of others.

There's an old saying, "Write what you know." In other words, situate your stories in locations and areas of life in which you have some expertise. That might work for a novel or two, maybe even three. But at some point, if an author is being honest, they will come to the end of *things they know.* What happens then?

What most do, including this author, is a lot of research. You spend quality time learning from people who really do know what they're talking about. You realize that the input they provide is invaluable and adds a much-needed measure of credibility and realism to your story. They provide details which would be impossible to obtain without their help.

On this page, I get to thank the people who've helped me make *Rescuing Finley* a much better book. If you happen to be an expert in any of the areas I touch on in the book and you find any mistakes—blame me, not them. I'm sure I just got something wrong or misunderstood something they said.

With this disclaimer out of the way, let me begin by thanking the one person who has helped me the most. Without her help, this book could not have been written (this is no exaggeration). It's not uncommon for authors to thank loved ones and spouses for all their support while writing the book. My wife, Cindi, contributed so much more than mere support.

As I mentioned in my Author's Note, she is a certified dog trainer and graduated from Animal Behavior College with a 4.0 GPA. She's trained hundreds of dogs over the past few years through her job as the Animal Behavior Manager at our local Humane Society. To put it simply, she is a wizard with dogs and really understands how they think. Her input on the chapters with Finley was priceless. She also provided significant editorial input regarding the characters themselves and the flow of the story.

I also want to thank the management, staff and volunteers of Halifax Humane Society (HHS), located in the Daytona Beach area where we live. The shelter you read about in the book is *not* a replica of HHS, but I've learned much from the folks over there. They do an amazing job every day taking in, caring for and finding homes for these precious animals. I especially want to thank Miguel Abi-hassan, the CEO of HHS, for his vision in seeing the necessity of dog training and adding an animal behaviorist to his staff. He created Cindi's position and gives her his strong support. He realizes the critical role training plays in helping owners experience a lasting and fulfilling relationship with their pets.

My wish is that every animal shelter would follow his example. Most pet-owners wind up bringing their dogs to shelters because of problems that could easily be fixed if they'd only spend some time with a certified trainer.

I would also like to thank Marge Blomquist and Allen Weigel, who pioneered the *Prison Pups and Pals* program at the Tomoka Correctional Institute, the state prison nearest our home in Florida. And I want to thank Officer Gail Irwin, who oversees the program from inside the prison. This program takes shelter dogs from our Humane Society and teaches prison inmates how to train the dogs to serve others, including military veterans. The program shown in *Rescuing Finley* bears some similarities to this program, but it's not an exact match. I actually researched dozens of similar programs taking place in prisons throughout the US and borrowed things from several different programs.

Let me encourage you to check them out. You will find it time well spent. But be forewarned, you might want to have a tissue handy. I cried several times as I watched a number of videos that show the amazing difference these dogs have made in the lives of the inmates and the military veterans they served. You can find programs very similar to the fictitious one seen in the book by Googling: *"Prison programs training shelter dogs for vets."*

Do everything you can to support them. These dogs and the people training them really are saving lives, both the dogs' lives and the lives of our veterans, especially those struggling with PTSD.

I'd also like to thank my team of proofreaders, for helping to catch all the things I and my editor missed: Deborah Keith, Donna Tinsley, Patricia Keough-Wilson, Jann Martin and Tonya Brown. Finally, I want to thank Kendy Wooden for giving me the idea for the series sub-title for these books: "A Forever Home Novel." This book is now officially: "Rescuing Finley – A Forever Home Novel – Book 1. Keep your eye out for Book 2 (*Saving Parker*) and Book 3 (*Finding Riley*).

Both should release sometime in 2016.